MW00438424

Scatman Dues

Freaky Florida Mystery Adventure, Volume 6

Margaret Lashley

Published by Zazzy Ideas, Inc., 2021.

Copyright

What Readers are Saying about Freaky Florida Mystery Adventures...

"The story lines are crazy, and all you want is more!"

"Hilarious, weird and entertaining."

"The X-Files has found its funny bone!"

"I read a lot, and Kindle suggested your book. This book is laugh out loud funny. Is everyone in Florida crazy?"

"I have read Tim Dorsey, Carl Hiaasen, and Randy Wayne White. Those writers are funny but they need to watch out for you."

"Not too many writers can make me laugh out loud, but Margaret Lashley is now officially on my short list of favorite laugh-out-loud authors. With witty sarcasm and stupid odd characters who make it so easy, I'm an official new fan."

"A funny cozy, science fiction, thriller, mystery all rolled into one great story!"

"I read the whole book in two days, something I've never done before! I just couldn't wait to find out what was going to happen next!"

Dedication

In loving memory of Randall James Hamilton Zwinge, better known as The Amazing Randi. 1928-2020.

I hope you were wrong about life after death—and a couple of other things.

Prologue

I'm Bobbie Drex, and I have a confession to make.

Becoming a private investigator wasn't exactly a profession I chose. At least, not *intentionally*—and certainly not while in complete control of my faculties.

If you want to know the truth, I'd been knee-deep in a vodka bottle when I'd ordered an online P.I. training course from a cheesy, late-night infomercial. I'd been even more out of my mind the next morning, when I'd sobered up and discovered the credit-card charges were non-refundable.

Fueled by frustration, stubbornness, and an inability to throw away hard-earned cash, I'd gone ahead and completed the course. I'd figured what the hell—it might've come in handy for my glamorous job as a part-time mall cop.

As it turned out, I never got the chance to find out.

A few days later, a ricochet bullet popped me in the forehead, putting an end to my glorious security-patrol gig. I'd returned home from the hospital with my head shaved, my health insurance cancelled, and my family's auto repair business in the crapper.

Awesome.

The only bright spot had been finding my training course certificate in the mailbox. But after reading the fine print, that bright spot had turned as dark and unwelcome as a suspicious mole.

I'd discovered that, in and of itself, my new "Private Investigator Intern Certificate" was barely worth the paper it was printed on. In order to become a full-fledged Florida private eye, I'd also have to complete *two years* of on-the-job training with a licensed investigator.

(Insert expletive of your choice here.)

Anyway, I was wadding up the stupid certificate and hurling it into the bin when something *even more* aggravating happened.

An oddball named Nick Grayson showed up at my door.

The mysterious, green-eyed stranger sported a vintage fedora and a shiny private-eye badge—and he was on the hunt for two things.

One was repairs to his ratty old RV. The other was ... uh ... *Mothman*.

And he'd wanted my help with both.

At the time, I couldn't tell if Grayson was a gift from the Universe or another sick joke at my expense. But back then, my life was so deep in the dumpster I'd decided to take him up on his offer.

I'd joined his weird crusade tracking down cryptids for cash.

As Grayson's P.I. intern, I've spent the past seven months roaming the dirty backwaters of the Sunshine State in a rundown Winnebago—with a guy whose own human pedigree was as sketchy as the creatures we investigate.

If all that weren't bad enough, we operate our research deep within the stomping grounds of Florida Man—where it's doubly hard to tell a monster from a maniac.

Sometimes, it's darn-near *impossible*.

They say hindsight is 2020. Well, let me tell you what. That infamous year's got *nothing* on the unbelievable crap that's gone down since I climbed aboard Grayson's magical mystery motorhome.

Little did I realize, I hadn't seen anything yet ...

Chapter One

I cracked open a sleepy eye and groaned. It was official. I was the only grown-ass woman in the entire universe who was "sleeping" with her boss—*literally*.

As in, "snoring-in-your-face, no-sexy-time" *literally*.

Worse yet, I couldn't decide if that was a good thing or a bad thing.

Ever since my big lug of a cousin came and wrecked the sofa-bed I usually slept on, I'd been forced to share the queen-sized bed in the back of the RV with my irritatingly handsome boss and partner, Nick Grayson.

My cousin Earl had headed back to Point Paradise a week ago. He'd left me with a mangled mattress and a horrible headache. While the headache came and went, the ruined sofa persisted. Unfortunately, so did Grayson's fixation on using *me* to fine-tune his weird brainwave monitoring device.

According to my mad-scientist partner, Grayson's modified EEG machine was supposed to measure my brain's alpha-wave activity in response to threatening stimuli. What that meant for *me* was regular sessions of having my skull plastered to the contraption via electrodes, then having my eyes blasted with images designed to scare the living crap out of me.

I mean, how lucky can one girl get?

Believe it or not, there was actually a method to Grayson's madness. Through sheer willpower and deep-breathing techniques, I was supposed to learn to override my instinctual flight-or-flight responses and remain calm in the face of fear. The higher my alpha waves remained on his monitor, the better I was doing.

Fun times...

Besides learning how to not freak out in the face of carnivorous cryptids and cantankerous crazies, as part of my internship Grayson was also instructing me on ways to deflect unforeseen attacks by vile, blood-sucking creatures.

Not that I needed the practice.

After swimming in the deep end of Florida's dating pool for the past two decades, I'd joined his team fully equipped with my own armor-plated life raft—and an arsenal of moves that could blow an entire army of despicable, handsy parasites clean out of the water.

But as for Grayson *himself*, he hadn't once tried to put the moves on me.

It was a fact that both duly impressed me *and* annoyed the living hell out of me. Was he being a gentleman? Or—horror of horrors—was he just not that into me? The man was a master of mixed signals. But then again, I wasn't sure if I wanted him myself.

Mainly because I wasn't totally convinced Grayson was a card-carrying member of the *Homo sapiens* genepool.

You see, during the two weeks we'd become unintentional bedmates, the closest thing to a romantic gesture I'd witnessed from Grayson was when he'd gone and cleaned the toilet without me asking.

As a bona fide Earth woman, that action *alone* had been enough to make me question whether Grayson was a real human male, or some kind of mutant clone.

Not that I didn't already have enough reasons to be suspicious about the guy. Given Grayson's strange diet, encyclopedic vocabulary, and secondary bellybutton, I had some pretty serious doubts about his family tree. Was the weirdo a mere mortal? Or was he some lost, alien life form trying desperately to find a payphone to call home?

I sat up in bed and glanced over at Grayson's empty side of the bed.

Here I am, about to turn 38, bunking with a mild-mannered Martian hiding behind a Freddie Mercury moustache. Not exactly a situation designed to send a girl over the moon...

I sighed and scratched my cheek. Half of me was dying to find out the truth about Grayson. The other half of me was worried about dying *if* I found out.

Still, there was a chemistry between us that was undeniable.

We just had to perfect the formula.

I ROLLED OUT OF BED and padded barefoot to the main cabin of the old Winnebago Grayson and I traveled in together. As usual, my bedmate and boss was wide awake—annoyingly alert and neatly dressed in his perennial uniform of black T-shirt, black jeans, and black boots.

Perched in his favorite spot at the small banquette booth across from the kitchen, Grayson's short-cropped dark hair matched his moustache. His face was ruggedly handsome. And he had the kind of wiry body that comes from intense focus on something other than food. As usual, that focus was now being directed to the only thing more annoying than his apparent prime directive of lifelong celibacy—

—that stupid EEG brainwave machine of his.

"Ah. You're awake," Grayson said, never looking up from his precious contraption. He fiddled with a few knobs on the device, making the needles on the monitors jerk around like a Richter scale in an apocalypse.

"If you want to call it that," I quipped.

"You're just in time," he said, ignoring my comment.

A frown pinched the corners of my mouth. I scrounged in the kitchen cupboard for a clean coffee cup. "Just in time *for what?*"

"To test my theory."

I shot Grayson some caffeine-deprived side-eye and poured myself a cup of coffee from the carafe on the stove.

"Theory?" I asked, then took a life-giving sip.

"Yes." Grayson finally looked up from fiddling with the monitor. "Drex, you've been displaying unusually high alpha waves on the last few tests. I'm trying to determine if this means my program is truly desensitizing you to strange phenomena, or if the test itself is influencing the results."

I groaned. "Grayson, if you don't let me drink this coffee in peace, *I'll* be determining the results *of your lifespan.*"

Grayson's eyebrow formed a Spock-like triangle. "Duly noted."

I ripped open a package of Pop-Tarts with my teeth and slammed them into the toaster. As I waited for them to heat up into warm, life-saving rectangles of blueberry-flavored salvation, my curiosity got the better of me.

I turned and stared at Grayson. "What did you mean when you said the EEG test *itself* could be influencing my results?"

Grayson's cat-like, green eyes locked on mine. "Non-objective anticipatory response, of course."

I stifled another groan. I should've been used to this by now. "More human-like speak, please, robot man."

Grayson studied me for a moment, then winced slightly when I took a savage bite of Pop-Tart.

"I merely meant that your *anticipation* of viewing shocking images on the test program could be subconsciously tempering your response," he said. "Your expectations could be putting you into a sort of 'prepared state,' thus influencing your reactions to the images themselves."

I sucked blueberry goo from my front teeth. "It's seven a.m., for crying out loud. Could you dial down the Mr. Science spiel one more notch?"

Grayson chewed his bottom lip for a moment, studying me as if I had white fur and whiskers. "How's this?" he said. "You know what's coming, so you mentally brace for it."

"Ah," I said, and flopped down across from him at the banquette. "Forewarned is forearmed."

"Exactly."

Grayson's cheek dimpled. It was the only way I could tell he was smiling, because his lips were perpetually obscured by a bushy black moustache that looked like the mothership that had delivered his bushy, shuttlecraft eyebrows.

He curled his long fingers around his coffee mug. "This 'mental preparation' could be skewing your alpha-wave results to a falsely high level."

I sighed. "Or, it could mean I'm finally getting the hang of dealing with otherworldly creeps."

"Hmm." Grayson rubbed his chin. "I suppose that's *one* of the other possibilities."

"*One?*" I set my coffee cup down and tried to gather pertinent facts from my groggy brain for my rebuttal dissertation, but got sidetracked. A manila folder was tucked under Grayson's laptop. The edge sticking out had the words *Experiment #5* written on it.

I frowned at the folder suspiciously. "Okay. What other possibilities *are* there?"

Grayson shrugged. "Quite a few, actually. Elevated alpha waves could be a causal symptom of the vestigial twin lodged in the center of your brain."

I sat back, surprised. "You think my *twin* has something to do with my high alpha waves?" I shook my head. "Sure. Why give *me* any credit?"

"Drex, I'm merely stating that the mass could be exerting pressure on your pineal gland, inducing a feeling of bliss."

"Bliss?" I laughed jadedly as an image flashed in my mind from a week ago. I'd been yanking the spikey legs off cicadas for a casserole at a *Duck Dynasty* bug barbeque.

"Well, Grayson, whatever 'bliss' I feel sure isn't coming from job satisfaction."

Grayson locked eyes with me. "The bliss I'm talking about would be totally unassociated with your current reality."

I smirked. "It'd *have* to be."

I jabbed a finger at the folder peeking out from beneath his laptop. "What's experiment number five?"

Grayson covered the label with his hand, then studied me for a moment. "That's on a need-to-know basis, Drex."

Frustration shot an arrow directly into my temple. "Come on, Grayson! I thought we were supposed to *trust* each other!"

Grayson cocked his head and raised an eyebrow at me. "Is that why you broke into my locked cabinet last week?"

I winced. "I already apologized for that. Besides, Earl did it first."

Grayson eyed me coolly. "If Earl jumped off a bridge—"

"Fine!" I blurted. "You're right. I shouldn't have done it. I'm sorry."

Grayson looked down his nose at me. "Apology accepted."

I glanced down at the mysterious folder and chewed my bottom lip. I couldn't stand not knowing what the hell *Experiment #5* meant. "Aw, come on, Grayson. Just give me a hint, okay?"

Grayson sighed. "Very well."

I smiled and took a victory sip of coffee.

Grayson cleared his throat. "It involves *hot bodies*."

Coffee spurted from my mouth like a busted lawn sprinkler. "*Porn?*" I hacked, wiping my chin.

Grayson studied me clinically, then put a spidery hand on my forehead. "Drex, do you have a headache?"

I blanched and yanked his hand away. "No. Why?"

Grayson stared at me oddly, but said nothing.

Suddenly, a thought stabbed my brain. My ears flamed with heat. "Grayson, is this your attempt at ... *foreplay?*"

Grayson's handsome head tilted slightly to the left. "*Four* play? Impossible, Drex. We're not equipped for that."

My eyebrows met. "What? Why not?"

"Because there are only *two* of us."

I collapsed back into my seat, stunned to silence. Either Grayson had stolen a joke from Leslie Nielsen, or he was indeed utterly clueless when it came to intergalactic relationships.

As I ground my teeth to powder contemplating whether Grayson was of this Earth or not, I realized there was only *one thing* I knew about him with absolute certainty.

The guy really knew how to pull my chain.

Chapter Two

A high-pitched wail echoed down the hallway of the RV. I glanced up from my laptop and winced. Either Grayson was giving an extremely reluctant cat an enema, or he was singing in the shower again.

My lips curled diabolically. I rubbed my hands together. *Yes!*

It was time to get to work.

WHILE GRAYSON CRUCIFIED *Jesus Christ Superstar*, I ransacked the RV like a flying squirrel on crack. I couldn't help myself. My mind was literally twitching with curiosity. I *had* to know.

What the hell is Experiment #5?

"On a need to know basis, my ass," I muttered as I rifled through the hallway cabinets like a meth-head craving a fix. So far, I'd come up empty-handed.

A hasty shuffle through Grayson's shelves of secret potions produced no results either—just another gander at his oddball collection, including the *Alien Parasite Remover* he kept in a Windex bottle. Behind it, floating in a jar of gross, pale-brown liquid, was the Nubian fertility statue my dingbat cousin Earl had mistaken for the extra appendage removed from Grayson when he was a kid.

Grayson's adoptive mother had given her new son the nickname "Nubbin" because of his extra appendage. Its surgical removal had left a scar on Grayson's stomach that looked remarkably like a second bellybutton.

Or, at least, that's the story Grayson had told me.

"Damn. No file," I muttered to myself.

I closed the cabinet and headed for the bedroom. But even after pilfering through Grayson's underwear drawer, ten minutes later I still had absolutely squat to show for my efforts.

Wedging my hand into every crack in the broken sofa-bed and scrounging through every kitchen shelf and drawer had produced nothing except the BabyRuth candy bar I'd stashed away in an empty macaroni box two months ago. You know, in case of emergency.

And as far as I was concerned, this was a freakin' emergency.

I flopped onto the bed, ripped open the silver foil, and sunk my teeth into the peanuts and firm, chocolate-coated caramel. As I bit off a huge hunk, a thought struck me.

Grayson said the folder contained "hot bodies." Where would a man of questionable genetic origin hide his porn stash?

A peanut tumbled off the candy bar, bounced off my shoe, and rolled under the bed.

Of course! Under the mattress!

I shoved the last hunk of BabyRuth into my mouth, then heaved up the queen-sized mattress.

Nothing. Crap.

Down the short hallway, Grayson crooned out another excruciating series of off-key notes. Caught off guard by his oral assault, I gasped and nearly choked to death on the logjam of nuts and caramel stuck to my upper palate.

Then another thought made me gag.

Did Grayson take the folder into the bathroom with him? Is he looking at the photos right now and... Ugh!

I cringed and let go of the mattress. It landed atop the box-spring with a soft thud. Caramel-coated disgust churned in my stomach. I called off my search for the folder and began covering my tracks.

First stop was the bed. I stretched and tugged on the black bedspread until it was creaseless and taut. Satisfied it was back to Grayson's military-precision standards, I swallowed the remnants of my contraband BabyRuth, then licked my teeth in the mirror above the bureau until every chocolatey speck of evidence was removed.

That done, I glanced around the bedroom. Everything appeared in order. I turned to leave, then remembered the AWOL peanut and froze in my tracks. If it had been anyone else I was sharing a room with, I'd have ignored the wayward legume. But I knew if Grayson found it, he'd put two and two together—and come up with five.

Ugh!

I got on my hands and knees and looked under the bed. Of course, the stupid peanut had rolled all the way to the front right corner, out of reach. I crawled over to the front side of the bed and fished it out, bumping my head on the nightstand in the process.

"Ouch," I grumbled, rubbing my head.

Aggravated, I stood up and kicked the nightstand. The drawer popped open an inch. The edge of a manila folder came into view. I glanced around the room. The coast was clear. I yanked open the nightstand drawer.

The folder marked *Experiment #5* lay right on top.

Ka-ching!

I reached for it.

"Baarriinnngg!"

An alarm rang, scaring the bejeebers out of me!

I jerked my hand back, slammed the drawer shut, and whirled around on my heels. I fully expected to see Grayson standing in the doorway, ready to turn me to dust with laser blasts from his alien-green eyes.

He wasn't there.

The alarm sounded again. A thought burst to the surface of my paranoid mind.

That alarm isn't Grayson's. It's mine.

It was the special "emergency" ringtone of my best friend back in Point Paradise. Beth-Ann was calling my cellphone!

I sprinted out of the bedroom, down the short hall, past the bathroom, and into the main cabin. I snatched my phone from the banquette table.

"Beth-Ann!" I yelled into the receiver.

"Wow. You can still recognize my voice." Her deadpan tone dripped with sarcasm. "I was just about to mark you off my best friend list."

Guilt washed over me. "Sorry. I've been busy."

"Doing what?" she asked.

I envisioned Goth-girl Beth-Ann milling about inside the quirky beauty shop she'd created inside her garage. In my mind's eye, she was leaning against a broom, filing her black-lacquered nails, a Cheshire-cat smirk on her black-painted lips.

"Uh...private eye stuff," I fumbled.

"Uh-huh."

I let out a sigh and padded back down the hallway toward the bedroom. I knew from experience there was no fooling the savvy woman on the other end of the line.

"Well, to be honest, Beth-Ann—"

I stopped talking—I could no longer hear my own voice. It was being obliterated by a horrendous wail emanating from behind the bathroom door. Outside, a couple of dogs began howling.

"What in the world is that godawful noise?" Beth-Ann asked.

"Its ... uh..." I fumbled.

"Wait!" Beth-Ann gasped. "You've got some crazy creature snared in that bedroom, don't you? You know. In that monster-trap thingy!"

"No," I said. "That's Grayson."

"In the trap?"

"No! In the..." I cringed. "He's in the..."

"Geez, Bobbie! Spit it out! Where is he?"

"He's in the bathroom."

"Oh." Beth-Ann's voice sounded three octaves deeper.

Grayson belted out another otherworldly yowl, making me envision C3PO being crushed between two flaming asteroids. I grimaced with embarrassment. "Look. It's not what it sounds like. He's not—"

"Stop!" Beth-Ann demanded. "Don't. Say. Another. Word."

I chewed my lip and listened to my best friend breathe for ten seconds. Finally, Beth-Ann broke the silence.

"Bobbie, I don't know how you two can live together in that crappy RV without driving each other crazy."

I blew out a jaded laugh. "Who says we *haven't*?"

I could almost *hear* Beth-Ann's jet-black eyebrows rise an inch.

"Oooh. Do I detect trouble in paradise?" she cooed.

I winced. "Kind of."

"What's wrong?"

I frowned. "Grayson doesn't trust me."

Beth-Ann snorted. "Imagine that."

My eyebrows crunched together. "I thought you were my friend."

"Sorry. But you know how you are."

I scowled. "What's *that* supposed to mean?"

"Never mind. Look. Why do you think Grayson doesn't trust you? Have you tried talking to him about it?"

"Come on. You know guys' ears are like their nipples, Beth-Ann. They don't actually work. They're just there to make them appear more human."

Beth-Ann laughed.

I opened my mouth to say something, but the sharp squeak of the water faucet cut me off. Grayson had finished his shower. A surge of panic shot through me. Would Grayson know I'd snooped through his stuff?

"Hold on a sec, Beth-Ann."

"Okay."

I held the phone in one hand and feverishly scanned the hallway, then the bedroom, searching for any telltale signs of my ransacking rampage. I scurried over to the nightstand to make sure I'd shut the drawer all the way. Then I tugged once more on the corner of the taught bedspread for good measure.

"Okay. I'm back," I said, then let out a sigh of relief. "Uh...what were you saying?"

"I asked you why you think Grayson doesn't trust you," Beth-Ann said.

"How the heck should *I* know?" I said, shooting a paranoid glance back down the hallway.

"Did he *say* he doesn't trust you?"

I frowned. "No. But he keeps stuff from me. *Important* stuff. And most of time, when I ask him a question, he tells me, "That's on a need-to-know basis.""

"That's his *right*, Bobbie. You don't tell Grayson everything *you* do, do you?"

I winced. "No. But since we've been sleeping together—"

"*What?*"

"Argh! I didn't mean it like that—"

"You're *boinking* Grayson?"

"No! We're just ... uh ... sharing a bed."

Beth-Ann laughed. "Sounds like boinking to me."

"It's not! Listen. Last time Earl came to visit he busted the couch, okay? I started bunking with Grayson until we can get a new sofa-bed. Anyway, I just thought by now that he'd, you know, be sharing more about himself with me."

"Oh, *no*, Bobbie," Beth-Ann said. "Don't tell me you're *falling* for the guy!"

I winced. "I'm *not*! But. I mean...would it be so bad if I *was*?"

"Girl, you've got one short memory. So let me remind you. You did the same thing with your last boss. Carl Blanders. Remember him? How'd *that* work out for you?"

A familiar pain shot through my head at the mention of my ex's name. "It turned into a total crap show."

"*Exactly*. Listen here, Bobbie. Grayson may be a 'sexy detectsy,' but he's your *boss*, not your *boyfriend*. There *is* a difference, you know."

I blew out a sigh. "Crap. You're right, Beth-Ann."

"Damned straight I'm right! Don't screw it up with Grayson." She paused for a moment. "Or, is it too late already?"

"No. It's not too late."

"Good."

I chewed my lip and listed to Beth-Ann breathe. When she spoke again, her tone had softened a notch.

"I saw the big jerk the other day," she said.

"Earl?" I asked.

Beth-Ann choked. "No! *Carl Blanders*."

"Oh."

"He and Candy Vincent broke up."

A streak of sadistic pleasure melded with the throbbing pain in my head. "Boo hoo. Couldn't have happened to a nicer couple."

"Look, Bobbie. I know the jerk cheated on you with Candy. But give him some credit. At least he asked about you."

I blanched. "You *talked* to him?"

"I had to. He came by my shop for a haircut. He's been on some European antiques buying trip for the last six months. The dumbass thinks you're still working at the auto shop with Earl. He didn't have a clue that you're actually off chasing monsters with the nutty professor."

I cringed so hard I nearly cracked a molar. "You didn't *tell* him, did you?"

"Hell, no! You know me. I've got your back. Besides, you made me promise not to, remember?"

I blew out a huge sigh of relief. "Thanks."

"You're welcome."

Suddenly, my face puckered with resentment. "So Carl took Candy to Paris, then forgot I existed. Geez, Beth-Ann. Are you telling me this to cheer me up?"

"Maybe," Beth-Ann said. "Because there *is* a bright side to it."

I scowled. "Really? I'm all ears."

Beth-Ann giggled. "Just between you and me, I edged around Carl's bald spot in the back. Thanks to me, he's now sporting a hole in his ozone layer the size of a softball."

Despite my best efforts, a smile cracked my lips. "You, Beth-Ann, are a true friend."

She laughed. "And don't you forget it. So, that's all the news from Point Paradise. What are you and Grayson up to—besides being bunkmates? Working on some new, exciting case?"

I glanced down the hall to see if Grayson was still in the bathroom. The door was shut. "Uh ... nothing at the moment."

"Well crap, girl. If you're not busy, get Grayson to swing that old hunk of junk back here to Point Paradise."

"Who you callin' a hunk of junk?" I teased.

"I meant that old motorhome of his! Aw, come on, Bobbie. I'd love to see you. And if you come, I promise I'll see what I can do with that crazy hair of yours."

"Uh, considering what you just did to Carl, I think I should wait until I'm sure you're not harboring any passive-aggressive feelings toward me."

Beth-Ann burst out laughing. "Don't worry. I reserve my 'special trims' for 'special people.' I'd never do that to *you*, girlfriend."

"I know. But honestly, Beth-Ann. I don't think my hair's grown out enough for even *you* to work one of your miracles on it."

"Let me be the judge of that. I can't promise I can make it look *fabulous*, but I guarantee I can make it look *intentional*."

I glanced in the mirror in the hallway and ran a hand through my spikey red locks. "At this point, anything would be an improvement. I barely look human."

The bathroom door squeaked open. Grayson passed me in the hallway without a word.

Really? What a jerk!

"Good grief, Beth-Ann," I grumbled into the phone. "Whether Grayson finds me attractive or not, the guy could at least acknowledge my existence, right?"

"You know the old saying," she said. "'If you can't bring Mohamed to the mountain, bring the mountain to Mohamed.' Or was it, 'Don't make a mountain out of a molehill?'"

"Ha ha," I said sourly. "Thanks for all your sage advice, Beth-Ann. I can always count on you."

Chapter Three

I slipped into the RV's tiny bathroom, wiped the steam from the mirror, and examined my hair. If Beth-Ann had taught me *anything*, it was this: If your hair doesn't look good, *you* don't look good.

I, personally, looked as if I'd just survived a last date with Old Sparky.

Geez. No wonder Grayson doesn't find me sexy.

I needed a Beth-Ann styling miracle, and I needed it bad. But how could I convince Grayson to take a detour to Point Paradise? Grayson was head of operations. To get my way, I was going to have to turn his head...

I plucked my eyebrows and applied pink lip gloss. With no other options coming to mind, I splashed water onto my hands and slicked my spikey auburn locks hair behind my ears. Forget *Experiment #5* for the moment. I had to find out where I stood in the *love* department.

Is Grayson interested in me that way? Or am I just his doormat sidekick?

I padded to the main cabin. As usual, Grayson was snugged into the banquette, tapping away at his laptop.

I stood tall, cleared my throat, and went fishing for compliments. "Umm ... Grayson?"

He looked up. "Yes?"

"Uh ... as your P.I. intern, what would you say is my best attribute?"

Grayson surveyed me with his all-seeing green eyes. "I'd say it's that you're not a typical woman."

My brow furrowed. "What do you mean by that?"

"You're not consumed by frivolous activities designed solely to enhance your physical appearance."

My ears caught fire. "Is that supposed to be some kind of joke?"

"Joke?" he asked.

"You heard me," I grumbled. "Wait. Were you listening in on my phone conversation with Beth-Ann?"

His left eyebrow arched. "That would be a breach of trust."

"Trust!" I laughed jadedly. "It's *you* who doesn't trust *me*!"

Grayson's shoulders straightened beneath his black shirt. "Why would you say that?"

"*Why*? Because of *this*!" I stuck my nose in the air and imitated Grayson's voice. '*That's on a need to know basis, Drex.*'"

Grayson's face lost all expression.

"I see," he said finally, and let out a slow breath. "Let's review, shall we? I hired you as my intern, Drex. You live with me in this RV. You have access to everything in it. And when your cousin Earl broke your bed, I let you sleep with me in mine. Yet for some reason, you still think I don't trust you. This may come across as ironic, but it may be *you* who has the serious trust issues."

My gut flopped.

Crap! Maybe he's right...

I cringed. My mind swirled, searching for a way to backpedal out of this mess. "I just meant tha—"

Crrssttcrk. Crrrchh.

From the driver's cab, the sound of static crackled through the air. As my mouth hung open mid-syllable, a familiar voice buzzed over the ham radio.

"Operative Garth to Mr. Gray. Come in, Mr. Gray. Over."

I glanced at Grayson. He appeared as relieved as I was.

"Hold that thought," Grayson said, then scrambled out of the banquette toward the driver's seat. I followed behind him, then flounced into the passenger seat a few feet away.

"Gray here," Grayson said, clicking a button on the microphone. "Come in, Operative Garth. Over."

"Mr. Gray! Thank God!" Garth almost shouted.

His normally nerdy, laid-back voice sounded awash with urgency—and something else. Panic, perhaps?

"Is Pandora with you?" he asked. "Over."

"Yes," I shouted.

"She's here," Grayson said. "Over."

"I need your help. Over."

"What kind of paranormal activity are we talking about?" I asked. When Garth didn't reply, I added a hasty, "Over."

"My brother Jimmy. Something's wrong with him. Over."

Grayson's eyebrow crooked into a triangle. "Has he sought medical treatment? Over."

"I ... I don't know. Four days ago, he and a friend of his went fishing. I found out today that his friend is missing." Garth's voice trailed off. "Jimmy's been acting really weird ever since. Over."

"Weird how?" I asked. "Over"

His voice cracked. "It's hard to explain. Over."

"We need more specifics," Grayson said. "Over."

"I can't. Not over the radio. Over."

Those last words from Garth caused my own eyebrows to shoot up an inch.

From what I knew of Operative Garth, he'd never had a problem yammering over the ham radio about everything from vampires to alien invasions. What could possibly be so weird about Jimmy's behavior that Garth couldn't mention it over the airwaves? I exchanged glances with Grayson. He seemed to be wondering the same thing.

"Is Jimmy in danger? Over," Grayson asked.

Garth cleared his throat. "If what I think is true, we *all* are."

"What do you mean?" Grayson asked. "Over."

"Uh ... hold on," Garth said, his voice suddenly hoarse. "Jimmy just—"

The signal went dead.

"Operative Garth?" Grayson prompted.

No reply.

"Operative Garth?" Grayson barked again into the microphone. "Come in, OG. Over."

We sat in the cab in silence for a full minute. Static was the only response we could raise on the radio.

I locked eyes with Grayson. "Is your radio broken?"

He fiddled with a few buttons on the black box mounted under the dashboard. "No. It's operating normally."

I bit my lower lip. "Then Garth's radio must've died."

"Let's hope it's as simple as that." Grayson pulled his cellphone from his shirt pocket and dialed Garth's number. "He's not answering."

"Let's give him a couple of minutes," I said. "He sounded *off* somehow. Maybe he's just ... you know ... indisposed."

"That must be it," Grayson said, clicking off the phone. "I'm sure he's all right."

But in the silence that followed, neither one of us believed it.

Chapter Four

The toothless old woman in green polyester pants stared at us like we were crazy, then clutched her purse tighter to her body and steered her shopping cart toward the other side of the Walmart parking lot.

"Hush!" I hissed at Grayson. "You're scaring the locals."

"All I said was that aliens are—"

"Hush!"

After Operative Garth had gone mysteriously radio silent, Grayson had been unable to reach him, despite numerous attempts. The strange little prepper wasn't answering his cellphone, either.

At the time, Grayson and I had been camped out in the Walmart parking lot in Chiefland, Florida. Needless to say, neither of us had required further encouragement to pull stakes and head out of town. After leaving a message on Garth's phone, we started packing up and setting our sights on Plant City—home of a giant strawberry water tower and Garth and Jimmy's junk-filled prepper compound.

I smiled apologetically at the old lady as she hobbled by, pushing her unwieldy, wobbly-wheeled shopping cart. She shook her head at us and avoided eye contact.

Great. I'm the weirdo here.

I hissed at Grayson. "For the last time, Garth was *not* abducted by aliens!"

"I disagree," Grayson said, hoisting a cooler up the steps of the RV. "Like Schrodinger's cat, it's a plausible theory until proven otherwise."

"No, it's not!"

Grayson shoved the cooler inside the decrepit Mini-Winnie. "Then what's your explanation for Garth suddenly going incommunicado?"

"It could be anything," I grumbled. "But say 'alien abduction' one more time and I'll render *you* incommunicado!"

Grayson's eyebrow rose an inch. "I don't see why you have to get all huffy about it. I'm merely speculating on possible scenarios."

"Ugh!" I snatched up a cheap lawn chair. Grayson had set up a pair so we could dine alfresco amid the ambiance of asphalt and exhaust fumes. I folded it savagely, then handed it to Grayson.

"Those boys live in a junkyard," I said. "Any number of things could've happened to either one of them. Maybe a rusty refrigerator fell on their heads, for all we know."

"Don't be preposterous," Grayson said, tossing the lawn chair inside the RV.

I blanched. "*I'm* the one being preposterous? Let me remind you—the only reason we're in this stupid parking lot in this stupid town is because you wanted to search for stupid 'secret Native American treasure.'"

Grayson shrugged. "I fail to see what's preposterous about that. Chiefland calls itself 'The Gem of the Suwanee Valley.'"

My upper lip hooked skyward. "So?"

"Think about it, Drex. *Chief*land. *Gems*. I was merely following the intellectual thread hidden in plain sight. You know. Like they did in *The Da Vinci Code*."

I closed my eyes and took a deep breath. Since arriving in Chiefland two days ago, the closest thing to an "intellectual thread" we'd discovered was the town's quirky quilt museum. And the closest thing to an "ancient relic" was the person running it.

I grabbed the second lawn chair and kicked it until it collapsed. "Get this straight in your head, Grayson. There are no *chiefs* in Chiefland, and no *aliens* in Plant City!"

Grayson sniffed. "You're entitled to your opinion, Drex. And *I'm* entitled to mine."

I opened my mouth to argue, but Grayson silenced me with the wag of a spidery index finger. "Without additional facts, there's no point in postulating further about either subject. Agreed?"

I let out a breath. "Agreed."

"Good. Are you ready to go?"

"I couldn't *be* any readier."

"Grab the lantern over there and let's roll."

"Why don't *you* grab—" I began, then stopped myself. Remembering my covert mission to get to Point Paradise for a haircut by Beth-Ann, I sweetened my tone. "I mean, 'Got it, chief.'"

I grabbed the lantern and smiled at Grayson. "You know, since we're heading out, do you think we could make a pit stop in Point—"

Grayson's cellphone rang. He glanced at the display. "I better get this."

"Who is it?" I asked. "Garth?"

Grayson shot me a quick glance. "That's on a need-to-know basis, Drex."

Then he turned and disappeared into the RV—totally unaware that I'd missed whacking him in the ass with that lantern by less than three inches.

I WAS STILL GRINDING my teeth when the RV's half-bald tires spun up a cloud of dust across the Walmart parking lot.

After clicking off his mysterious phone call, Grayson hadn't had the courtesy to offer me a single word of explanation. Instead, he'd jammed the keys into the ignition and peeled out of the lot like he'd just gotten word the last taco stand on the planet was closing in two minutes.

"What the heck's going on?" I demanded, my arms folded over my chest. Miffed at being ignored and left out of the loop, I was determined to make Grayson trust me—even if I had to use every deceitful trick in the book.

"He's dead," Grayson said, tucking his cellphone into his shirt pocket.

I gasped. Then I wilted with horror. "Dead?"

"Yes, I'm afraid so." Grayson shook his head and pulled onto the highway. "What a tremendous loss to paranormal research."

I sat back in the passenger seat, stunned. A tear came to my eye. I scrounged in my purse for a Tootsie Pop to console my aching heart.

Garth had been a harmless, goofball nerd. Sure, he'd been a weirdo conspiracy chaser. And he hadn't exactly given Brad Pitt anything to worry about, either. Garth had been short and wiry, with thick, black glasses, a frizzy, bleached-blond mullet, and buck teeth that would've made a donkey cringe in shame. But all in all, he'd been a pretty decent guy.

Plus, he'd always thought I was a babe.

"Poor guy. How'd he die?" I asked.

Grayson sighed. "Age-related causes."

I stuck the Tootsie Pop into my mouth, barely able to conceive of the notion. "He seemed so young. I thought he was in his late twenties, tops."

Grayson nodded solemnly. "The truly inspired do often seem to defy the effects of time."

"So, how old *was* he?"

"Ninety-two."

I choked on my sucker. "Garth was *ninety-two*?"

Grayson shot me a look. "Garth? No. I'm talking about The Amazing Randi."

My eyes shot twin death-rays at Grayson. I'd have hurled my Tootsie Pop at him if it hadn't been my last watermelon-flavored one. "Who the heck is Amazing Randi?"

"What?" Grayson gasped and nearly ran the RV off into the ditch.

After regaining control of the vehicle, he turned and stared at me as if I'd come from another planet. "Not Amazing Randi. *The* Amazing Randi. He's only the greatest scientific skeptic and paranormal debunker who ever lived!"

"Debunker?"

Grayson let out an indignant grunt. "Really, Drex. I'm sure I mentioned him before. He co-founded the Committee for Skeptical Inquiry?"

I shrugged. "Uh...not ringing any bells."

"Don't you remember? The Amazing Randi's mission in life was to challenge and disprove paranormal and pseudoscientific claims from around the world."

My upper lip hooked skyward. "Uh, no offense. But from what I've seen, there's a *ton* of guys out there doing the same thing. You and Garth included. What was so great about Randi?"

"*The Amazing* Randi," Grayson corrected again. "Well, for one, he put his money where his mouth is."

I smirked. "That must've made it hard for him to eat."

Grayson eyed me as if I'd just had a seizure. "I'll give you a pass this time. But only because of your utter ignorance."

"Gee, thanks." I stifled an urgent eye roll and decided to play nice. "So tell me, Grayson. How did *The Amazing* Randi put his money where his mouth is?"

"By creating the James Randi Educational Foundation. It offers a million dollars to anyone who can prove their own supernatural powers or the presence of a supernatural being."

The million dollars prompted something in my brain. "Oh, yeah. I remember you saying something about that not long after we met." I smirked. "I bet the thought of getting a million bucks really brings the kooks running."

"They've examined a few claims over the years," Grayson conceded.

"Let me guess. No winners yet?"

Grayson let out a sigh so deep his chest sunk inward. "No. Over the last sixty years, thousands have tried for the prize. But no one has ever gotten beyond the master's unsurpassed ability to spot tricks and fakery."

"What makes—I mean *made*—Randi so good at spotting fakes?"

"Simple," Grayson said. "He was a master magician."

I laughed. "Oh. Of course. That explains everything."

Grayson's face grew stern. "I'm serious, Drex. The Amazing Randi was every bit on par with Houdini."

"Seriously?"

"Yes. He knew every trick in the book. In fact, one of his most famous acts was escaping from a locked coffin submerged in water. He also got out of a straitjacket while dangling over Niagara Falls."

"You don't say," I said. "So, is that how you got out? Escaping from a straitjacket?"

Grayson glanced over at me. "Ha ha."

"So Randi was an escape artist," I said. "What's the big deal? I've gone out with at least half a dozen guys who disappeared when the check arrived. Nothing magical about that."

"That was kind of his point," Grayson said.

"What do you mean?"

"The Amazing Randi traveled the globe doing feats that appeared to require otherworldly powers. But at the end of each performance, he always concluded his show with this simple statement,

'Everything you have seen here is tricks. There is nothing supernatural involved."

"Oh." I sat up in my seat. "So, in other words, Randi used magic to prove there was no such thing as magic."

Grayson's left eyebrow flat-lined. "Well, yes."

"And that's what made him famous?"

Grayson shrugged. "That and his obsession with debunking people who claimed they could read minds and whatnot."

"You don't think mind-reading's possible?"

"No."

For some reason, I felt oddly relieved. I smiled. "So, how'd Randi get so famous?"

"Back in 1972, The Amazing Randi was invited to *The Johnny Carson Show* to oversee the props used by Uri Geller."

"Uri Geller? What power did he claim to have?"

Grayson turned his head from the road and stared at me, a pained expression on his face. "You're kidding. Uri Geller? He was only the most famous psychokinetic practitioner of his time."

"Psycho *what*?"

Grayson winced. "Psychokinesis. It's the ability to manipulate physical matter without physical intervention."

"Oh. Cool. What did Geller do to prove his claim?"

"He bent spoons with his mind."

I sneered. "*Bent spoons*? Geez. I can think of a few better things to do with a talent like that."

"*If* such a talent exists," Grayson said. "During that episode of *The Johnny Carson Show*, Geller failed."

I smirked. "Are you saying no utensils were harmed in the making of that show?"

"I suppose. But you're missing the point."

"No, I'm not. He proved Geller was a fake, right?"

"More or less. The show was basically twenty-two minutes of Geller staring at spoons."

I laughed. "So, how'd Randi stop him?"

"He wouldn't say. The Amazing Randi was first and foremost a magician. And, being a gentleman, he never revealed his secrets."

I noticed a dimple form in Grayson's cheek. "You admired This Amazing Randi guy, didn't you?"

"Absolutely. He was one of a kind."

I cocked my head. "Isn't that rather ironic?"

"What do you mean?"

"The Amazing Randi was a paranormal *skeptic*. I figured you'd consider him your enemy. Or at least your rival."

Grayson's eyebrow arched. "Why would you think that?"

"I dunno. I guess because *you* want to prove the paranormal *exists*. Randi wanted to prove it *didn't*."

Grayson shrugged. "I don't see the conflict."

"You *don't*?"

"No. Drex, to prove something scientifically, one must be willing to examine all the facts and accept the conclusions they yield. The same set of facts that might lead to proving something's existence might instead lead to proving the exact opposite."

"Okay, but—"

Grayson turned his gaze toward me again. "Don't you see? Only by eliminating human bias—including fraudsters, cheaters, charlatans, and other falsifiers—can we arrive at the unadulterated *truth*. And, ultimately, the truth is what we seek, is it not?"

"Uh...sure," I said, then laughed.

"What's funny?"

"You sound like you're channeling Buddha or something."

"Not possible. The Amazing Randi proved channeling is a hoax."

I smirked. "Perhaps he just never met a *real* channeler."

"Perhaps. And now he never will." Grayson let out a sigh and stepped on the gas.

I could tell the news of his death had affected Grayson deeply. "Where did Randi die?" I asked softly.

"In Plantation, Florida," he said. "It's not that far from Plant City. I thought we might pay our respects while we're in the area."

"Sure. Why not?"

As I turned to face the road ahead, my thoughts wandered back to Garth's voice on the ham radio. He'd sounded strangely hoarse. Panicked, even.

Geez. I hope Randi's grave is the only one we'll be visiting on this trip...

Chapter Five

A s Grayson steered the old Winnebago off the I-4 exit ramp toward Lakeland, the anxiety that had been gnawing at the pit of my stomach for hours amped up its pitch. In a few more minutes, we'd be at Garth's prepper compound.

What could've happened to him and his brother Jimmy?

As opposite as bookends, Garth was a goofy-looking, *Wayne's World* wannabee. He was the kind of nerd you'd expect to find holed up in a basement playing *World of Warcraft* with his imaginary online "friends."

Even so, Garth was no dummy. The first time we'd met, he'd managed to weasel a hundred bucks out of Grayson for pictures of Lester Jenkins, a UFO nut who'd allegedly been turned into man-pudding.

In contrast, Jimmy Wells, Garth's brother, was the quintessential all-American boy. Handsome. Athletic. Clean-cut. And a rookie policeman. When he'd caught me and Grayson entering a taped-off crime scene, Jimmy had arrested us on the spot—at gunpoint. He'd cuffed us and read us our rights, doing everything exactly by the book.

But Jimmy had proved to be as naïve as he was straight-laced. Grayson and I'd quickly turned the tables on him. And later, Jimmy had gone off the deep-end, believing some pretty wild things based on some pretty sketchy evidence.

The odd-couple brothers lived together in a so-called "survivalist" compound that appeared, ironically, as if it had been ground zero for a recent apocalypse. Given the massive quantities of junk filling both their premises and their minds, any number of improbable things could've happened to the pair—from botulism to blowing themselves to smithereens.

If they *were* both dead, I wondered what would happen to their massive guard dog, Tooth. I pictured the huge, black hound and shook my head. It wasn't likely another prepper would adopt him.

Although Tooth appeared as intimidating as one of the hounds of Hell, the poor pooch was all bark and no bite. In fact, when visitors came, Garth had to put Tooth in a cage—not to keep the dog from attacking, but so he wouldn't pee all over the floor from sheer fright. Not that it would matter. Their place would make a pig cry for his sty.

"Not much longer," Grayson said, interrupting my thoughts. He turned off the main road. "We should be there in a few minutes."

"Right." I unhooked my seatbelt and climbed out of the passenger seat.

"Where you going?" he asked.

"I gotta pee."

"We're almost there. Can't you wait?"

"And use *their* bathroom? Are you kidding?"

"You're right," Grayson said. "Good thinking. We wouldn't want to disturb any evidence."

"Yeah." I smirked. "My thought process exactly."

AS I SCURRIED BACK to the passenger seat, Grayson turned onto a narrow, asphalt lane. I recognized it as one bisecting the rural suburb Jimmy and Garth called home.

The brothers' compound was one of a dozen or so prepper-type properties that dotted the otherwise undeveloped stretch of native palmetto-and-pine woodlands. Most of these rural homesteads featured modest single- or doublewide trailers situated on four or five acres. All were tucked safely behind chain-link security fences that probably cost more than their aluminum-clad homes.

As we drew near the brothers' property, I rolled down the passenger window and stuck my head out for a better view.

At first glance, everything seemed in order at the Wells' country establishment. The algae-covered double-wide trailer was still standing where it always had—partially hidden by trees, overgrown bushes, and an assortment of rusty household appliances. Next to the trailer sat a satellite dish so huge I suspected it probably once belonged to a TV station.

"Anything seem out of place?" Grayson asked, eyeing the compound himself.

My nose crinkled. "If it *were*, how could we tell?"

"By *that*," Grayson said, and nodded toward the front gate.

To the left of the dirt driveway, a metal flagpole displayed a black flag flying at half-mast, sagging sadly in the anemic breeze.

It took me a few seconds to make out the neon-green form flowing from its dark background. It was a skull and crossbones—only the skull was elongated, and its empty eye sockets were double the normal size.

I grimaced. "Don't tell me E.T. died, too."

Ignoring me, Grayson maneuvered the RV up to the gate. It was the only entry point in the eight-foot-tall, chain-link fence surrounding the compound. He rolled down the window and reached out to mash a button on the intercom mounted on a thick, metal post.

There was no response.

"That's odd. Garth usually answers right away," I said.

"Hmm," Grayson grunted, and mashed the intercom button again.

From somewhere inside the compound, I thought I heard the faint sound of a dog barking.

Tooth!

I chewed my bottom lip. "What do we do now?"

Grayson locked eyes with me. "The only logical thing left *to* do."

I grimaced. "Call the cops?"

"Crash the gate."

"But—"

Grayson shifted the RV into reverse.

I grabbed his arm. "Wait! Are you serious?"

"Absolutely," he said, jerking his arm free. "Garth's in trouble. It's our duty to come to his aid."

"Who goes there?" a raspy voice crackled over the intercom. It sounded like the ghost of Garth.

Grayson scrambled to mash the intercom button again. "Gray here. Pandora, too."

"Mister Gray!" the voice hacked. "Thank God you came!"

Chapter Six

When Garth opened the front door to his trailer, it became clear to me that the impending apocalypse he'd been prepping for had finally come to pass. Not only did he *sound* like his own ghost, he looked the part as well.

"Come in," he croaked, waving us inside with a pale, boney hand.

He shuffled a few hobbling steps backward to let us enter, then blinked at us through crusty, bloodshot eyes magnified three times their size by the thick lenses of his Poindexter-brand glasses.

Garth's normally frizzy blond mullet was a tan-colored oil slick. His sweatpants and T-shirt appeared to have come straight from the laundry hamper—and I didn't mean the clean one. Worst yet, he looked like he'd aged fifty years since I last saw him.

I cringed. My breath suddenly froze inside my lungs—not from the temperature, but from *fear*. I glanced around his hoarder hovel, images of *The Andromeda Strain* dancing inside my head.

Where's a damned hazmat suit when you need one?

Grayson seemed to be thinking the same thing. He took a step back and asked, "What's going on here? Biological warfare?"

"No," Garth said, then proceeded to have a coughing fit. "I think it's just a bad cold. Maybe the flu. Can't hold anything down. But never mind about me. It's Jimmy I'm worried about."

Garth hacked up a lung like a seasoned chain-smoker, making me double down on my wish for a hazmat suit. "Ginger tea?" Garth asked, then coughed again into a tissue.

I glanced around at the kitchen. It was obvious the two brothers lived alone without adult supervision. I hadn't seen a place so beyond repair since the *Times* did that full-color spread on Chernobyl.

"Uh, no thanks," I said. I clasped my hands together to avoid touching anything.

"How about a donut, then?" Garth proffered an oil-stained bag. Through the smudged cellophane window, deep-fried clumps of dough languished greasily.

I smiled, and shook my head.

Not a chance on this Earth.

"We just ate," Grayson lied. "But I'll take some coffee if you have it."

Garth coughed into his hand. "Coming right up."

I shot Grayson a horrified stare.

"I'll do it," Grayson said, getting the message. "Sit down, Operative Garth. Save your strength and tell us what's going on."

Garth's shoulders slumped with relief. He flopped onto the sofa like a dirty dishrag.

I sat in a chair on the opposite side of the room. On the coffee table between us, amid empty tissue boxes and heaps of soiled Kleenex, I noticed a framed photograph. It was Garth standing next to some short, bald guy in a wizard hat. The old man looked like a garden dwarf, complete with bushy white eyebrows, a beard, and gold-rimmed glasses.

I nodded toward the picture. "Who's the gnome?"

Garth blanched as if I'd slapped him. "That's not a *gnome*. That's my Svengali."

I picked up the photo and studied the guy's face. His eyes seemed to twinkle like jolly old St. Nick's. "Is this Gandhi?"

"No," Garth croaked. "But close. They both believed in truth and non-violence."

I glanced up at Garth, losing my patience. "Okay. So, who's the old dude?"

He blew his nose and almost smiled. "Pandora, you're looking at a picture of Randall James Hamilton Zwinge."

My nose crinkled. "Who?"

"What?" Grayson yelled from the kitchen. He sprinted into the living room and nearly knocked me over as he grabbed the photo from my hand. He stared down at picture, then up at Garth.

"You met The Amazing Randi?" Grayson asked.

Garth nodded. "Well, yeah. He's actually my uncle, twice removed. Jimmy was named after him. So was I."

My nose crinkled. "I thought your name was Gary."

"That's my middle name. My first name is Randall."

I winced. "My condolences."

Garth nodded sadly. "So you heard about him passing, then."

"Oh." I sat up straighter. "Well, yes. And I'm also sorry you got named Randall."

He shrugged. "Could've been worse."

"How?"

"Ask my cousin, Zwinge."

I grimaced, then shifted uncomfortably. "Uh ... I heard Randi died of natural causes."

"Yeah," Garth said. "He didn't have any choice in the matter." He turned to Grayson and winked a bloodshot eye. "As you know, he didn't believe in *unnatural* ones."

He and Grayson grinned at each other, then laughed like a pair of nerdy hyenas.

Seriously?

"Sorry to break up the fun," I said. "But what's going on with your brother Jimmy?"

Garth's grin evaporated. "That's just it. I can't say for sure."

Garth coughed again. I covered my mouth with my hand. "Does he have the same plague you do?"

"No," Garth said, shaking his head vehemently. "Jimmy's not sick. I mean, not the way *I* am. He's just been...I dunno...acting *weird* lately."

"Weird like what?" Grayson asked. "We need specifics."

Garth shrugged. "I dunno. He's been acting all *sneaky*."

"Sneaky?" I asked. "We drove all this way because Jimmy's acting *sneaky?*"

"Something's wrong with him, I know it!" Garth said. "He's been making secret phone calls. Sneaking out at night. Stuff like that."

I smirked. "Maybe he's got a girlfriend."

Garth's greasy eyebrows rose an inch. It was obvious the idea had never occurred to him.

"Maybe you're right, Pandora," Garth said. "But, I mean, who would go out with *him?*"

I drew a mental image of Jimmy. He was a slim, well-built young man with all his facial features in the right place. For rural Florida, he was a hunk.

"I don't know," I said. "Lots of women are suckers for a man in uniform."

"Maybe," Garth coughed. "But I think it's something else."

"You told us over the radio a friend of his disappeared," Grayson said.

"You think Jimmy killed his friend and is trying to cover it up?" I blurted.

"What?" Garth gasped. "No! I think he's joined some secret club or something. Maybe even a cult."

I nearly blanched. Uptight, by-the-book Jimmy in a toga, dancing and chanting in some kind of cult? No way!

On the one hand, it didn't make sense. But then again, Jimmy teetered on the edge of two worlds. By day, he was a rookie cop. By night, he shared a prepper compound with a known conspiracy nutter. That was a pretty huge seesaw to ride—both socially and professionally.

Then I remembered that during our last investigation, Garth's loose lips about our alien abduction theories had gotten back to the police station where Jimmy worked. The poor guy had gone from golden child to laughingstock in under sixty seconds.

"A cult?" Grayson asked. "Why do you think that?"

"Because he's not the same person anymore," Garth said.

"What do you mean?" Grayson asked. "Has he experienced a sudden personality change?"

Garth winced. "Sort of."

"Hmm," Grayson said. "Perhaps Pandora's right. Murder suspects often exhibit—"

"He didn't do it!" Garth yelled. "I know my brother!" He shrunk back in his seat. "Sorry, Mr. Gray. No disrespect, but I know something's wrong with him. I don't know how else to explain it."

"We're trying to help," I said. "What other evidence do you have?"

"Only this." Garth picked up a remote and clicked on the TV monitor. "Here. Take a look at this surveillance footage."

The TV set pinged on. Fuzzy, black-and-white static filled the screen. A few seconds later, the pixelated snow cleared and the wide derriere of a pudgy, shaggy-haired guy hoisting himself into a battered old pickup came into view.

"Isn't that Jimmy's old truck?" Grayson asked.

Garth sniffed. "Yeah."

"Who's the fat guy? A thief?" I asked.

"No," Garth croaked. "That's *Jimmy*."

My jaw dropped. "You're kidding."

Jimmy's once square jawline had gone round and jowly. His dimpled chin had duplicated itself. In the months since I'd seen him, Garth's brother had to have packed on forty pounds, minimum.

"Intriguing," Grayson said. "What do you think he's gotten involved with?"

I sneered. "It certainly ain't Weight Watchers."

"He won't tell me," Garth said. "Jimmy only said that he'd found a 'life-changing opportunity.'"

Yeah. To get diabetes...

"Play the video again," Grayson said.

Garth fumbled with the remote and reset the video. "He hasn't come home for days. I need you two to find him. Figure out what he's up to."

"I'd say about two-fifty," Grayson said.

I elbowed my partner, then turned to Garth. "Why don't you just contact his friends on the force?"

Garth blanched. "And get Jimmy fired? They already think he's a flake, thanks to me." He shook his head. "No. I need *your* help. Jimmy blew up like that practically overnight."

Grayson studied the video. "If that's true, there's definitely something abnormal going on. Any ideas where Jimmy's been going or doing?"

Garth sighed. "None. I asked him a couple of times. All he would say was he was 'Going out.' I've been too sick to tail him."

My nose crinkled. "How are *we* supposed to find him without any clues?"

"I did a thing," Garth said.

My upper lip hooked skyward. "What?"

Garth sat up a little straighter. A determined look formed on his face. "I LoJacked his ass."

"Indeed," Grayson said, his eyebrow arching. "I thought LoJack was only available to members of law enforcement."

Garth slumped back into the couch. "Busted, Mr. Gray. But I did tag him, sort of."

"How?" Grayson asked.

"The last time Jimmy came home, I slipped my cellphone into his gym bag."

"Why?" I asked.

"You know, so I could track the GPS signal."

"Good thinking," Grayson said.

"So what's with all that 'LoJacked his ass' business?" I asked.

Garth shrugged. "I dunno. It guess it just sounded a lot cooler."

"Understandable," Grayson said. "So, were you able to track your brother?"

"Yes and no." Garth sneezed. "That was the last time I saw him. Wherever he's been going, it's in the boondocks. The signal skips out after he passes Turkey Creek Road."

"Hmm," Grayson grunted. "That gives us a good point to start. Anything else you can tell us?"

Garth grimaced. "Well, maybe. A couple of days ago, Jimmy left a message on the land line." Garth blinked up at us blankly.

"Well, let's hear it," I grumbled impatiently.

Garth frowned. "Christ. It's Frickin' Krull."

I blanched. "I didn't think I was *that* crabby."

Garth's bloodshot eyes widened. "No. Not *you*, Miss Pandora. That's what *Jimmy* said. 'Christ. It's Frickin' Krull.'"

My mouth fell open. I glanced over at Grayson.

"Krull?" Grayson said. "Are you absolutely positive?"

"Yeah." Garth honked at the snot building up in his nostrils.

"Hmm." Grayson rubbed his chin. "I don't recall Krull being mentioned in my cryptid research or in ancient mythology."

"Me either," Garth said. "The only thing I could find on it was a *Star Wars* knock-off movie called *Krull* made back in 1983."

"What's it about?" I asked.

Garth sighed. "It's one of those interplanetary, swashbuckling schmaltz fests."

I smirked. "How many times did you watch it?"

Garth winced. "Eighteen."

"So, who was Krull?" Grayson asked.

Garth shook his head. "That's just it. Krull was nobody."

Grayson's brow furrowed. "What do you *mean*, nobody?"

Garth pushed his black glasses up on his puffy red nose. "In the movie, Krull wasn't a person. Krull was a *planet*."

I glanced over at the TV. The video was freeze-framed on Jimmy's fat butt bending over the bench seat of his truck. "Well, that makes perfect sense, given the fact that Jimmy's ass is the size of an asteroid."

"Please, guys," Garth said. "You gotta help me—and quick. I think something big is about to go down, and soon."

"What makes you believe that?" Grayson asked.

"Because I've never seen Jimmy with a sword before."

I nearly swallowed my tonsils. "*A sword*?"

"Yeah," Garth sniffed. "It got delivered two days ago. He unpacked it and took it with him. I haven't seen him since."

I shook my head. "How is any of this possible?"

Garth shrugged. "Easy. Nowadays, you can get anything on Amazon."

Chapter Seven

Dusk had fallen on the rural outskirts of Plant City, mercifully softening the hard edges of the rusted out truck chassis and decaying trailer homes that served as points of interest in Garth's backwoods neighborhood.

We'd waited until dark to begin our search for Jimmy for two reasons. One was for fear Jimmy might recognize Grayson's old RV and get spooked. The second was that, try as he might, Garth couldn't get a GPS bearing on Jimmy. Either his brother had driven out of signal range, or Garth's cellphone battery had died.

While we'd waited to see if the signal would reappear, Grayson and Garth had discussed pertinent geeky details of the case. As for me, I'd taken the liberty to run some errands, including picking up chicken soup and Nyquil for Garth—and disinfectant wipes and zinc lozenges for me and Grayson.

When I'd returned, so had the GPS signal emanating from Garth's covert cellphone. Grayson and I had dropped off the groceries, then jumped in the RV and headed out before the signal petered out again.

"Which way should I turn?" Grayson asked as he came to a stop at an intersection marked only by a stop sign full of bullet holes.

"I don't know. How do you work this thing?" I asked, then bitch-slapped the side of the plastic gizmo in my hand. It looked like a transistor radio—without any knobs.

"What are you trying to do?" Grayson asked.

"Track Jimmy's cellphone, like you said."

"Drex, that's a bug sweeper."

"Eww!"

I flung the device onto the floorboard, then kicked it back under the seat where I'd found it. "Gross! Where's the hand-sanitizer I bought?"

"Not *that* kind of bug."

"Oh." I grimaced, then smiled sheepishly. "You meant the, 'Do you think you're being *bugged*,' kind of bug."

Grayson pursed his lips. "Exactly."

I frowned. "Well, *do* you?"

"Do I what?"

"Think you're being bugged!"

Grayson's eyebrow arched. "I will if you continue with this line of questioning."

"Hardy har har." I crossed my arms, stared out the window, and gnawed resentfully on the Tootsie Pop in my mouth.

"What made you think the bug sweeper was the GPS tracker?" Grayson asked.

I reached down under the seat, snatched up the gizmo and shoved it in my partner's face. "Maybe because it says, *R F Signal Detector* on it?"

"R-F stands for radio frequency, not wifi signal."

"Oh." My brow furrowed. "What's the difference?"

Grayson stared at the road ahead for a full minute, then muttered, "There are subtle differences."

I smirked. "Ha! You don't *know*, do you? Finally, a question 'The Great Grayson' doesn't know the answer to! Ha ha!"

Grayson blew out a breath. "Okay. *Now* you're officially bugging me."

"Not according to this thing," I said, grinning and wagging the device in the air. "See? The light's green."

Grayson shook his head. "That means the signal is clear. No one's listening in."

"Oh." I turned down the sarcasm a notch. "Why do you have this thing, anyway? Who would want to listen in on our conversations?"

"You'd be surprised."

Anger poked a hot finger into my brain. I studied Grayson for a moment, a scowl forming on my lips. "I *might* be, if you'd ever *tell* me anything."

Grayson sighed. "This is a discussion for another time, Drex. Right now, we need to get a bead on the phone Garth hid in Jimmy's bag."

I shifted uncomfortably. "Fine. How we gonna do that?"

"With the very latest in detection equipment. Maybe you've heard of it?"

Grayson shot me a sour face and reached into his breast pocket. "It's a newfangled gadget called a 'cellphone.'"

"Oh."

Grayson punched a key on his phone and handed it to me. "Here."

I snatched the phone from his hand, my face burning with embarrassment. "I thought they just *gave out* GPS signals. Who knew you could track somebody else's cellphone with a stupid phone app?"

Grayson's eyebrow shot up. "Everyone except *you*, apparently. Weren't you listening to anything Garth and I said?"

I cringed. I really *had* tried to. But their geek-speak was like chloroform to my attention span. "I guess I kind of lost it when I saw that video of Jimmy."

"It was shocking," Grayson said. "What could make someone gain forty pounds in a matter of days?"

I shook my head. "That's such a guy question. I once gained five pounds just looking through a bakery shop window."

Grayson stared at me blankly. "So, which way do I turn?"

I stared at the phone, trying to figure out the app. "Sorry. How's this thing work?"

"I already input Garth's phone number," Grayson said. "All you have to do is press the little green button marked 'Go.'"

My ears went up in flames. "Oh."

I clicked the button. A map popped onto the display. "Wow. That's pretty cool."

"Handy, isn't it?"

"Oh, look!" I said. "A red dot. And it's moving!"

"Excellent. We've got a bead on Jimmy. Which way is he headed?"

I grabbed some cheater glasses out of the glove compartment and slapped them on my nose. "Uh ... south. Out of town. Take a right."

Grayson turned the steering wheel to the right, maneuvering the old Minnie Winnie onto a rural state road not much wider than the one we'd just left.

I glanced down at the phone again. "Okay, good. Go straight ahead for a mile or two."

"Is Jimmy stationary, or still moving?"

"Moving, I think."

Grayson gave a quick nod, his gaze glued to the road ahead. "Keep an eye on the signal. Let me know when we're close."

"I will."

But as I watched the dark woods flit by the passenger window, anxiety began to grow in my gut. I studied Grayson for a moment, then posed a question.

"Are you sure it's such a good idea to be doing this without backup?"

Grayson straightened in his driver's seat, but kept his eyes on the road. "Why would we need backup?"

"Uh...let's see. We're alone. At night. On some backwoods road to Hicksville—tracking a young, possibly plague-ridden cop who happens to be armed with a service revolver and a freakin' *sword*. Did I mention he's been acting unstable lately?"

Grayson shrugged. "There has to be a reasonable explanation for Jimmy's behavior, Drex. And remember, we're doing this in the service of a friend. Garth asked us to keep the cops out of it for his brother's sake."

I blew out a sigh. "I know. Take the next right."

Grayson shook his head. "There is no right."

I rolled my eyes. "This is no time to get philosophical."

"No," Grayson said. "There is nowhere to turn right."

I glanced back down at the display. "There should be. It says on the map here that Jimmy's vehicle is off to the right about three hundred feet ahead."

Grayson strained to see the road ahead. "If he *is*, he's gone off-road."

I stared at the woods in the fading sunset. Grayson was right. There was nothing to the right *or* left of us but an uninterrupted thicket of palmettos, cypress, and pines.

"What the?" I pressed my nose to the window pane for a better look. Suddenly, the RV veered off onto the shoulder, causing me to bang my head on the window.

"Ow!" I grumbled. "You could give a girl some warning, you know."

"You're the one who's holding the tracking device," Grayson said calmly. "What did you expect me to do? Fly over the trees like ET?"

Well, now that you mention it...

"I dunno," I grumbled. "I guess we'll have to go the rest of the way on foot."

I jerked open the door and tumbled out of the RV. "Yuck!" I squealed as I sunk up to my ankles in mud.

"What is it?" Grayson asked.

"Forget it! This place is a bog!" I said as I climbed back in. "We'd better get out of here before we get—"

"Stuck?" Grayson said, then punched the gas.

The tires spun.

The RV shimmied.

But we weren't going anywhere.

"Great. Just great!" I yelled, and kicked the floorboard with my muddy boot. "We're gonna need a tow to get out of this mess."

"Excellent deduction, cadet," Grayson said. "Call your cousin Earl."

"What?" I gasped.

Grayson eyed me dully. "You said it yourself. We need a tow."

"Come on, Grayson! It'll take Earl *hours* to get here. We should call someone local."

"Then Jimmy will find out about our investigation."

I frowned. "How do you figure that?"

But I already knew the answer. In small towns like these, the local grapevine didn't have very far to swing. Jimmy would know what we were up to before we could make it back to Garth's compound.

Still, Earl?

"B...but—" I stammered.

Grayson cut me off. "Given the swampy terrain, we're going to require Earl's monster truck to track down Jimmy anyway. It's a win-win, Drex."

"Sounds more like a lose-lose, if you ask me."

Grayson's cheek dimpled. "The sooner you call, the sooner he'll get here."

I swatted a mosquito and groaned. "I know. That's what I'm afraid of."

Chapter Eight

"Earl says it'll take him a couple hours to get here," I said, clicking off the phone.

I glanced over at Grayson. He was busy adding antennae to the smiley faces he'd drawn in the condensation on the windshield.

Not exactly what I'd call a "confidence booster."

While my partner scrawled a few final flourishes on his windowpane masterpiece, I checked the cellphone display. The blip indicating Jimmy's location blinked, then faded out before my eyes.

"He's gone!" I gasped, nudging Grayson with my elbow.

His long, tapered finger jerked on the windshield, spoiling the curlicue on an otherwise impressive alien moustache.

"Earl's gone?" he asked.

"No," I said. "*Jimmy.* He just ... vanished!"

"That's odd," Grayson said. "The cellphone reception must not reach much further than those woods."

"Or Garth's phone just gave up the ghost." I handed Grayson his cellphone. "So, what are we gonna do now, Da Vinci?"

Grayson tucked the phone into his shirt pocket. "What all good detectives do on stakeouts, Drex."

Curiosity furrowed my brow. "Discuss the case?"

"No. Break out the snacks."

Grayson's gaze shot downward. I followed his line of vision and found myself staring at a scruffy little Igloo cooler on the floorboard beside my seat. Garth had handed the cooler to Grayson as we were leaving his trailer.

My spidey senses tingled. "What's in there—besides flu virus and salmonella, I mean."

Grayson smirked. "Open it and find out."

I bristled. "Why don't *you* open it?"

"Because *I'm* the boss."

Ugh! That's the same stupid line Carl used to say.

"*Fine*," I hissed. "But if some stupid alien puppet pops outta there, I'm whacking you upside the head with it."

Grayson laughed. "It's nothing like that."

"Sure, it's not." I reached over and cautiously slid open the lid, keeping the cooler at arm's length. I blinked at the contents once. Then twice.

"Twinkies and Pepsi?" I asked.

Grayson grinned. "Well done, Garth."

"Seriously?" I said sourly. "I think we just solved the mystery of why Jimmy's as big as a hippo."

"No," Grayson said. "You don't understand. That's a tribute to his uncle."

My nose crinkled. "His uncle's a hippo, too?"

"No." Grayson pulled a can of Pepsi from the cooler and cracked the tab with a *whoosh*. "You don't know the story?"

"Obviously not," I said, grabbing a pack of Twinkies and wiping down the cellophane to get rid of the cooties.

"Ah," Grayson cooed. "Then I'll tell you."

His eyes glowed with a faraway look—an expression I'd only seen on his face once before, when he was talking about a chance encounter with Gene Roddenberry.

"Ah, what?" I griped.

"You see, Drex," Grayson waxed philosophically, "legend has it that once—when The Amazing Randi was staking out the trash cans of a purported faith healer—he spent days in his car, surviving on nothing but Twinkies and Pepsi."

My gut flopped.

Good grief. I hope it doesn't come to that...

I'D JUST CRAMMED THE last Twinkie in my mouth when I saw it. A faint, pinkish glow emanating from the swamp—right in the general area where Jimmy's old truck had been when the GPS signal disappeared.

I checked my watch, figuring it must've been around midnight. It was 8:39 p.m.

I groaned, then nudged Grayson, who was draped over the steering wheel, passed out in a sugar coma.

"Wake up," I whispered.

He grunted, then cracked open an eye. "What?"

I nodded toward the woods. "What's that?"

Grayson shot up in his seat. "What's *what*?"

"See it?" I pointed a finger at the passenger window. "That weird glow over there. Coming from the woods."

Grayson leaned across me for a better view. "Yes. I see it!"

The hair on the back of my neck stood up.

Damn. I hadn't just been imagining it.

I grimaced. "Uh ... what do you think it is?"

Grayson snatched a pair of binoculars from the dashboard and pointed them in that direction. "Swamp gas?"

I nearly fell out of my chair. "*Swamp gas*? Seriously? *You* of all people?"

Grayson hung the binocular strap around his neck and reached for the door handle. "There's only one way to find out for sure."

I cringed. "I thought we were going to wait for Earl."

Grayson turned to face me. "*Earl*? Seriously? *You* of all people?"

My face collapsed like a lemon soufflé.

"Touché," I said. "Let's go."

Chapter Nine

" **T**he glow looks like it's coming from that direction," I said, my cowboy boots slogging through the ankle-deep mud a few paces behind Grayson.

I took a last glance back at the RV as we left the cleared shoulder edging the road and slipped into the surrounding forest.

Immediately, my senses were overwhelmed.

The fresh, sharp smell of pine mingled with the odor of rotting cabbage to fill my nostrils. My ears pricked to a cacophony of frog calls and insect chirps. Their orations nearly drowned out the gloppy, sucking sound our boots made with each footstep as we cautiously picked our way around cypress knees in the dark, shin-deep muck.

The cypress canopy blotted out the moonlight. I could barely see a thing. In my haste to keep up with Grayson, I'd forgotten my flashlight. I'd fired up the one on my cellphone, but he'd quickly ordered me to turn it off to conserve the battery.

Stumbling behind Grayson, just out of range of the circle of light cast by his flashlight, the thought of what else might be lurking in the swamp made me edge closer to him until I was almost riding on his back.

In the woods to our left, a loud, baritone call rang out in the darkness, like the belch of a drunken giant. The sound stopped Grayson cold. I ran straight into the back of him.

"Sorry!" I whispered.

"I wonder what would cause that?" Grayson asked.

"I can't see. If you'd let me turn on my cellphone—"

"Not *you*," Grayson said. "*That.*"

He directed his light beam down the trail about fifty feet ahead of us. Then he turned off the light.

I grabbed him. "What'd you do that for?"

"Shh. Wait and see. Let your eyes adjust."

I held my breath and reached for my Glock, expecting a pair of glowing red eyes or a set of sharp, yellow fangs. Instead, slowly but surely, an oval ring of light appeared in the trees. It glowed with a faint orange-red light, and appeared to be hovering six or eight feet off the ground.

"Intriguing," Grayson said.

I dug my nails into his shoulder. "Intriguing my ass! What the hell *is* it?"

"I don't know."

Grayson took another step toward the mysterious, glowing ring.

"Wait!" I said, unable to take my eyes from the object. The center of it was dark as night, and about the size of hot-tub turned on its side.

"You're right," Grayson said. "We should exercise caution. Shame I didn't bring my radiation detector."

"Radiation?" I gasped. "Are you saying we're getting *nuked*?"

"I don't know. It's possible."

I tucked my Glock in my pants and put my hands on my hips where I thought my ovaries might be.

Geez! My eggs are already middle-aged. Are they getting microwaved *now, too?*

I tugged Grayson by the arm. "Come on! Let's get out of here!"

"Not yet," he said, and yanked free of my grip. He straightened his shoulders and tromped two more steps toward the unidentified glowing object.

"Don't!" I cried out, not wanting to follow, but not wanting to be left behind in the dark, either.

I stared at the mesmerizing, yellow-orange glow. It flickered on the tree trunks, turning them into ghostly visions of pointy-fingered goblins. Every molecule in me wanted to flee—not just to save myself, but my unborn children, too.

"Grayson," I said, trying to find him in the dark.

He was gone.

"Ack!" I cried out. "Where are you?"

I reached for my cellphone and clicked the button for the flashlight. An anemic yellow light flickered once, then died.

Darkness swallowed me up—just as it had my partner.

"Grayson!" I screamed.

Suddenly, a horrible claw-like hand grabbed my arm. As I struggled for my Glock, I caught a glimpse of its eyes in the moonlight.

They were green.

"Geezus, Grayson!" I hissed. "You scared the crap out of me!"

"Keep it down!" he said, grabbing my cellphone.

"If you're looking for the flashlight, don't bother. It's dead," I said.

"So's my flashlight," he said. "I don't understand. I just changed the batteries."

"Seriously?" I hissed. "We're about to become hors d'oeuvres for some intergalactic microwave, and you're worried Walmart cheated you with expired batteries?"

In a sliver of moonlight, I could just make out Grayson cocking his head. "No, Drex. You don't understand. Power drains like this are commonly reported by those encountering interdimensional phenomena."

I gulped. "So it's an *interdimensional* microwave?"

"Not exactly. Here. Hold this."

Grayson pressed his dead flashlight into my hand. Then he reached into his breast pocket and pulled out his cellphone.

Suddenly, the glowing orange ring began to pulse.

My mouth fell open. "Uh-oh. What does *that* mean?"

Grayson studied the pulsing orb. "Uncertain," he said. "It could be powering up."

"Powering up?" I gasped. Deep inside me, I thought I felt an ovary shrivel. "Look, Grayson. I don't know what's going on here, and I'm not hanging around to find out."

I turned to run, but my boots tripped up in the muck. I lost my balance and was heading for a date with a mud bath when Grayson's arm caught me around the middle, just in the nick of time.

"Thanks," I gasped.

"You're welcome," he said, pulling me face-to-face with him.

"Now please, can we get the hell out of here?" I begged.

"Shhh!" he said, laying a finger to my lips. "You might disturb it!"

"*I* might disturb *it*?" I yelled, pulling free of him. "Are you *nuts*? We gotta get out of here, Grayson. We need backup!"

"Fine," he said. "Just let me get a couple of quick shots of it first."

"Are you cra—"

I froze mid-sentence as a hot, white light seared my retinas. But it hadn't come from that freaking space microwave. It was the flash from Grayson's stupid cellphone camera.

"Are you kidding me?" I hissed, blinking back the white dots swimming before my eyes in a sea of red.

Another flash went off.

I stumbled forward, trying to punch Grayson in the face. My ovaries were at stake!

Then, suddenly, just as mine had, Grayson's cellphone display faded and blinked out. Darkness again zoomed in on us like a black fog.

"Great," I muttered. "Now what?"

All of a sudden, a low grumbling began emanating from the direction of the glowing ring. Then an inhuman, high-pitched whine filled the air, making every hair on my body stand on end.

"It sounds like it's gonna blow!" I squealed.

"Intriguing," Grayson said. "Listen. The frogs and insects have gone dead silent."

He was right. All I could hear was my pulse thrumming in my ears.

Man, oh, man, this is sooo not good...

Then I heard it.

Something was crashing through the underbrush.

Something big.

And it was heading right for us.

"Huh," I heard Grayson say some paces behind me. "Whatever it is, it must be sensitive to light."

"You think?" I hissed between gritted teeth as I crashed through the forest like a wigged-out wildebeest.

Chapter Ten

I was exhausted and panting like a panther in heat when I scrabbled my way out of the woods and into the cleared shoulder of the road. I gasped for air, noticing the stars above provided just enough light to turn the landscape into a charcoal rendering of itself.

A branch snapped in the forest behind me.

I spun around, still wheezing.

I strained to see into the dark woods. There was no sign of the glowing form I'd just run from. But there was no doubt about it. Something was crashing through the cypress swamp in my direction. I recognized his heavy breathing.

"Grayson!" I yelled as he stumbled toward me and the clearing. "You made it out!"

"Yes," he gasped. "No thanks to *you*, by the way."

"*Me*?" I wheezed. "I'm not the one who flashed the damned monster!"

Suddenly, a flash of bluish light blinded me.

"Not again!" I yelled.

"That wasn't me," Grayson said.

I looked around and realized we were both caught in a laser beam of light. I froze in place like a fish in liquid nitrogen.

"Ha!" a voice rang out. "Flashed the monster, did ya? So you two finally went and done the deed!"

Annoyance thawed my brain in half a millisecond.

Earl!

If I hadn't been so happy to see my dumb cousin, I'd have slapped him bald-headed.

"Howdy, Mr. G!" Earl hollered, then lowered the beam blasting from his industrial-sized flashlight.

Grayson sprinted toward Earl. I followed, hot on his heels.

"It may be fortuitous ...," Grayson gasped, still trying to catch his breath, "to expeditiously dispatch ourselves ... from the immediate premises."

Earl cocked his shaggy head. "You mean on account of the premises that you two was gettin' it on?"

"No!" I yelled. "He means we need to get the hell out of here. *Now!*"

Earl chuckled. "Don't get your panties in a wad, Cuz. While you two was off gallivantin' on yore romantical stroll, I done got the RV hooked up and ready to tow."

"Thank God!" I yelled, and ran for my cousin's monster truck. As I hauled myself up inside, I started to yell through the window for them to hurry up, but nearly choked on my own spit instead.

From my vantage point six feet above the ground, I could see the edges of that weird, glowing orb.

Good lord! It's still there!

I waved frantically at Grayson and Earl. "Good, grief! Come on, you two! Get a move on!"

Earl shrugged. "What's the rush?"

"Can't you see?" I screeched. "The sky over there. It's lit up like a freaking *aurora borealis*!"

Earl scratched his head. "You mean that ugly gal at church what had the mole on her eyelid?"

"No! That was Aurora Borillis. Now get your ass behind the wheel and get us the hell out of here! *Now!*"

"WHAT'D Y'ALL DO? NOT pay your parking tickets, or what?" Earl asked as he piled in behind the wheel of the huge, black monster truck he'd nicknamed Bessie.

"Not even close," I grumbled, straddling the gear shift while Grayson got the passenger window. "Just go!"

Earl chuckled. "You got it, Cuz."

I braced for liftoff, but Earl shifted Bessie into first and eased his foot gingerly on the gas pedal.

"What the?" I said.

"Hold onto your hat," Earl said, then stomped the gas pedal like it was a fleeing cockroach.

Bessie's engine roared to life. Above the din, I heard Grayson's old RV groan like a geriatric dinosaur.

For a moment we all sat motionless in suspense, as if time had stood still. Then, suddenly, we jolted forward as if we'd been rammed from behind by a Mack truck.

Bessie had just yanked the old RV loose from the muck.

"Here we go," Earl said, easing up on the gas. Slowly and carefully, he maneuvered the dilapidated Winnebago off the muddy shoulder and onto the asphalt of the narrow backroad.

"We're free," I said, breathing a sigh of relief. "Now punch it, Earl!"

Earl eyed me curiously, the way a tortoise might inspect a suspicious lettuce leaf. "I still don't see what all the rush is about."

"There's some kind of weird ring of light in the woods," I hissed, my hysteria rising again. "It could be dangerous. Right, Grayson?"

Grayson shrugged. "Possibly."

"Well, what exactly is it?" Earl asked.

I scowled and lifted my left foot. If my idiot cousin wasn't going to hit the gas, *I* was!

"I'm not sure," Grayson said. "I need to do some testing to be certain. But I believe we may have just discovered an intergalactic portal."

My left leg went limp.

What the hell?

Earl shook his bear-like head. "They got port-a-lets in space?"

I stared at Grayson. "A *portal*? Are you serious?"

Grayson shrugged. "Only time will tell."

My lip snarled. "Is that some kind of sick geek joke?"

"So, which way we headed, y'all?" Earl asked.

"To Operative Garth's compound," Grayson said.

"Woohoo!" Earl hollered. "Wait'll that ol' boy finds out we done found us an outhouse in space!"

"No!" I said, elbowing Earl in the gut. "We can't tell Garth a word about this."

Earl looked down at me. "Why not, party pooper?"

"Because he'll broadcast it all over that ham radio of his," I snarled back.

Earl shrugged. "So what?"

I turned to Grayson. "If Garth gets wind of this, every nutcase in the world will be tromping all over the woods trying to find your so-called 'portal.'"

Grayson locked eyes with me. "And your point is?"

"Seriously?" I said, anger rising in my throat. "I've got *three*. For one, any evidence at the scene will be trampled. Two, if we're wrong, we'll all become laughingstocks—including Jimmy. And thirdly, if this thing really *is* a portal like you say it might be, we don't want it falling into the wrong hands, right?"

"Excellent," Grayson nodded.

"Geez. It's just basic reasoning," I said.

Grayson's cheek dimpled. "I know. And you rose to the challenge. Good job, cadet."

I frowned. "Happy I could jump through your hoops."

"Still, we have to report *something* back to Garth," Grayson said. "What should we tell him?"

"The truth," I said. "That we got stuck in the mud and had to be towed by Earl."

Grayson eyed me like a proud professor. "Hmm. A lie of *omission.*"

"A *mission?*" Earl said. "Hot dog! We're on a mission!"

Please. Someone shoot me now...

Chapter Eleven

I flushed the toilet, then stared at my face in the miniscule mirror in the RV's tiny bathroom. I felt slightly nauseated. My face seemed pinker than normal.

Holy crap! Did I get radiation poisoning last night?

"I don't get paid enough for this shit," I muttered.

I took a deep breath, braced myself, then yanked open the door. I padded down the hall and into the main cabin, where I could hear Earl and Grayson in the middle of some sort of discussion. Since Earl was involved, I knew it wouldn't be an intellectual one.

"And that's how Sally, my two-headed turtle, got her name," Earl said.

Nailed it.

"Look who finally dragged herself up outta the sack," Earl said with that cheerful, happy-go-lucky tone of his that, without sufficient caffeine, made me want to punch his teeth in.

"Drex suffers from dysania," Grayson said.

Earl snorted. "Then I sure hope she flushed twice."

A divot formed in Grayson's cheek. "Dysania is the chronic inability to get out of bed in the morning."

"Oh," Earl said, and shot me a wink. "My momma called that being a lazy ass."

"Ha ha, wise guys." I shot them a sneer and grabbed for a coffee cup. "Anyway, I'm not feeling right this morning. Does my face look red to you?"

Earl chuckled. "No more'n normal. But then again, if'n I looked like you, I'd be permanently embarrassed, too."

I picked up the carafe of coffee and snarled, "Might I remind you, I haven't had my first cup yet?"

Earl winced. "Oops. My bad." His eyes darted to Grayson, who was sitting in the banquette booth across from him. "So, Mr. G., what's on the agenda for today?"

"The agenda?" he asked, putting a pinch of salt in his coffee.

"Yeah," Earl said. "You know, our *mission*. To find out what happened to ol' Jimmy boy."

"Right," Grayson said, tapping a finger on his mug. "Well, before we began discussing bi-cranial amphibians, I was researching interdimensional portals."

"Why?" Earl asked. "You think ol' Jimmy got sucked up into that thang?"

I laughed. "With any luck, you will, too."

Earl grinned. "Cool!"

"I need to run some tests of the area's electromagnetic field," Grayson said, ignoring us. "But given the visual anomaly we observed last night, plus the fact that Jimmy has apparently vanished, an interdimensional portal seems to best fit the evidence at hand."

My nose crinkled. "Wait a minute. You *agree* with Earl? You think Jimmy got sucked up into that glowing microwave hole?"

A knock sounded at the side door. I slammed my coffee cup down on the counter and shot Earl and Grayson my best *wait till your father gets home* evil eye. "Not a word about this to Garth. You hear me?"

Before I could take a step, the side door opened. A frizzy blond mullet attached to a buck-toothed head poked itself inside.

"Miss Pandora," Garth said, sounding like Kermit with emphysema. "Good morning, m' lady."

"Hi," I replied, noticing, with gratitude, that he'd washed his Kentucky waterfall. "Looks like you're feeling a little better today."

Garth smiled weakly, then coughed until he nearly strangled. "Some, thanks."

"Come in," Grayson said.

Garth wiped his nose on his sleeve and shuffled inside. I handed him a cup of coffee, then remembered my red face and the slight case of nausea I had that morning. I scowled.

Could I have caught this twerp's creeping crud?

"So, what happened last night?" Garth asked, holding his cup with both shaky hands. "Did you find Jimmy?"

"Not exactly," Grayson said. "He may have slipped into another dim—"

I sealed Grayson's lips with a death ray, then turned and gave Garth an apologetic smile. "What Grayson meant to say is that Jimmy gave us the slip."

Garth's shoulders slumped. "Oh."

"Howdy, Garth," Earl said. "You look like you're wrastlin' with the flu bug."

"Oh. Hi, Earl. Sorry," Garth said, pushing his glasses up on his red nose. "I didn't know you were helping out with the investigation."

Earl grinned proudly. "Well, you know—"

"He's not," I said. "We got stuck in the mud last night and had to be towed. That's the only reason Earl's here."

"Stuck in the mud?" Garth asked, flopping onto the broken couch like a damp sack of dirty laundry. "Where'd you lose his trail?"

"His signal blinked out about five or six miles south of here, off Turkey Creek Road."

Garth winced. "Crap."

"Agreed," Grayson said. "Battery drainage is a sign—"

"That you can't trust cellphone reception around here," I finished.

"You're right," Garth said, crestfallen. "But it was the only thing I could think of to do. Jimmy only came home for a few minutes at a time—mostly to check the mail and get a shower. I didn't have time to rig anything more elaborate. Plus, I'm not exactly at my mental or physical best at the moment."

I would certainly hope not.

"Any word from him last night?" I asked.

Garth sighed. "No. I was hoping he'd come home again before my phone batteries died. Or at least long enough for me to recharge them." Garth blew his nose into a hanky. "So, where were you on Turkey Creek Road when he gave you the slip?"

"I'm not exactly sure," I said.

"I seen a sign," Earl said. "Somethin' about a mallard park, I think."

"Oh," Garth said, perking up a bit. "I bet you were out by the old Hi-Ho area."

"Could'a been," Earl said. "But I didn't see no ladies of the evenin' out there."

Garth's head cocked to one side. "That's a local nickname for Edward Medard Park. It's an old phosphate mining area. Full of hills and holes—hi ho. Get it?"

"Oh," I said. "Cute. But right now, we need to focus on our next steps."

Garth bobbed his head like a low-rent gangster. "*Ward*, man."

I cringed. "I believe the ghetto slang term is '*word*,' Garth, not '*ward*.'"

Garth cocked his head at me. "No. I meant WWARD. As in, 'What Would Amazing Randi Do?'"

"Ah!" Grayson said. "Of course!"

"Seriously?" I muttered, shaking my head. "If I was Randi I'd run away and join the circus."

Garth snorted, blowing a snot bubble. "Good one, Pandora."

Grayson laughed, too.

"Uh ... sorry guys," I said. "I don't get it."

Garth's mouth fell open. "I thought you *knew*, Pandora. Uncle Randi never finished high school. He dropped out and joined a traveling carnival."

My gut fell four inches. "You're kidding."

Garth wiped his nose on his sleeve. "Nope."

I shook my head. "But I thought Randi was this big cheese in the scientific world."

"He *was*," Garth said. "But he never went to college, either. When he was in his late fifties, he was awarded a MacArthur fellowship. You might know it as a 'genius grant.'"

Earl gasped. "Your uncle was a bona fide genius?"

Garth beamed with pride. "He was when it came to debunking paranormal and pseudoscientific claims."

"Well, I'll be," Earl said, nodding in admiration. "What got him all stoked up over provin' ghoulies and haints was fakes?"

Garth shrugged. "I'm not sure. I guess we've all got to believe in something. Uncle Randi decided to believe in not believing."

"Huh?" Earl's head tilted sideways like a confused puppy.

Grayson sat up in the banquette and rubbed his chin. "You know Garth, your uncle said something during one of his last public interviews that's always stuck with me."

I snorted. "What? Don't forget the Crazy Glue?"

Grayson carried on, ignoring my quip. "The Amazing Randi told the reporter, and I quote, 'I suffer from this obsession that I have something important to do.'"

Garth grinned. "And what could be more important than proving the paranormal doesn't exist?"

Grayson locked eyes with Garth, then the two men spoke in unison: "Proving that it *does*!"

I shook my head.

It's true. Great dopes do *think alike.*

Grayson pulled out his cellphone. "On that note, I took—"

Oh, no! Not the photos from last night! If Garth sees those...

"Look," I said to Garth. "I think it's time you left."

"But I want to help," he protested as I yanked him up off the couch.

"You need your rest," I said, giving him the bum's rush out the door. "Grayson and I'll go back to Hi-Ho this morning and check everything out."

"You need my help," Garth said. "There's a lot of unmarked trails out there. People ride dirt bikes and dune buggies on them. Horses sometimes."

"Thanks, but we can manage," I said, shoving him out the door.

Garth hung onto the doorframe like a cat on a washtub rim. "But!"

"Look," I said. "No offense, but if you keep hacking all over us and we get us sick, *no one* will be able to help your brother Jimmy."

Garth stopped struggling. "Sorry, Pandora. You're right."

"Of course I am. Now go get some rest. And leave your flu bugs in that trailer with the rest of the arthropods."

"Garth," Grayson called out. "There *is* one thing you can do. Keep monitoring the ham radio for any intel about missing persons or communications from Jimmy. If you hear anything, report back to us immediately. We'll do the same."

Garth's wimpy shoulders straightened. "Yes, sir, Mr. Gray."

I stood in the doorframe and watched Garth stumble back along the dirt driveway toward his trailer. As the chain-link gate began to close, I turned to Grayson.

"Why'd you tell Garth that? He needs to be in bed, getting well."

Grayson shrugged. "A man needs to feel useful, Drex."

"Oh. Right." I turned the tap on the kitchen sink and waited for the water to heat up. "I only hope he hasn't already contaminated us." I glanced around. "Speaking of unwanted germs, where's Earl?"

"In the restroom."

I grimaced. "Great. Let's add a Walmart stop to today's plans."

"Why?" Grayson asked.

I sighed. "Let's just say I've got a hunch we're gonna need a bigger can of Febreze."

Chapter Twelve

"What 'cha lookin' at?" Earl asked. He'd emerged from the bathroom and shuffled over to the banquette where Grayson was seated. He stood beside the table like a bear in jeans, staring over Grayson's shoulder.

Grayson swiped the display on his cellphone. "These are pictures I took last night of the strange phenomenon we encountered."

"Whoa!" Earl said. "That's purty *strange*, all right."

He grabbed the phone from Grayson and shoved it in my face. "Lookie here, Bobbie! It's a dad-burned blue-tongued devil!"

"What?"

I dropped the plate I was washing, grabbed the cellphone, and slapped on my cheater glasses. The image of a ghostly, wild-eyed creature came into focus. Its tongue was the color of blueberries.

I let out a groan. Somehow, Grayson had managed to capture a partial headshot of me in total freak-out mode.

Great. That's the last time I eat a blue-raspberry Tootsie Pop before a stakeout.

I shot Earl a sneer. "Har har. Very funny."

He tried to snatch the phone back, but I was too quick for him. "Nothing doing," I said, shoving it into my shirt pocket, out of his grasp.

"Interesting," Grayson said, tapping on his laptop keyboard. "A Google map of the vicinity around Edward Medard Park shows a veritable network of unpaved roads."

"So?" I said.

Grayson looked up from the screen. "That could explain Jimmy's disappearance. Some of these side roads go pretty deep into the woods, perhaps out of wifi range."

"Or maybe it's like you said," Earl replied. "He got sucked up into that porta-potty thing."

"*Portal*," I said.

"Hmm." Grayson rubbed his chin. "I guess we won't know for sure unless we get another signal blip from Garth's phone."

"How do you figure that?" I asked.

"Elementary," Grayson said. "Another signal would prove Jimmy was still in range, and therefore still on Earth."

"No," I argued, a smirk forming on my lips. "It would only prove Garth's *phone* was still here."

Grayson's dimple reappeared. "Fair point, Drex. But either way, we should explore the entire area today. See if we can locate him, his vehicle, or at least some tire tracks. With any luck, we should also be able to pinpoint the site of the strange phenomenon we saw last night."

Earl smirked. "I thought she was right over there washin' dishes."

I shot my cousin a glare that could fry eggs in a cold skillet. He winced and turned to Grayson. "Uh ... what's Jimmy drivin', anyways?"

Grayson chewed his lip. "An old pickup. GM, I think."

I shook my head. "Jimmy drives a 1966 light-blue Chevy C-10 with factory four-by-four."

Earl's eyes lit up. "Sweeet!" He turned to me. "They don't make four-wheel drives like they used to. Is it mint?"

I laughed. "Not even close. The chassis looks like it's been in an avalanche."

Earl winced. "Dang. So you reckon he's stuck out there? He could a blown a gasket or somethin.'"

I shrugged. "It's possible. But from what I remember, Jimmy kept the engine in excellent working condition. You know, just in case of an apocalypse."

"Apocalypse?" Earl asked. "That don't sound like no fun."

"Jimmy's a doomsday prepper like his brother Garth," I said. "That's the whole reason he drives that old truck. No electronic ignition. You know. In case of an EMP."

Earl scratched his head. "Elephant making poop?"

I closed my eyes and let out a long breath. "Electro-magnetic pulse, genius." I looked over at Grayson, feeling quite smug I'd remembered his lecture from a couple of months ago.

Grayson nodded at Earl. "No worries. It's a common mistake."

Wha?

"You see," Grayson continued, "a strong-enough electromagnetic pulse, whether from a solar flare or man-made signal, would knock out every vehicle with an electronic ignition."

"Oh, sure. Gotcha," Earl said.

"Unfortunately, the fact that Jimmy's truck has no electronics also means there's no built-in GPS for us to track him with."

I frowned. "So, how are we gonna find him if Garth's phone signal dies?"

"What about tracking Jimmy's own phone?" Earl asked.

"No. He's too smart for that," Grayson said. "Garth told us Jimmy turned his locator off. That's why we need to start searching for him as soon as possible. Hand me my phone, Drex. We can start our search from where we got stuck last night."

"And how do we find *that* location?" I asked, pulling the phone from my pocket.

Earl snatched the phone from my hand and wagged it in my face. "Easy, Cuz. We'll just look for your skid marks."

RAINDROPS AS BIG AS grapes splatted on Bessie's windshield as we sped down Turkey Creek Road, the truck's tractor-sized tires whining on the wet asphalt.

"Great," I grumbled. "Rain. Just what we need."

"What you worried about, Bobbie?" Earl said. "You ain't made of sugar."

I sneered at my cousin. "I was thinking of you, Earl—but not of sugar. What's that other thing that melts in the rain?"

Earl grunted. "Har har."

The sky opened up like a high-velocity carwash, reducing visibility to the split-second between wiperblade swipes.

I frowned. "Slow down, Earl. If this keeps up, we're never gonna be able to find where you pulled us out of the muck."

"Never mind that," Grayson said. "Look for the sign."

"Juanita's Casa del Tacos?" I asked, reading a giant billboard as we passed by at fifteen miles an hour.

"I meant the sign for Edward Medard Park," Grayson said. "I think it's just up ahead on the right."

Sure enough, the forest-green-and-brown sign for the state park appeared at the edge of the woods like a soggy beacon in the gray monsoon. Directly across the street on the left, above the door of what appeared to be a repurposed gas station, a neon sombrero blinked like an acid-flashback from a trip long ago and far away.

Eat here and get gas...

Grayson frowned and pursed his lips. "I'm making an executive decision. Earl, take a left into Juanita's parking lot. We'll grab a snack and wait until the rain eases up."

"Tacos?" I shot Grayson a sideways glance. "This was your plan all along, wasn't it?"

Grayson adjusted his fedora and sat up a bit straighter. "No. Just a fortunate coincidence."

I shook my head. "You're lying, Grayson."

Grayson glanced over at me. "Why do you say that?"

"Because I know you. And you don't believe in coincidences."

Chapter Thirteen

It had been exactly twenty-seven hours since Grayson last pulled over for tacos. I glanced up at the neon sombrero and resigned myself to impending heartburn. It wasn't even *Tuesday*, for crying out loud.

"Good thing you've got your priorities in order," I said, yanking open the door to Juanita's Casa del Tacos. "We fill our guts with chips and salsa while Jimmy's tire impressions get washed away in a monsoon."

"The rain's already done its damage," Grayson said slipping past me and into a booth by the fogged-up front window. "Besides, scientific evidence supports better brain function with proper nutrition."

I stifled an eye roll and scooted in across from him. "I don't think tacos count as one of the four basic food groups."

"They do around here," a plump, middle-aged woman said with a laugh.

She swiped at her dark-brown bangs as she shuffled up to us, then paused to shift the gum she was cracking to one side of her mouth before she spoke again. "So, y'all know what you want?"

"Let's keep it simple," Grayson said before Earl or I could speak. He nodded to a chalkboard sandwich board propped up by the front door like a "wet floor" sign. "We'll have today's special, the *Familia Grande* Taco Extravaganza."

Our server's left eyebrow flat-lined. "For just the three of you? Normally, that feeds a family of five."

"I hope it's enough," I quipped. "These two count as two people each. Maybe three."

The waitress laughed. "Sounds like y'all got yourselves a big appetite. Any big plans to go with it?"

"Yep," Earl said, grinning proudly. "We're on a case."

The woman grin skipped a beat. "A case? You guys cops?"

Earl smiled smugly. "No ma'am. *Detectives.* We're lookin' for us a fella went missing in the ol' Hi-Ho out yonder."

"Earl!" I hissed, and kicked him under the table

The waitress studied us for a moment. "I see. Anything to drink with that?"

"Three Dr Peppers," I said, smiling up at her weakly.

"I'll get your order in," she said, and headed for the kitchen.

"Did you see that reaction?" Grayson said. "Something's up with her."

I shook my head. "I wouldn't read much into it. Earl has a negative effect on women."

"Perhaps," Grayson said. "But I believe she knows something."

"What?" I quipped. "That Earl's full of crap? Every gal with half a brain knows that."

Grayson's jaw tensed. "I meant about the disappearances."

"Shh," I whispered. "Here she comes. Earl, keep your trap shut!"

Earl frowned. "What'd *I* do?"

"Here you go," the waitress said. "Three Dr Peppers." She unloaded a trio of quart-sized, red-plastic glasses from her tray, then lingered as we each grabbed a drink.

"Uh ... y'all need straws?" she asked, poking three paper-wrapped straws at us.

"No," I said. "We're fine."

"Uh ... okay." she said, tucking them back into her apron pocket. "This fellow you're looking for. His name isn't Wade, is it?"

"No," Grayson said. "Why would—"

"It's Jimmy!" Earl said, earning him another kick in the shin from me.

"Why do you ask?" Grayson said to the waitress.

She glanced out the window, then back toward the kitchen. Then she leaned over and whispered, "Your friend Jimmy ain't the first to go missing from the old Hi-Ho."

"No?" Grayson said. "Who else is missing?"

The waitress chewed her lip. "I can't say for sure. But you know, usually by this time a day we're half full up with customers. Over the past week or so, a bunch of our regulars have quit showing up."

My upper lip hooked skyward. "Uh ... how often do you change the grease?"

Grayson shot me a look, then turned back to the waitress. "These regular customers. Did they have anything in common?"

"Yeah," she said. "They ate here."

Grayson took a breath. "I mean besides that."

"Oh. Well, they liked to hunt and fish around here."

"In the Hi-Ho?" I asked.

"Well, yeah," she said. "I mean, it's right across the street."

"Have you heard any stories of strange phenomena going on in the park?" Grayson asked.

"Like what?" she asked.

"Like a port-a-potty from outer space," Earl blurted.

I kicked him again. "Hush!"

The waitress' drawn-on eyebrows raised like McDonald's arches. She glanced around the empty restaurant again, then leaned over our table. "Just old Indian legends and whatnot," she said. "They say that place is an ancient Native American burial ground."

"Technically, this whole country is," Grayson said dryly. "Anything else?"

"Just what my cousin Wade told me," she said. "He said he saw some weird lights out there last weekend. He was gonna check it out and let me know what he found out. But he didn't come back. I haven't seen him since. I'm afraid something bad's happened to him."

"Thelma!" a man's voice yelled from the kitchen.

The waitress froze like a deer in the headlights.

"Order up!" the cook yelled.

Thelma turned and left without a word.

"Interesting, Grayson said, watching her leave. "Sounds like a lot of people are going into the Hi-Ho, but not all of them are coming out."

"What you think's the culprit causing it?" Earl asked.

I picked up greasy fork and grimaced. "I can't speak for the rest, but I've got an idea."

Grayson locked eyes with me. "Fluctuations in electromagnetic frequencies?"

I wiped the fork with a napkin. "Nope. *Botulism.*"

Chapter Fourteen

"Ugh," Earl groaned and rubbed his belly. "I done et me so many tacos I think I sprung a gut."

"Crapulence," Grayson said.

"You think it'll help?" Earl asked, reaching for his Dr Pepper.

Grayson's eyebrows inched a little closer together. "Crapulence is the term for that sick feeling you get after eating or drinking too much."

"Oh," Earl said, patting his swollen belly. "Well, lemme tell you, Mr. G., I got me a crap-load of crapulence goin' on in here."

"Thanks for *that* imagery," I said, and tossed my paper napkin over my half-eaten taco.

"Speakin' a crap, where's the john around here?" Earl asked.

"By the front door," Grayson said.

Earl wiggled his bear-sized body out of the booth. "I'll be back."

I sneered up at him. "Thanks for the warning."

As Earl waddled in the direction of the men's room, Grayson called out, "Be sure to do a courtesy flush."

I snorted. "In his case it's more like a *mercy* flush."

"Why do you say that?"

I smirked. "Because otherwise, it's not survivable."

Grayson's brow furrowed. He pushed away his empty plate and studied me with his mesmerizing green peepers. "A lot of things survive being flushed, Drex. Rats. Alligators. Aquarium fish. It's not the flush, but the *toxic sewer fumes* that kill."

"My point exactly," I said. "Anyway, while numb-nuts is in the can, tell me something. What did you mean when you said fluctuating electronic magnet thingies could be the cause of people disappearing around here?"

"Electromagnetic fluctuations," Grayson said. "It's one of the theories being put forth by a former police detective named Dave Paulides."

"What's he got to do with this?"

"Well, for the past twenty years, Paulides has been investigating cases involving thousands of people who've vanished from state parks around the US."

I choked on my Dr Pepper. "*Thousands? Vanished?*"

Grayson nodded. "Yes. Without a trace."

"But anything could've happened," I argued. "Bears. Serial killers. Dumb luck."

"Paulides only takes a case after thorough conventional investigations have ruled out every possible explanation, including murder, suicide, natural disaster, and animal attacks. Drex, these people disappeared without leaving a single trace. Not a shoe, a cellphone, a body part, *nothing.*"

"Oh." I slumped back into the booth. "So what does that leave?"

"Nothing we know currently," Grayson said. "Paulides proposes that the only answers remaining must be unconventional ones."

I locked eyes with Grayson. "Like these electromagnetic fluctuations you're talking about?"

"Yes. Their called EMFs, for short."

"So, tell me," I said. "How's this EMF theory work?"

Grayson opened his mouth. I grabbed his arm. "The non-geekified version, please."

Grayson nodded. "To start, EMFs themselves aren't responsible for the disappearances. They're just a remnant—a fingerprint, if you will—left behind by an Einstein-Rosen Bridge."

I stopped slurping my Dr Pepper. "I said the *non*-geek version."

Grayson drummed his fingers on the table. "I'll try. How about this? Many physicists agree with the premise that strong fluctuations in electromagnetic fields may create areas where conventional physics breaks down, thus allowing for unexplained phenomena to occur."

"So where there's fluctuations, there's funky stuff going on?"

Grayson sighed. "Yes."

I shrugged. "Like what?"

"Bends in time and space. Wormholes, if you will."

My eyebrow met my hairline. "I thought you were kidding. Are you saying that glowing microwave thing we saw out there last night really *is* a wormhole? And that people are getting sucked into it?"

"In a nutshell, yes."

"Grayson, that's insane!"

Grayson sighed and shook his head. "The thing about smart people is they seem like crazy people to dumb people."

My face puckered. "That's the stupidest thing I've ever heard."

Grayson locked eyes with me. "Tell it to Steven Hawking. He's the one who said it. A direct quote, I might add."

Crap. I couldn't argue with Hawking, for crying out loud. But I didn't have to be happy about it. "Fine," I said, grinding my molars. "How would this wormhole thing suck people up?"

"It's elegantly simple," Grayson said. "The wormhole itself is merely a portal where time is passing differently in one spot versus another. Those who enter it simply step into another time or dimension."

My jaw dropped open. "That's impossible."

Grayson shrugged. "Your disbelief is irrelevant, Drex. The theory that time and space can be folded to meet in other dimensions of time and space stands up to scientific scrutiny."

I stared sullenly at Grayson. I still didn't get what he was yammering about. If that made me stupid, so be it. But it also made me as surly as a gal with no prom date.

"Whatever," I grumbled.

"Look," Grayson said. "Take this taco shell, for instance." He picked up a soft flour tortilla. "The distance from this edge to the other is what? Five inches?"

I shrugged nonchalantly. "More or less."

"Okay. But if I fold it in half, like this, those same edges are now touching. There's no space between them. Right?"

I perked up a little. "Yeah."

"That's kind of how a portal works, Drex. You bend time and space, creating a shortcut from one point to another. That's an Einstein-Rosen Bridge, or wormhole."

I sat up. "So, what happens when the tortilla—I mean the wormhole—bends back?"

Grayson's cheek dimpled. "It takes with it whatever's crossed to the other side."

My nose crinkled. "I'd be lying to say I totally get it, Grayson. But let's say it's possible. Is there any way to tell when it's gonna happen? You know, before it's too late?"

"As far as I know, there's no way to tell when a wormhole is going to open up. But you *can* tell if there's been one there in the past."

"Not especially helpful to avoid getting sucked into one," I said sourly. "But okay, how do you tell one was there?"

"By looking for distortions in the area's electromagnetic field," Grayson said. "When a bend in time and space occurs, it leaves a distortion in the EMF—that's the electromagnetic fingerprint I mentioned earlier."

I chewed my bottom lip. "So, how do we find these EMF wormhole fingerprints?"

Grayson grinned. "With an electromagnetic field detector. I just happen to have one handy." He reached into his jacket and pulled out a rectangular, black device that looked a lot like the bug sweeper I'd found under the floorboard.

"You guys ready for the check?" the waitress called out from across the restaurant.

"Uh ... sure," I called back.

"Pay the woman," Grayson said, patting his pockets. "I don't have any cash on me."

"What?" I grumbled. "You forget your wallet, but you remember to bring *that* stupid gizmo. Unbelievable!"

Grayson shrugged. "Consider it more proof that coming to this restaurant wasn't part of a premeditated plan."

"Yeah, right." I reached for my purse. "The theory's still out on that one, mister."

I pulled out a couple of twenties while Grayson fiddled with the knobs on his shiny EMF-detector toy.

"How's that thing work?" I asked.

Grayson's green eyes lit up like a kid's at Christmas. "See this needle gauge? It moves if it detects changes in either the electric or magnetic fields. It also lets out an alarm tone."

"Huh." I glanced up and spotted Earl heading our way from the men's restroom. "It doesn't happen to detect deadly gas, too, does it?"

Chapter Fifteen

B y the time our waitress Thelma came back with my change, the
sun was breaking through the clouds, shining beams of golden
light on the greasy front window of Juanita's Casa del Tacos.

"Sun's out. Y'all heading over to the park?" Thelma asked, pock-
eting the eight dollars I'd left her for a tip.

Earl snorted. "Hi-Ho, Hi-Ho, it's off to work we go!"

I groaned and shot Thelma an apologetic grimace. "I'm sure you
haven't heard *that one* before."

"Oh, come on," Earl said. "You were *thinkin'* it."

"Maybe," I said, shoving Earl toward the edge of the bench. "But
at least *I* had the decency not to say it."

Thelma shot us a pained smile. "No harm done. Y'all come back
now, you hear?"

"We will," I said absently.

I stood and followed Earl and Grayson toward the door. Thelma
grabbed my arm.

"Wait," she said, her face marred with concern. "I meant that *literally*. Y'all come back."

I blanched. "What do you mean?"

Thelma glanced around nervously, then spoke in a whisper.

"Like I tried to tell you before. It could be *dangerous*. This past
Saturday, my cousin Wade left his truck here in the parking lot and
walked over to the Hi-Ho for a stroll, like he always did after lunch
on the weekends. But this time, he never came back. I haven't heard
from him since." Thelma shook her head. "It's been four days, now.

Wade hasn't been home. He hasn't picked up his phone. Something's wrong. It's just not like him to do that."

"Did you contact the police?" I asked.

"Yeah," Thelma said. "Lot of good it did. They said there was no evidence of foul play, so they couldn't do anything. They told me to mind my own business—that a grown man can do what he wants."

"Thanks for the warning," I said. "I promise we'll be careful."

"Could you keep an eye out for Wade while you're over there?" Thelma asked, following me out the door. "That's his Dodge over there. The blue one by that big old monster truck."

"Sure," I said, the tears in Thelma's eyes playing my heartstrings. "What's he look like?"

"Kind of like him," she said, pointing over at Earl. "Tall, dark and—"

"Hairy?" I quipped, trying to lighten the mood.

Thelma smiled weakly. "Yeah. If it helps, Wade was partial to walking the Whirlwind Trail."

"Okay. How can we find it?"

"There's a small sign for the trailhead off the main road," Thelma said. "Keep an eye out. It's easy to miss if you don't know it's there."

"I know what you mean," I said, watching Earl kick a pinecone across the shell parking lot. "Kind of like my cousin's charm."

EARL MANEUVERED BESSIE back and forth down Turkey Creek Road twice, but we couldn't spot the place where the RV had gotten stuck in the muck last night. Heavy rain had washed away all traces.

There were also no GPS signals pinging from the cellphone Garth had stuffed in Jimmy's gym bag. That meant either Garth's phone battery had died, or Jimmy had moved out of wifi range.

I looked up from the phone app. "Nothing pinging on the radar, either. What do we do now?"

"Well, we're here," Grayson said. "We might as well take a look around for Jimmy and Wade. We have a known route for Wade. Whirlwind Trail. Let's start there. His disappearance is too close geographically and time wise not to be related somehow to whatever's going on with Jimmy."

"Agreed," I said.

Earl shrugged. "Works for me."

We spotted the sign for the trailhead on the second pass. Earl pulled off onto the gravel shoulder and up to the marker for Whirlwind Trail.

"I'll lead the way," Grayson said. You two keep close. Don't get separated, whatever you do."

"Why not?" I asked, annoyed that I'd have to stay within earshot of Earl.

"I forgot to mention it," Grayson said, climbing down out of the monster truck. "But that was one of the things all of Paulides' missing person cases have in common."

My nose crinkled. "*What* is?"

"Each person who vanished had either been hiking alone, or they'd gotten separated from their group. Some disappeared without a trace just a couple hundred yards down the trail from their companions."

I gulped. "Seriously?"

"Yes. Seriously."

As I climbed down out of the truck, Grayson clicked a button on the EMF detector. It whirred to life.

"In fact, Drex," Grayson said, "some vanished almost before their companions' eyes."

"What's he talking about?" Earl asked, walking around the front of the truck to meet us.

Grayson shot me a glance. "Explain it to him while I calibrate the detector. Make it quick."

My jaw dropped.

Oh, sure. Explain the time-space continuum to a guy whose best friend is a two-headed turtle. This should only take a sec.

Earl had been in the can when Grayson explained to me how fluctuations in electromagnetic fields could represent the "fingerprints" of past wormholes and other disturbances in time and space.

Grayson had dumbed it down for me with a taco shell. Now I had to dumb it down another hundred notches for Earl.

God help me.

"Uh ... Earl?" I said, snapping my finger to get his attention. He'd picked up a handful of mud and was rubbing the black muck between his thumb and forefinger.

"Yeah?" he said, wiping the black smear on the thigh of his camo hunting pants.

I sighed.

I guess I should be glad he didn't eat it.

"Listen," I said. "Grayson thinks there may be a hole in time out there in the woods that people are falling into."

Earl's eyes narrowed. I could almost hear the rusty cogs in his brain crunching.

"You mean like in *Back to the Future*?" he asked, then looked up at the sky like a turkey in the rain.

"Yes," I said. "Exactly like that. Only there's no DeLorean required. You just walk into it. That's why we need to stick close to each other. You know. So we don't end up sucked up into space."

Earl surprised me by grinning. "I think that'd be kind a cool, Bobbie."

"No," I said, shaking my head. "You wouldn't like it."

Earl frowned. "Why not?"

"They don't have fried chicken in space."

Chapter Sixteen

E arl and I hiked alongside each other for about a half mile up and down the undulating slopes of Whirlwind Trail. Accustomed to Florida's usually flat terrain, I was having a hard time keeping pace a few yards behind Grayson, who was in the lead, waiving his EMF detector in front of him like some space cadet in a low-budget sci-fi flick.

The only thing missing was the red shirt.

Back at the truck, Grayson had told us there was safety in numbers. I begged to disagree. As far as I was concerned, the fewer people who witnessed this ridiculous parade of idiocy, the better my odds were of not dying of embarrassment.

Still, a niggling little part of me worried Grayson was right. What if there really was a wormhole out there, vacuuming people up like some ravenous space Hoover?

I hedged my bet and tugged Earl along as my human shield—just in case.

Whirlwind Trail wound its way through patches of palmetto and pine flatland, interspersed with small hills covered mainly in stunted, gnarled scrub oaks. It was obvious the land had, in the not-too-distant past, undergone an upheaval of apocalyptic proportions. The terrain was hilly. And, with the exception of a scant handful of places, Florida simply didn't have hills.

From what I'd gathered in a Google search, the hills and valleys covering Edward Medard State Park were manmade—a byproduct of decades of phosphate mining by the American Cyanamid Company. The digging had ended in the late 1960s. The company had donated the land to the county back in 1969, and the area had been revegetated with trees and shrubs.

From what I could see, since then Mother Nature had been hard at work trying to heal the damage. She was doing her level-best to make the land, well, level again. Rains like the one that fell earlier in the day were slowly eroding the man-made hills, exposing the roots of the towering oaks that had sprouted atop them decades prior.

Like the child's fable of the little pigs who built their houses of straw, the unfortunate trees that chose to sprout on the hilltops could do nothing but watch and wait as the soil they'd sunk their roots into washed out from underneath them.

At the top of a particularly high hill, I stopped to take in the view. The grey-white sand comprising the mound was still damp from the rain, and left fairly detailed impressions of Grayson's boot treads. Other than a few bird footprints, no other marks marred the cleanly washed trail.

I sighed. This expedition wasn't turning into the clue-finding bonanza I'd hoped for. But on the bright side, I didn't have to keep such a keen eye on Earl. After all, he couldn't destroy evidence that didn't exist, right?

Ringing the base of nearly every sandy hill we descended, dark, muddy puddles burbled like miniature moats. Leaves and twigs washed in by the heavy downpour floated on the blackish-brown surfaces of the backwash pools, making them resemble ponds of brewing tea.

About an hour into our journey, nothing out of the ordinary had yet to happen. Grayson's gizmo hadn't gone off. And Earl had remained unusually silent and thoughtful, making me begin to wonder if we'd stumbled into another dimension without me noticing.

I shook my head, fighting against the enticing calm of the tranquil woods. If that detector thing of Grayson's *did* eventually go off, I needed to remain vigilant—my Glock at the ready. I planned to shoot that hyperactive Hoover in the nads before it could sweep us up in its cosmic vacuum hose. But then again, would that work?

"What's Grayson doing, Bobbie?" Earl asked, sending my crazy train of thoughts colliding off their tracks.

"What do you mean?" I asked, glancing up from where I'd been kneeling, staring at my reflection in a puddle as black as slate.

Earl nodded to his left. I followed his gaze to see Grayson about twenty feet away, waving his EMF detector around the edges of a pond.

"Think he found that space hole?" Earl asked.

"I dunno," I said. "Let's go find out."

"WHAT'S GOING ON?" I asked Grayson.

He looked over at us and stopped waving his EMF detector over a pond about the size of a swimming pool. He adjusted his fedora, then rubbed his chin.

"Intriguing," he said as we approached.

I could see the water in the pond wasn't black, but an odd, crystal blue. It almost appeared to be glowing. At the bottom of the crystalline water, massive clumps of creepy, greenish-blue slime lurked, making me think of crocodiles lying in wait along the Nile for their prey.

A shiver ran up my spine. "Is that the portal?" I asked.

Grayson shook his head. "No."

I frowned. "Then why is it glowing?"

"Phosphorous can give the water that appearance."

"Huh," Earl grunted. "What about that swamp cabbage crap growin' down there in the bottom of it?"

"Blue-green algae," Grayson said. "A byproduct of excessive phosphate contamination."

"Phosphate," I said. "Makes sense. Isn't it an ingredient in fertilizer?"

"And bombs," Grayson said. "But not portals, apparently. I'm not getting any fluctuations in electric or magnetic readings. The pond may look odd, but it's perfectly normal."

"Hey!" Earl called out. "What about this over here, Mr. G.?"

"Earl!" I yelled. "You're not supposed to go—"

"Don't move!" Grayson yelled.

Earl froze like a scarecrow hanging on the North Pole. "Am I gonna die?" he asked, barely moving his lips.

"Yes," Grayson said as we sprinted over to the small clearing Earl had wandered into.

"How long have I got?" Earl asked, remaining stiff as a board.

"Who knows?" Grayson said. "We're all going to die someday, Earl. But I don't think today is your day."

"That's good to know, Mr. G," Earl said between his teeth like a bad ventriloquist. "Then why can't I move?"

Grayson pulled his cellphone from his shirt pocket. "I need to get some pictures of this area without your size thirteen boot prints all over it."

"Ah, gotcha," Earl said. "Sorry 'bout that."

While Grayson documented the scene with his cellphone camera, I took a minute to figure out why he thought the place was noteworthy. After all, it was just a clearing in the woods.

Then I figured out what the fuss was about. In the center of the clearing was what appeared to be a circular patch of scorched earth. And the vegetation in the clearing itself wasn't naturally short. It had been pressed down, as if an elephant had been rolling around on it.

As I glanced around, I realized the flattened area was perfectly round—just like a primitive crop circle.

My gut flopped.

"What could've done this?" I asked, only half wanting to know the answer.

"You thinkin' them space-hole critters landed here?" Earl mumbled through pursed lips, voicing my secret fear.

"Perhaps," Grayson said, snapping off another shot. "By the way, you can move now."

"Whew!" Earl said, and shook out his shoulders as if he'd just bench-pressed a cow.

Grayson tucked his phone away and pulled out his EMF detector. "Now I just need to get a reading on the area."

As Grayson walked the perimeter of the clearing, scanning it with the detector, I held my breath in anticipation. Then I spotted something in the grass that made me laugh out loud with relief.

"Ha!" I cried, giddy with relief. "A cigarette butt!"

"Hmm," Grayson said, walking over. He knelt down for a closer examination. "That's odd."

"What?" I quipped. "That a space alien would smoke cigarettes?"

"No. That a lifeform intelligent enough for interdimensional travel would choose unfiltered cigarettes when there are so many other healthier options."

My shoulders went slack. "Are you serious?"

As I watched Grayson pluck the cigarette butt from the ground with tweezers and drop it into a baggie, my faith in intelligent lifeforms faded away.

"Does Jimmy smoke?" Grayson asked.

I frowned. "Not that I know of."

"How about Thelma's cousin? What's his name?"

"Wade," Earl said.

"Right," Grayson said. "So, does Wade smoke?"

I shrugged. "I don't know. I didn't think to ask Thelma."

All of a sudden, a weird whine filled the air. My eyes darted up at the sky. Were we about to be beamed up?

"Dear God! What is that?" I whimpered.

Grayson's cheek dimpled. He waved the EMF detector around in a circular motion. "Well, boys and girls. It appears we have ourselves a fluctuation."

"What's he talkin' about?" Earl asked me.

Grayson took another step toward the center of the clearing. The needle on the device jerked to the right. "We could be looking at the telltale signature of a tear in the time/space continuum," he said. "But I'll need to measure for time dilation to be sure."

My nose crinkled. "Time dilation? How do you do that?"

Grayson tipped his fedora with an index finger. "Well, first one sets up a laser to measure the speed of light in a given location, thus creating a catch point, or target. Then one sets up the laser in a secondary location and shoots the beam through a prism set up at the catch point. The prism bends the light beam and projects it back to the second site. If there's been an anomaly or ripple in time and space, the speed of light will differ from one location to the other."

"Huh?" Earl and I grunted simultaneously.

Grayson sighed. His arms went limp at his sides. "A discrepancy in the speed of light would mean time is passing differently in one spot versus the other. Like I told you before, this opens up the possibility for unconventional physics, where any number of unexplained phenomena can occur—including wormholes."

"Golly, Mr. G.," Earl said. "Seems like a lot a work just to find some old worm's butthole. I know a guy sells baitworms for three bucks behind the Piggly Wiggly."

"Not a worm's hole, you dingbat!" I growled. "A worm*hole*."

Earl frowned. "What's the difference?"

"Ugh! Never mind." I turned to Grayson. "Look, do you have one of these time-measuring gizmos?"

"By gizmo, you're referring to an oscilloscope, I presume," Grayson said. "And no. I'll have to borrow one."

My eyebrows collided. "*Borrow* one? From *who*?"

Grayson shook his head. "Sorry to break it to you, Drex, but Dr. Who isn't real."

My jaw pressed down at fifty million pounds per square inch. "I *meant—*"

Just then, a raindrop splatted on my forehead like cosmic birdshit.

"No time for long discussions," Grayson said, looking up at the sky. "I need to collect soil samples from around this ring before the scene is completely compromised."

"What difference does it make?" I argued. "It's already rained on it at least once."

Grayson nodded toward the clearing behind me. "Not *that* kind of rain, it hasn't."

I turned around and nearly swallowed my tongue. Earl had unzipped his pants and was peeing directly into the center of the blackened patch of earth.

"Earl!" I screeched. "For crying out loud! Stop it! Stop it right now!"

Chapter Seventeen

B y the time Earl's monster truck rolled back into Garth's compound, it had stopped raining again. Grayson and I jumped out
of the truck and headed to the RV. It was time to process the evidence we'd gathered at the mysterious, circular clearing we'd discovered along Whirlwind Trail.

"I'm sorry about Earl," I apologized again as I unloaded the sample vials from Grayson's field kit. I laid them on the banquette table
and rummaged around for a test-tube stand amid a cardboard box
full of science-looking junk Grayson had hauled from a cabinet in
the hallway. "I had no idea he was gonna piss all over the evidence."

"You can't be held responsible," Grayson said, plucking the stand
from my hand. He dumped the contents of each vial into individual
test tubes and stuck them, one by one, into holes in a clear-plastic
tray. "It's not Earl's fault. He hasn't been properly trained."

"I guess you're right." I sighed and glanced out the small window
above the table. Earl was hosing the mud off Bessie's huge tires. "You
know it took my aunt six years to potty-train him. Teaching him to
be a detective could take decades."

When Grayson didn't respond, I looked back over him. His face
was stone-cold serious as he opened the eyedropper cap on a small,
brown bottle and began adding drops to the open test tubes.

"You think that circle we found was made by some kind of electromagnetic force?" I asked.

"Possibly," Grayson said absently. He picked up one of the test
tubes and swirled it around. "Then again, Native Americans believe

places exist where the veil between the spirit and man are at their thinnest."

"What do you mean?"

"Vortexes, Drex," Grayson said, his eyes darting briefly to me, then back to the test tube. "Doorways to the realms of the Star People."

I swallowed hard. "*Star* People?"

"Yes. Ancestors of humanity who brought us here from the stars and continue to visit us today."

My nose crinkled. "You sound like some New-Age kook, Grayson."

He shrugged. "I like to keep an open mind."

"Really? What happened to your 'swamp gas' theory from last night?"

"I traded it in for phosphorus."

My right eyebrow rose. "I'm not following you."

"See this sample here?" Grayson held up a test tube containing water as blue as Ty d Bol. "It indicates high levels of phosphate."

"Wow," I deadpanned. "You discovered phosphate in an old phosphate mining area. Shall I alert the media?"

Grayson blew a breath out his nostrils. "I have a point."

"Okay," I said, folding my arms across my chest. "I'm all ears."

Grayson eyed me skeptically. "Take that pond we saw. It was dug from phosphate rock. Phosphate contains *phosphorous*. And phosphorous is the key element needed to create phosphorescence—the stuff that makes glow-in-the-dark stickers glow."

My brow furrowed. "Are you saying that's what made the glowing ring we saw in the forest last night? Phosphorous? I thought you said it was a *portal*—made of intergalactic microwave ovens, or something like that."

Grayson winced as if I'd just pinched his brain. "The two have to be related somehow. I need to take readings of the glowing phenomenon. We should go out again tonight and see if it makes another appearance."

"And get sucked into another dimension, like that Paulides guy says? Uh ... no thanks."

"The probability of that happening is extremely unlikely, Drex."

"Really?" I argued. "You said yourself that *thousands* of people have disappeared without a trace. Face it, Grayson. You can't guarantee it won't happen to us, too."

"True. But Paulides took the time to map out the major locations of the disappearances. Florida didn't make the list."

My arms fell to my sides. "Are you saying there's finally something crazy going on that *isn't* happening here in Florida?"

Grayson nodded. "Yes."

I smirked. "How's that possible?"

Grayson shrugged. "We don't have any quartz."

I blanched. "*What?* Is that some kind of cosmic go-juice or something?"

Grayson sighed. "Did you not attend a single science class in school? I'm talking about *rocks*, Drex. Quartz *rocks*. According to Paulides, one of the commonalities of the sites where people disappeared was the presence of rocks or boulders with significant quartz content."

I chewed my lip and tried to look smart. "What's so special about quartz?"

"It's a natural conductor."

I smiled. "You mean like Yo-Yo Ma?"

Grayson shook his head and handed me the tray of test tubes. "Here, empty these and wash them out. There's nothing remarkable about the soil—unless you count the ash from the cigarettes."

I took the tray and noticed one of the tubes had turned bright yellow. "What about this one?"

"Oh. That's just urea."

"Urea?"

"Earl's urine."

"Gross!"

I headed toward the sink. A knock sounded at the door. It cracked open and Garth's head popped inside.

"Any news about Jimmy?" he asked, then coughed.

"Sorry. No," I said.

I set the test-tube tray on the counter and my cellphone rang. "Hold on," I said, and walked over to the banquette table where it lay. I glanced at the display. "Huh. Looks like a local number."

"That's Jimmy!" Garth wheezed over my shoulder.

"Put it on speaker," Grayson said from across the room.

I mashed the button. "Hello?"

"Bobbie?" a man's voice asked.

"Yes. It's me. Jimmy? Where are you?"

"No time to talk," he whispered. "Listen carefully. Whatever you do, don't—"

"Cough, cough, cough!"

Garth had chosen that exact moment to hack out half a lung.

"What was that?" I said into the phone. "Sorry, Jimmy. Could you repeat that?"

The line clicked off.

"Crap!" I said.

"Hit redial," Garth sputtered.

I mashed the button and the three of us stared silently at the phone, listening to it ring until it clicked to voicemail. A mechanical voice told us Jimmy's mailbox was full.

"He's not picking up," I said.

Garth looked up with pleading, watery eyes. "What do you think that means?"

"I dunno," I said. "But on the bright side, Jimmy's still alive."

"Yes," Grayson said. "But from the sound of it, he's in more trouble than I thought."

Chapter Eighteen

Jimmy's mysterious call had put our investigation back to square one. He hadn't been swallowed up by a wormhole—unless intergalactic rights allowed you one phone call home. Instead, it was more likely a game of hide and seek. Jimmy was alive and well—but for some reason he didn't want us to find him.

At least, that's the impression I'd gotten from his tone over the phone, anyway. Instead, Jimmy had tried to warn me of something. But what? Garth's cough had obliterated his message.

"What do you think Jimmy was talking about?" I asked Garth. "He said, 'Whatever you do, don't—' Don't what?"

"I dunno," Garth said, then wiped his nose on his flannel sleeve.

"Why'd he hang up?" I asked.

"Perhaps he thought his message had been received," Grayson said. "Being a cop, Jimmy's savvy enough to know his location could be tracked via his phone, so he made it short and quick. He's obviously turned off the GPS tracking option so we can't find him. But we still have one advantage, while it lasts."

"What's that?" Earl asked.

"Jimmy still isn't aware that Operative Garth's planted his *own* phone inside his brother's gym bag."

"How do you know that?" Earl asked.

"Because he had to get within wifi range to call Bobbie," Grayson said, then flashed Earl the display on his cellphone. "As soon as he was within range, the GPS app began signaling again."

I glanced at the red blip moving across Grayson's phone display. "Where is he?" I asked.

"He's heading south on Turkey Creek Road," Grayson said, slipping the phone into his shirt pocket. "Bingo. Let's roll."

THE SUN WAS HANGING low in the sky as we peeled out of Garth's compound and sped down the rural backroad in the direction of the red blip marking Jimmy's position.

"What's the game plan, Mr. G.?" Earl asked, swerving to avoid a flattened roadkill possum.

"Ward," Grayson said, staring out the windshield and tapping his chin with a long, tapered index finger.

My nose crinkled. "What would Amazing Randi do?"

Grayson stopped tapping and stared at me. "No. I meant that waitress' cousin. What's his name?"

"Wade," I said.

Grayson gave a quick nod. "Right. We should keep an eye out for him. I feel more certain than ever he's involved in whatever Jimmy's gotten himself tangled up with."

I winced at the thought. "You thinking drug dealing or something like that?"

Grayson pushed up the brim of his fedora with the same spidery index finger. "Intergalactic drug trade. I hadn't considered that."

"Pill-pushin' pimps from Pluto!" Earl blurted with glee.

I shook my head. "Speaking of tangled up in problems, why on Earth did *Earl* have to come with us this time?"

"We need Bessie," Grayson said. "Unless you want to get stuck in the mud again. I told Earl we might have to go in the back way, like we did last night."

Earl snickered.

I turned and shot him a glare that could explode molten lava. I raised my fist. "Say *one word* and you're gonna be the next missing person on that Paulides guy's list."

Earl sucked his lips inside his mouth and shifted Bessie into overdrive.

Grayson checked the GPS tracker again. "Slow down, Earl. Looks like we're closing in on Jimmy."

"You got it, Chief," Earl said, easing up on the pedal.

Suddenly, Grayson slapped the dashboard with his palm. "Dammit!"

"What's wrong?" I asked.

"Beat's me," Earl said. "I didn't hit a turtle nor nuthin."

"The signal vanished," Grayson said. "Pull over, Earl. Now!"

Earl hit the brakes and eased Bessie on to the soggy shoulder of the road. Grayson rolled down the window.

"The last point the GPS tracker indicated was somewhere over it that direction," Grayson said, pointing to a patch of cypress swamp.

I grimaced at the marshy muck on the side of the road. "What do we do now?"

Grayson tucked the phone into his pocket. "Elementary. Put on our duckies and wade."

"Great." I reached for the insect repellent sitting in the holder by Earl's YETI drink cup. "Stay here and guard the truck, Earl."

Earl pouted. "But I wanna see me one a them angora boar's asses."

"*Aurora borealis*," I said through gritted teeth. "And that *wasn't* what we saw last night!"

Earl eyed me skeptically. "Then what was it?"

"Most likely an emission of natural phosphorescent," Grayson said.

"You mean like that over there?" Earl asked, and pointed out the windshield.

I glared at my cousin. "I'm not falling for that stupid joke, burrito breath."

"Yes, exactly like that," I heard Grayson say.

I turned and stared. There in the woods to our right was the same reddish-orange glow I'd seen last night.

My mouth fell open.

"Good spotting, Earl," Grayson said. "Looks like we've found the right spot."

"All right!" Earl hollered, reaching for the door handle. "Let's roll!"

"No," I said. "I told you. You're staying here. Right, Grayson?"

Grayson shrugged. "Let him come."

"Why?" I whined.

"Like I said before. There's safety in numbers."

"Yeah," I grumbled. "But you forget. Earl doesn't count."

Chapter Nineteen

"**D**o we really have to do this tonight?" I asked, pulling on a pair of rubber galoshes I'd had the foresight to bring after ruining my cowboy boots tromping through the mushy terrain last night.

"It's called an investigation for a reason," Grayson said. "You know. We *investigate* stuff."

"I *know*," I grumbled. "But you said last night this thing could be emitting microwave radiation. Shouldn't we be wearing some kind of protective gear? I'm not exactly in the mood to have my ovaries turned into Hot Pockets."

"That was just a working theory I espoused at the time, due to lack of data," Grayson said, tucking the EMF detector into his jacket. "It's far more likely we're looking at some sort of natural phosphorescent phenomenon."

I shot him a skeptical look. "So now you're saying phosphorous can drain cellphone batteries, bellow like a mad cow, and then come charging after us?"

Grayson shrugged. "The batteries could've malfunctioned."

"Mr. G.'s right," Earl said. "And as far as the bellerin', you could a just been chased by an ugly old boar."

I sighed.

Well, it wouldn't be the first time.

AFTER TWENTY MINUTES of slogging through the swampy cypress woods in galoshes, the glowing spot we were searching for was beginning to seem like a mirage. Despite our best efforts to locate it, the thing remained elusive and out of sight.

If only *Earl* had.

My cousin had made it his mission to pester the living daylights out of me since we'd left the truck. Correction—since he'd left the birth canal.

"If you snort like a pig one more time, Earl, I'm gonna skewer you clean through and serve you with fried green tomatoes."

Earl sidled up to me and whispered, "That last one weren't me."

My heart pinged with fear. Was something out here with us? I glanced around at the dark woods, then realized I'd been had yet again.

"Yeah, right," I said sourly.

"I mean, it *was* me," Earl said. "But it weren't voluntary. That was my stomach a growlin.' I'm about slap starved to death."

"Ugh!" I said, relief filling my lungs. "Why didn't you eat a snack or something while we were at the RV?"

"You kiddin' me?" Earl said. "I checked y'all's fridge. You ain't got nothin' in there 'cept ingredients."

"Quiet!" Grayson hissed. "I think we're getting close."

I shot Earl some side eye. "We'd better be, for your sake."

Grayson climbed a steep ridge about ten feet high, then stopped at the top.

"See anything?" Earl whispered.

Grayson didn't answer.

Earl turned and looked at me, his eyes wide. "Maybe he's done got zapped by aliens."

"Right. Or maybe he just didn't hear you, boy genius," I said, trudging past him up the ridge.

BY THE TIME I REACHED Grayson, the climb up the ridge had my heart beating in my throat. But what I saw at the top nearly stopped it cold.

I stared, mouth agape, at what looked like the ghost of a solar eclipse. It was that weird, orange ring again. It hovered, silent and stationary, a few feet off the ground.

"What in *Hell* is that?" I squeaked, my lungs so tight I could barely breathe.

"Uncertain," Grayson replied robotically, his gaze never leaving the radiating orb. "But whatever it is, it's not from Hell."

"How do *you* know?" I said.

"Easy," Earl said, coming to stand beside me. "No horns."

Stupefied by the strange orb and my cousin's otherworldly stupidity, I stood motionless beside Grayson as he shone his flashlight into the dark middle of the orb. From within its center shadow, the vague silhouette of an oblong, silvery object came into view.

"Hoo doggy!" Earl said. "What you think *that* is, Mr. G?"

Grayson rubbed his chin. "Based on the information Garth provided, I'd say it's most likely an ambassador ship from the planet Krull."

My knees began to shake with sheer terror.

Dear God! If these two idiots are who make first contact, we Earthlings are doomed!

Chapter Twenty

"**A** ... *sss ... spaceship?*" I stuttered, my brain frozen with fright.
"It would appear so," Grayson said, aiming his flashlight
beam at the metallic-looking object in the center of the glowing ring.

As a block of ice replaced my once-functioning brain cells, I noted a band encircling the craft. Strange hieroglyphic symbols adorned the raised strip around its middle.

I giggled as hysteria set in. Whatever the thing inside the glowing orb was, my haywire mind had decided it was the basic shape of a Tootsie Pop. But even in my impaired state of consciousness, I still had enough functioning synapses to know that I had no desire whatsoever to find out what awaited me in the center of that thing.

I put a hand on Grayson's shoulder and whispered, "Let's get out of here."

Suddenly, Grayson's flashlight went out.

"For God's sake! Turn the light back on!" I screeched.

"I can't," Grayson said. He slapped the bottom of the flashlight. "It's not working!"

"That's not possible!" I said, my knees wobbling so bad I nearly collapsed. "I put fresh batteries in it myself!"

"I should have anticipated this," Grayson said, shaking his head. "The vast majority of abductees report power drains to their equipment."

My knees nearly gave out. "Ab...ab...*abductees?*"

Just then, exactly like the night before, a strange, inhuman whine filled the air. Then came a thundering sound, like the pounding of a thousand horse hooves.

"Uh ... that sounds like a lot a boars, y'all," Earl said, his eyes as big as boiled eggs.

In the darkness, a tree branch cracked somewhere near the space-craft.

"Holy shit!" I squealed.

I grabbed my cellphone from my pocket and shot my reading light in the direction of the sound. To my utter horror, right before it blinked out, the beam landed on a white, triangular-headed form about six feet tall. Beside it, a dark figure loomed, sporting a headful of snake-like tentacles—a Medusa from Mars.

"Aaak!" I screeched. "It's freaking aliens from the planet Krull!" Then I turned around and blew past Earl like a floozy in a brothel raid.

Grayson yelled something at me as I whizzed by—but I couldn't hear him over the sound of my galoshes. They were squeaking like a flock of rubber ducks in a bathtub gangbanger.

"SO MUCH FOR THE THEORY that you've become desensi-tized to paranormal phenomena," Grayson quipped as we piled into Bessie like a tragic, redneck version of *The Three Stooges*.

Earl stomped the gas pedal before Grayson could even get the door closed. Bessie's tires spun, then grabbed the asphalt and lurched forward, plastering me to the bench seat with the G-force of a rocket launch.

Sandwiched between the two guys, I held on for dear life as Bessie hurtled down the narrow backroad, Earl's foot jammed to the floorboard like it had been Superglued.

"Desensitized?" I gasped, as soon as I could catch my breath. "Excuse me, but I didn't exactly see *you* hanging around to sign any peace treaty."

"Fair enough," Grayson said, pulling a device from his pocket. "But to my credit, I *was* able to obtain a fairly respectable reading on the EMF detector."

"Oh, goody," I said sourly, using my last speck of willpower to not slap the stupid gadget from Grayson's hand.

"What's that gizmo thang say, Mr. G.?" Earl asked. "Was them space critters for real?"

"To confirm that would be pure speculation at this point," Grayson said. "But according to the detector, there's definitely been some sort of EMF anomaly."

"No, shit," I said.

Earl laughed. "He didn't mean what you done in your pants, Bobbie."

"Hmm," Grayson grunted. "We need to regroup and work out a better plan."

"I repeat," I said. "*No shit.*"

Chapter Twenty-One

"**A**liens?" Garth said, his nose as burgundy red as the stripes on his flannel housecoat. Perched on the edge of the broken couch in the RV, he waved his damp hanky in the air like a NASCAR pro. "I knew it! What'd they look like?"

"Well ... uh," I stammered, still woozy from my extraterrestrial encounter. I was hunched over the banquette booth. My wobbly head rested in my hands, propped up by my elbows on the table.

"They kinda looked like them Coneheads to me," Earl said, taking a sip of Pepsi. "You know. What used to be on *Saturday Night Live.*" He opened a kitchen cabinet. "Hey, Garth, you got any more a them Twinkies up in that trailer a yore's?"

Garth's face went limp. He glanced over at me. "Is he serious? About the aliens, not the Twinkies."

I winced and hiked my shoulders up to my ears. "Uh ... from what I saw, one of them *did* have a pointy head. But it was dark. And the other one sure as hell didn't. It looked like it had snakes coming out of its—"

"Hold still, Drex!" Grayson barked.

I froze. "Come on, Grayson! Do we have to do this *now?*"

I reached up to scratch one of the pasty electrodes stuck to my forehead. On top of just getting the living crap scared out of me by a pair of ET goblins, Grayson had insisted on hooking me up to his stupid EEG machine as soon as we got back.

"Absolutely," Grayson said. "This is a rare chance to collect actual field data for comparison." He rubbed his chin and stared at the monitor. "Hmm. This thing must be broken."

I frowned. "Why do you say that?"

"Historically, your results have trended toward marked improvement in your alpha-wave levels. This is the lowest reading I've seen since we began testing."

"Well *excuuuse* me," I said, yanking an electrode off my forehead. "Can I help it if I'm allergic to alien life forms? Good grief. Are we *done* here?"

Grayson sighed. "I suppose."

"Lemme try it, Chief!" Earl said.

"Knock yourself out," I said, yanking off the remaining electrodes. "Sit over there."

Earl plopped down opposite me at the banquette and wiggled like a puppy waiting for a treat as I pasted my used electrodes to his Neanderthal brow ridge.

Grayson frowned at me. "If this machine is functioning properly, you're results are truly disappointing, Drex."

I shot him a sour face. "Then why don't you give your new protégé a shot at it? He's all hooked up."

Grayson glanced at Earl, blew out a sigh, then began resetting the dials on his EEG machine. "Fine."

"I mean, really, Grayson," I grumbled. "What kind of results did you expect? Who in their right mind could keep their shit together with aliens on their asses?"

Grayson's eyebrow shot up. "*Earl*, apparently."

I glared at Grayson. "I said in their *right* mind."

"Intriguing," Grayson said, staring at the monitor. "Earl, your alpha waves are impressively high."

I scowled at my cousin. "Seriously? Those aliens didn't scare you outta your stupid gourd?"

Earl shook his head. "Naw."

My jaw flexed. "Why the hell not?"

"I don't think they was after *us*," Earl said nonchalantly. "And that white one looked kinda friendly, if you ask me."

I shook my head. "That could only mean one thing."

"That Earl's a natural at this?" Grayson asked.

"No!" I hissed. "That Earl's a big *buffoon*!"

"Uh...I hate to interrupt," Garth said, raising a hand like a kid in class. "But these aliens. Do you think they might have my brother Jimmy trapped inside their spaceship?"

The three of us stopped our petty bickering and stared at poor Garth. Clad in a ratty flannel robe and coiffed in a bed-head mullet, the sad little dude looked like the star of a Nyquil ad—for new, Jack Daniels flavor.

"Uh ...," I fumbled.

"Inconclusive," Grayson said. "Our mission was cut short by unforeseen circumstances, Operative Garth. Due to the hasty retreat of one investigative member, we were unable to gather conclusive evidence one way or the other."

"So this is *my* fault?" I hissed. "Excuse me for wanting to *survive*. How thoughtless of me!"

Grayson's eyes darted to the ceiling, then returned to studying Earl's results on the monitor. "Uncanny," he said, then glanced up at Garth. "Hey, you wouldn't happen to have an oscilloscope, would you?"

Garth perked up. "You need to measure the speed of light?"

"Yes."

Garth nodded. "You a Cathode or digital man?"

I blanched.

Seriously?

"Digital, if you've got it," Grayson said.

Garth shook his head. "I don't. But my buddy Sherman's got a couple of sweet o-scopes back at his place."

Grayson's cheek dimpled beside his bushy moustache. "Excellent. Is your colleague nearby?"

"Just a mile or so down the street."

"Let's go, then." Grayson got up from the monitor and took a step toward the front of the RV. "I'll drive."

"Hold on a minute!" I said. "Shouldn't we be calling that Warren Engles guy at the FBI or something? I mean, we're talking about *space aliens* here!"

"And have them come and lock down the site?" Grayson said, his face aghast.

"And remove all the evidence, then say it never happened?" Garth added, equally horrified.

The two conspiracy nutters locked eyes for a moment, then turned and stared at me, a determined look hardening on their faces.

"Not on my watch," Grayson said.

"You got that right, Mr. Gray," Garth said, then had a coughing fit.

Earl yanked off the electrodes. "I'm with you fellers!"

Outnumbered by idiots, I glanced at the clock above the banquette. It was nearly midnight. I was exhausted, sweaty, sticky with electrode paste, and totally *not* in the mood to be probed by extraterrestrials.

Not *tonight*, anyway.

"What's the rush?" I asked, following Grayson to the front of the RV. "That spaceship's probably already portal-letted back to Krull by now, anyway."

"Perhaps," Grayson said, fishing the motorhome's keys from the visor above the driver's seat. "But even if it has, with the oscilloscope, we should still be able to more accurately determine if there indeed was a distortion in time and space, and help zero-in on the its location."

"How long does the distortion last?" I asked.

"Who knows?" Grayson said. "Perhaps millennia."

"Then what's the hurry?" I said, desperate to stall him at any cost. "Shouldn't we think this through a bit more? Come on. What's it gonna take to make you at least sleep on the idea?"

"A miracle," Grayson said.

He slid into the driver's seat and turned the ignition. The RV wouldn't start.

I smiled up at the heavens.

Thank you, Universe!

"Uh, Mr. Gray?" Garth said, sticking his red nose into the driver's cabin. "I hate to slow down the project, but Sherman's not allowed visitors after 9:30."

Seriously? You've outdone yourself, Universe!

I shot Garth a sideways smirk. "Let me guess. Psychiatric facility?"

Garth cocked his head like a bespectacled donkey. "Nope. His mom's basement."

I glanced over at Grayson and caught him wince as if he'd been shot through the temple.

"Gee. That's too bad," I said.

Grayson exhaled a long sigh. "Very well," he said, and pulled the keys from the ignition. "It appears we'll have to resume efforts in the morning. In the meantime, Earl, you're in charge of diagnosing what's wrong with the RV."

"I'm on it, Chief!" Earl said, sticking his head in the driver's cabin next to Garth's. He turned and smirked at me. "So who's the buffoon *now*, Bobbie?"

Given the prime choices around here? Tough call.

"You are," I said.

Earl showed me his *suck it* face. "That's right, Cuz. And don't you forget it!"

Like I ever could.

Chapter Twenty-Two

I stared blankly into a cup of coffee almost as black as Earl's face and hands. I'd been up since 4:13 a.m.—the exact time my brilliant cousin had decided to start taking apart the engine on the RV.

I'd been sitting at the banquette drinking coffee and listening to him bang around for over two hours when he finally poked his grease-covered head inside the door and leered at me.

"I found it!" he said, grinning from ear to ear.

"What?" I asked. "An oil slick?"

"Nope. That's just occupational hazard. I had to take the dang engine apart. It's the water pump what's busted."

I handed Earl a cup of coffee. "Where we gonna find a water pump around here?"

Earl took a steaming slurp. "Wake up and smell the junk, Bobbie."

Ew! I'd rather not...

Earl poked a hitchhiker thumb over the left shoulder of his blue coveralls. I glanced out the door. The sun was just beginning to cast a faint, pink glow on the mountain of rusted-out stoves and refrigerators littering the compound.

"Oh," I grunted. "*That* junk."

"We can pr'olly find an old water pump somewheres in this heap a garbola Garth lives in," Earl said.

"Ahem," a voice sounded from amid the apocalyptic debris. Garth stepped out from behind an old Buick chassis and cleared his throat again. "It's not *all* garbola."

Earl winced. "Uh ... no offense, buddy."

119

"None taken." Garth started to say something else, but instead sneezed so loudly my hand instinctually moved to cover my coffee cup. He wiped his bulbous red nose with a hanky, then nodded toward his trailer. "I'd say your best bet for a water pump that'd fit the RV is in the hangar out back of the doublewide."

"Thanks," Earl said. "I'll head over there soon as I finish my coffee."

"You want a cup?" I asked Garth.

He smiled weakly, giving me a glimpse of his bucktooth choppers. "That'd be great, Pandora." Then he blew his nose like a foghorn.

"I'll get the coffee," Grayson said from behind me.

The sight of Grayson already neatly dressed in his uniform of black jeans and black T-shirt made me cringe. It really raised the bar on my gray sweatpants and a *Who Farted?* T-shirt.

"Good morning, clan," Grayson said as he padded over to the stove. "Earl, I see you're already hard at work. Do you require assistance with your rudimentary operation?"

Confusion marred Earl's blackened brow. "I thought she was a Winnebago."

"He meant do you need help with the water pump," I said.

"Oh." Earl shook his head. "Nope. I got it all under control, Mr. G."

"I can see that," Grayson said. "Very good. Carry on."

"Will do, Chief." Earl saluted, drained his coffee cup, set it on the floor by the door, then disappeared into the junkyard like a redneck chimneysweep.

Grayson handed Garth a cup of coffee. "Let's go pick up that oscilloscope, shall we?"

Garth sat on the couch and blew on the hot brew. "Uh...sorry, Mr. Gray. It's barely past seven o'clock. Sherman usually sleeps till noon."

"You don't say," Grayson said dully. "Well, no bother. We have other things we can do in the meantime."

My nose crinkled. "Why don't you just go to Walmart and buy your own stupid Oscar Mayer scope thing?"

"Oscilloscope," Grayson corrected. "It's not exactly the kind of thing they carry at Walmart."

"He's right, Pandora," Garth chimed in. "And a good digital o-scope can set you back six or seven grand."

The two techno-nerds exchanged smirks, making me feel like a doofus.

"Fine," I grumbled, reaching for a box of Pop Tarts. "So what else is on the agenda?"

"Retrofitting the back bedroom to contain our alien quarry, for one thing," Grayson said.

I nearly dropped my blueberry toaster pastry.

"Retrofitting?" I asked. "I thought you said that room was already reinforced with monster-proof trapping stuff. In fact, I distinctly remember you telling me it was strong enough to hold Godzilla."

"*Physically*, yes," Grayson said. "But in *this* case, we'll need to add certain *accoutrements* to entice the space creatures in."

"Accoutrements?" I snarled. "Like what? A *Star Wars* bedspread?"

"Hmm." Grayson's eyebrow raised as if he were actually contemplating my suggestion. "I was thinking more along the lines of gustatory and auditory lures. Sweet treats and a homing beacon, if you will."

"Of course!" Garth said excitedly. "Just like in *ET the Extraterrestrial*!"

Grayson pointed a finger gun at Garth and pulled the trigger. "Exactly, my good man!"

"Huh?" I grunted.

Garth's bloodshot eyes aimed in my direction. "You remember. That kid used a trail of Reese's Pieces to get ET to follow him home. And then ET tried to phone home with that contraption he made out of toys."

Dear God! Have I had a stroke?

Grayson sighed thoughtfully, his gaze skyward. "A truly inspired movie, if you ask me."

Garth nodded violently, like a head-banging *Queen* fan. "Totally!"

I fought in vain against a sudden attack of involuntary eye roll. "Uh ... sorry to burst your space bubbles, dudes, but I've got a feeling it's gonna take a lot more than a bag of Halloween candy and a souped-up Speak & Spell to entice alien life forms into *this* ratty old RV."

Grayson rubbed his chin. "Of course it is, Drex. That's why I plan to supplement the trail of Reese's Pieces with induction coils."

Something inside me broke. I think it was whatever little hope I had left for the future.

I smiled weakly, resigning myself to my fate. "Oh, sure. I mean, there's not an alien out there who can resist a tasty *induction coil.*"

Garth snickered and shot Grayson another knowing glance.

"What's so funny?" I asked.

Grayson locked his green eyes on mine. "Drex, it's not the coils' *flavor* they'll be enticed by. It's the *frequency* the coils will be emitting."

Oh. Well that explains everything.

NOT!

I slapped on a studious look and tried to focus. Whatever those two science jerks were talking about, I had a feeling understanding it might come in handy soon for my ongoing survival.

"I'm sorry," I said. "I'm afraid I need a little bit more of an explanation."

"Let me make it easier for you," Grayson said.

He held up a black plastic box the size of a juice box. I recognized it as that stupid bug sweeper gizmo I'd found the other day under the passenger seat.

"During our expedition last night, I used the EMF detector to measure the magnetic frequency fluctuations being emitted by the alien craft."

Not exactly a sentence I thought I'd hear in my lifetime, but okay...

I smiled weakly. "Well, um ... well done!"

Grayson nodded. "Thank you."

"But Grayson, I thought that thing in your hand was a bug sweeper."

He smiled. "It *is*. This morning, I'm going to recreate those identical magnetic fluctuation patterns electronically, then retrofit this bug sweeper to serve as a transmitting coil." He smiled at the black gizmo. "This little baby is going to become a beacon, transmitting the identical electromagnetic signature as the alien craft."

I cringed with confusion. "Wait. I thought you said you were going to use *induction* coils, not transmitting coils."

Grayson's cheek dimpled. "Right again. I *did*. You see, by embedding *induction* coils into the back room of the RV, we can use them to pick up the bug sweeper's *transmissions* and amplify the signal for a broader reach—all while keeping the homing source localized to the back bedroom, or what you've so eloquently dubbed, 'the monster trap.'"

Geez. If that's the dumbed-down version, I'm a goner.

"Uh ... okay," I said.

Garth snickered. "Mr. Gray, it looks like your ETs are about to phone the wrong home!"

Grayson's eyes twinkled. "Exactly! And when they do, all we'll need to do then is entice them into the trap and slam the door shut on them!"

A sinking feeling came over me. I raised a finger. "Let me guess. That's where the Reese's Pieces come in?"

Grayson grinned. "Precisely!"

I shook my head.

All right, Universe. All we need now is a good extinction event.

Chapter Twenty-Three

"This is the last one," I said, putting a dab of glue on the only remaining induction coil.

I'd been surprised at how tiny they were—no larger than half a c-volt battery. Still, according to Grayson, they were supposed to be able to amplify electronic transmissions all the way to the ozone layer.

I pressed the coil onto the baseboard behind the nightstand in the back bedroom and held it for sixty seconds. "There. All done."

I heaved myself up of the floor. As I moved the nightstand back in place, my mind flashed to the mysterious folder labeled *Experiment #5*. It was right there—in that drawer—mere inches from my hand. But with Grayson in the room with me, it was as out of reach as if it had been on Mars.

Hot bodies. Is Grayson a perv?

I glanced over at my partner. He was sitting on the bed, happily filling a Mason jar with Reese's Pieces. I shook my head.

What am I supposed to do with that *information?*

I took a deep breath and carried on with my life like a hapless victim of Stockholm Syndrome. "So, how do these induction coils work?" I asked.

Grayson looked up from the jar brimming with pill-shaped, bright yellow, orange and brown candies. "By taking advantage of the Earth's natural electromagnetic field."

"You mean like radio waves?"

Grayson set the jar full of Reese's Pieces on the nightstand. "Same principle, different medium."

I nodded. "Wow. There must be a lot of technology packed inside those tiny little coils."

"Not really."

Grayson clamped a chip-clip on the open end of the industrial-sized bag of Reese's Pieces. "An induction coil is really nothing more than a core of metal with wires wrapped around it. The Earth's molten core means it's one big induction coil itself, radiating electromagnetic energy. We're just tapping into the motherlode, if you will."

I forced a smile. I still didn't quite get the technical mumbo-jumbo, but I guess it didn't matter. It was only my lousy life at stake.

"Uh, Grayson—"

"I talked to Sherman, Mr. Gray," Garth said, poking his head into the room. "He's prepared the digital oscillator as you requested."

"Excellent." Grayson rubbed his hands together. "We just finished up in here. Drex, do you want to come along?"

"Uh ... gee, thanks," I said. "But I just reached my nerd quotient for the day. Besides, Earl may need help installing the water pump. I used to be a mechanic, remember?"

Garth stared at me with what I assumed was his come-hither look. Either that or the poor dweeb was about to lose his lunch.

"You know, Pandora," Garth said, pushing his glasses up on his red nose, "with your skills you'd be the *perfect* post-apocalyptic mate."

"Gee. Thanks, Garth."

I forced a smile, recalling the last compliment the doomsday prepper had given me.

It had been about my nice, extra-wide breeder hips.

I COULD STILL MAKE out Bessie's tailgate on the asphalt road when I slammed the RV side door and headed for the back bedroom.

With Earl chauffeuring Garth and Grayson to Sherman's mom's house, I finally had a few minutes to myself.

Alone.

And I needed to make every second count.

Like a ninja on crack, I sprinted down the hall past the bathroom and nearly did a cartwheel over the bed. I landed with my keister parked on the mattress beside the nightstand.

Sweet!

I was about to get my hands on that mystery folder labeled *Experiment #5*.

"Come to mamma," I said, and yanked open the drawer.

The folder was gone.

"Nooo!" I wailed.

Either Grayson had no idea of my intentions and had simply moved the folder somewhere else, or he was totally aware of my busybody snooping and had decided to foil it.

"Crap." I needed somebody on *my* side.

I pulled my phone from my pocket and hit speed dial.

"Yeah?" a raspy voice grunted.

"Hey, Beth-Ann"

"Bobbie? Hold on. I gotta get Gladys under the dryer."

"Okay."

While I waited, I padded to the kitchen, unwrapped a Tootsie Pop, and began scrounging around the RV for the folder.

"What's up?" Beth-Ann asked.

I plucked the sucker from my mouth. "Beth-Ann, I think I may not have too long to live."

"What?" she gasped. "Is that tumor thingy in your head acting up?"

"Huh? Oh. No. But this crazy case we're working on. I don't know if it's survivable. Tonight, we're going out to investigate ... uh ..."

"What?"

I winced. "I'm not supposed to say."

"Come on. You can tell *me*."

I glanced out the kitchen blinds, then whispered into the phone. "*Aliens*."

"Did you say *aliens*?" Beth-Ann said. "As in little green men?"

"Yeah only they're not green. And they're not little."

Beth-Ann laughed. "Is that Tootsie Pop I hear clacking around in your mouth laced with LSD?"

"Ha ha. No."

"Okay. Seriously, Bobbie. Why do you think tracking down aliens is potentially deadly? To be honest, it doesn't sound any crazier than all the other stuff you've survived since you hooked up with Grayson."

My best friend's lack of surprise confounded me. "Well, *this* time is different."

"How?" she asked, her voice sounding like a challenge.

I frowned. "Well, for one thing, I just found out my life is the hands of people who think ET is *real*."

"Big deal. Lots of people think aliens are real, Bobbie. In fact, isn't that the whole point of your mission with Grayson?"

I frowned. "Well, sort of. But I'm not talking about believing in aliens *in general*, Beth-Ann. I mean these guys think the alien in that movie, *ET the Extraterrestrial* is real."

"Aww, come on, Bobbie!"

"I'm *serious*! They just left to go buy Reese's Pieces—to use to lure the space aliens into the RV."

"Oh."

"Exactly."

"Hmm," Beth-Ann said, hesitating before her next question. "So, you've *seen* the aliens yourself?"

I winced. "Sort of."

"And they looked like ET?"

"No! I mean ... I only got a quick glimpse of them before my phone battery died."

"So ... what did they look like?"

I swallowed hard. "One of them looked like a Conehead."

Beth-Ann choked. "From *Saturday Night Live?*"

"Uh ... yeah. Kinda. Geez, Beth-Ann. What should I do?"

"Uh ... consume mass quantities?"

"Thanks a lot," I said over her laughter.

"Come on, Bobbie. How should *I* know what to do with an alien?"

I shook my head. "I'm doomed, aren't I?"

"Cheer up. Maybe the Reese's Pieces will work."

"How do you figure *that?*"

"With any luck, these Conehead guys will turn out to be as addicted to sugar as you are."

I scowled. "What's *that* supposed to mean?"

Beth-Ann laughed. "Asks the girl with the ball of sugar in her mouth."

"Hey. Tootsie Pops help me think. And right now, I need to figure out a way to avoid a starring role in Grayson's production of *Aliens vs. Idiots.*

"Hey. Pony up, girlfriend. Give yourself more credit. You survived so far. You can survive this, too."

I sighed. "I don't know, Beth-Ann. I can only put on my big girl panties so many times before the elastic breaks."

"Broken elastic is okay," she said. "The only thing you need to avoid is showing your ass."

Chapter Twenty-Four

I never found that blasted file folder labeled *Experiment #5*. After I hung up with Beth-Ann, I was in the middle of rifling through Grayson's cabinet full of secret potions for the second time when I heard the crunch of tires on gravel. I peeked out the window. Earl's monster truck was rolling into the compound.

I straightened the bottle labeled *Alien Parasite Remover*, closed the cabinet, smoothed my spikey hair with my hands, then traipsed over to the side door. Then I flung it open and smiled demurely, doing my best June Cleaver impersonation.

"Hi guys!" I said cheerily as Earl, Grayson and Garth climbed out of the truck.

"You feelin' all right?" Earl asked, eyeing me with suspicion. "You don't look right."

I ditched the fake smile. "Did you get that water pump fixed?"

"Sorta. I rigged up somethin' using some spare parts I pulled off an old Chevy pickup I found around back."

"Hmm ... this thing you rigged up," Grayson said. "Are you sure it will function within normal parameters?"

Earl shrugged. "It ain't permanent, but it ought a hold till we can get the old jalopy back to the shop in Point Paradise."

"Why do we have to take it all the way back *there*?" Grayson asked.

"Well, that's where the gen-u-wine replacement pump is. Lemme tell ya. Parts for a 1967 Minnie Winnie don't grow on no trees no more."

Earl grinned and pointed a thumb at the chest of his own blue coveralls. "But lucky for you, Mr. G., I got ahold of one from the *JC Whitney* catalogue. I ordered the last one they had eight months ago, when you come to town and had me overhaul the whole engine."

"I see," Grayson said. "Why didn't you install it then?"

Earl grinned, apparently too stupid to even notice the trap he'd set for himself. His beady eyes darted first to me, then to Grayson.

"Well now, as I recall, you two was in kinda a rush to get outta town, remember? Put me in a tight spot, you did. I had to make me some executive decisions. The old water pump was workin' fine back then, so I let it be."

Grayson nodded. "Well, I hope I wasn't charged for—"

"Is that Sherman's precious oscilloscope?" I asked, gazing admiringly at the gadget in Grayson's hand. The rectangular gizmo looked a lot like the EMF detector. The only difference was it was a little bigger, and the plastic casing was the kind of garish yellow usually reserved for rubber bathtub duckies.

"Yes," Grayson said, holding up the oscilloscope for my inspection. "A beauty, isn't she?"

"Uh ... sure." I reached out to touch it. Grayson slapped my hand away.

"No touching," he said. "It's a loaner, after all."

I shook my head. "Unbelievable. You really *don't* trust me, do you?"

Grayson pulled the o-scope close to his body. "Drex, you broke the toaster this morning shoving a fork down it. You're not exactly what I'd call a technological savant."

I scowled. "Fine. But answer me this. We already found the spaceship. Do you really even *need* that thing anymore?"

"Yes," Grayson said defensively.

"For what?"

"For *documentation* purposes, okay?"

I sneered. "Whatever."

Boys and their toys.

I spun on my heels and headed back toward the RV. But then a thought hit me. I turned back around.

"Hey, Grayson," I said.

He looked up from fiddling with his new gadget. "What?"

"If we actually do manage to trap an alien in the RV, what are we gonna do with it?"

Grayson's moustache twitched. "Well ... we'll burn that Einstein-Rosen Bridge when we get to it."

My gut went slack.

That's exactly *what I was afraid of...*

I CAME OUT OF THE BATHROOM to discover Grayson duct-taping one of his stupid mystery gadgets to the back of Earl's camo hunting vest.

"What are you doing?" I asked.

"Getting ready for tonight." Grayson ripped a piece of duct tape with his teeth. "We're sending Earl in as first contact."

"What?" I gasped.

Confusion, fear, paranoia and envy played *Twister* in my head. "Wait a minute. Did you choose Earl because he did better than me on your stupid EEG machine?"

I knew I was arguing against my own best interests, but I couldn't stop myself. I didn't *want* the job of Martian Greeter. Far from it. But Earl and I had been rivals for thirty years. The force of habit was so strong in me that I didn't want my cousin to best me at anything—not even death by alien probe.

I scowled at Grayson. "You think Earl's better than me. Admit it!"

Grayson shrugged. "In some ways, yes. He's more—"

"Cool under pressure?" I grumbled.

"Well, Drex, I *have* noted you've shown a remarkable ability to defy conventional scientific theories."

I softened, feeling flattered. "Really?"

"Yes." Grayson smirked. "For every action you have an *un*equal and opposite *over*reaction."

I scowled. "Ha. Ha."

"But regarding Earl," Grayson continued, his voice fading to a whisper, "I was thinking more along the lines of him being more *expendable* than you."

"Oh." I winced with guilt, and glanced over at the banquette. Earl was snarfing down Reese's Pieces from a Mason jar—with a fork. *Maybe it really is for the best...*

"What'd he say?" Earl asked, looking up at me. "I couldn't hear him over the crunching."

"Uh ... Grayson said you're *indispensable*," I lied.

Earl grinned, revealing teeth stained in every color no one ever wants their teeth to be. "Is that true, Mr. G.?"

Grayson glanced at Earl, then back to me. "As far as you know."

"Ha ha!" Earl giggled excitedly. "Grayson thinks I'm better'n you, Bobbie! Na-na-na na-na!"

Resentment bitch-slapped my guilty conscience into submission. "Yes, Earl. *You* won this one, fair and square."

But this victory rang as hollow as my poor cousin's head.

If Earl really *did* end up becoming Earth's intergalactic ambassador, it could quite possibly spell the end of the world as we knew it.

And I didn't feel fine.

Chapter Twenty-Five

It was 6:15 p.m.

T-minus forty-five minutes and counting.

At seven o'clock, we would all be heading out to prank call a mixed race of alien creatures that were probably billions of years older than us and trillions of times smarter.

What could possibly go wrong?

For our last supper, I'd ordered Hungry Howie's Crazy Bread and six bottles of Boone's Farm Strawberry Hill. I'd figured, what the hell. If I was going to die, I wanted to go out with as many regrets as possible.

"I thought I told you to clean those up," Grayson said, reaching into a bag of Crazy bread on the kitchen counter.

He nodded toward the windowsill. I glanced at the rack of test tubes I was supposed to have washed yesterday. I'd stashed them up there to do later. Perhaps this time, procrastination really *would* pay. With any luck I'd be dead by dawn, and it wouldn't matter.

Score.

"Sorry," I said. "I've been a little busy given the—you know—alien invasion and stuff."

Grayson's green eyes studied me like I was a new species of algae. "Never mind. I'll do it myself tomorrow."

I poured another pink glass of wine and muttered under my breath, "If there *is* a tomorrow."

Grayson's eyebrow arched. "You don't think we're going to be able to pull this off?"

I sighed and glanced over at Earl, who was dutifully completing his TV "assignment."

"No offense, Grayson. But in what universe does watching reruns of *ALF* qualify as an in-depth course on communicating with aliens? We have no *real strategy*!"

Grayson grabbed me by the shoulders. "Listen to me, Drex. Historic moments can't be *orchestrated*—merely *experienced*."

"Really?" I said, a tinge of hope returning to my soul. "Who said that?"

Grayson locked eyes with me. "*I* did. Just now. Are you having trouble hearing?"

I closed my eyes and let the breath drain out of me.

It's official. We're doomed.

I CHECKED THE PROVISIONS in my purse again.

One Glock. Thirty extra rounds of ammo. Fourteen Tootsie Pops.

I closed my eyes, hoping against hope that this whole alien invasion thing was some kind of stupid misunderstanding. But if I was indeed going to be abducted and whisked off to planet Krull, well, by God, I was going out in style—and with a ready supply of high-fructose corn syrup.

"You ready?" I heard Grayson ask.

I opened my eyes. He was standing in the hallway of the RV, talking to Earl.

"Yes sir, Mr. G.," Earl said, and saluted.

My lip snarled. "What are you two doing?"

Grayson reached into his potion cabinet. "I'm giving our trooper here something to make him feel invincible."

My eyebrows inched closer. "Jack Daniels?"

"No." Grayson pulled out the Windex bottle and spritzed Earl from head to toe with *Alien Parasite Remover*. "Now you'll be untouchable, my good man."

"In my book, he already *was*," I muttered.

Earl grinned and studied his arms as if he'd never laid eyes on them before. "Cool!"

I shook my head. "You really think that's gonna work?"

Grayson shrugged. "It can't hurt. I give it a thirty percent chance."

"How do you figure that?" I asked, watching Earl flap his arms like a water turkey, trying to dry himself.

"I extrapolated from placebo research," Grayson said. "Like any sugar pill, if you think it will work, it works."

A twinge of pain shot through my head like a stray bottle rocket. I closed my eyes. Either the Boone's Farm was beginning to talk, or the little twin inside my brain was trying its best to kick me in the ass.

For once, I had to agree with it. This whole situation was a disaster looking for a place to happen.

I opened my mouth to voice my objection one more time, but was drowned out by an unearthly wail only slightly worse than one of Grayson's shower soliloquies.

"Okay, troops," Grayson said, lowering the bugle from his lips. "Let's move out."

Chapter Twenty-Six

I was surprised by the number of cars in the parking lot of the former 7-11 that was now Juanita's Casa del Tacos.

Then I remembered it was Tuesday night.

Straddling Bessie's gearshift, I shifted my weight to the right and glanced over at my typically taco-crazed commander in chief. His eyes were fixated on the road ahead. He hadn't even given the neon sombrero a passing glance.

I nearly choked on my Tootsie Pop. I'd never seen Grayson so ... *focused*. Either that or the green-eyed taco fiend had finally gone mad.

I sat in silent contemplation and listened to the monster truck's tires whine as we passed the restaurant and turned onto the dark, rural road leading to Edward Medard Park—the Hi-Ho.

Earl began humming an unrecognizable tune. I turned toward him and my jaw clamped like a vice grip. I was caught between a madman in black and a redneck in camo spritzed with alien parasite remover.

By any rational measure of sanity, all three of us were stark-raving nuts.

"Do you see anything?" Grayson asked, staring out the passenger window through a pair of binoculars.

Only my future skittering away like a three-legged dog in ice-skates.

"Nope," I said, even though I'd spotted the glow coming from the woods about five seconds earlier. I guess my will to live was stronger than I'd planned on.

"Hey! There it is!" Earl said, pointing a beefy finger at the windshield.

"Excellent," Grayson said. "Pull over here."

LIKE A LOW-BUDGET VERSION of *Survivorman* with an all-idiot cast, the three of us tromped through the swamp, filling our galoshes and feeding the mosquitos.

Silently, I prayed the ominous glow we'd spotted on the roadside would skip making an encore tonight. But against all odds—and forsaking all my hopes and dreams—that damned luminous ring and its glowing portal of doom had reappeared at the ridgetop, right on schedule.

I couldn't make out the spaceship in the center, and there was no sign of either the Conehead or Medusa alien life forms. I wondered if Earl's ALF training had been all in vain...

"You know the drill," Grayson said.

"Yep," Earl replied. "I'm ready, Chief."

"The drill?" I asked. "*I* don't know the drill!"

Before my eyes, my big, bear of a cousin saluted, drew himself up six inches taller, and flexed his muscles like King Kong.

"Step aside, Bobbie," he said. "I'm going in. If anything happens, save yourselves!"

"Wait!" I called after him.

But it was too late. Before I could stop him, Earl ran past me and headlong into the portal.

He disappeared with a metallic, gong-like sound.

"Earl!" I screamed, and took a step toward the glowing ring.

"Ouch!" Earl hollered. "Well, would you look at that!"

"What is it?" I yelled, running toward the intergalactic portal. "Are you hurt? Are you trapped in some kind of other dimension?"

"You might could call it that," Earl said. "Don't rightly know what to make of it."

"God help me," I screamed as I closed in on the portal. "Hold on, Earl! I'm coming after you!"

I took a step back, preparing to make a giant leap.

"Wait," Grayson said, grabbing my arm from behind.

"Let me go!" I screeched. "I've got to save Earl!"

"Shh!" Grayson said, putting his hand over my mouth. "Look over there."

He turned me around.

I gasped.

Then I couldn't breathe.

Chapter Twenty-Seven

Grayson and I stood side by side, stunned to silence, staring out from behind the thin strip of forest that hid us from an army of pointy-headed aliens.

I held my breath and watched helplessly as my camo-clad cousin stumbled down the ridge where the portal hovered, then barreled directly into a circular clearing at the bottom.

The tamped-down clearing was eerily similar to the one we'd discovered yesterday in the woods right off Whirlwind Trail. Except instead of a dark circle in the center of it, a bonfire blazed.

And it was occupied with an army of otherworldly beings.

All around the fire, Conehead-like aliens in white robes stood motionless, staring into the blaze like pawns in an intergalactic game of chess. They would've appeared harmless—perhaps even friendly—except for the fact that each of them was wielding a shiny, sabre-like weapon.

"Uh ... howdy," Earl said, standing up and dusting himself off. He waved a meaty paw and approached the alien toga party. "I come in peace."

Wordlessly, in perfect synchronicity every alien's head turned toward my cousin and raised their light-sabers high.

I cringed and whispered to Grayson, "What are they going to do to him?"

He didn't answer, and I didn't look over to read his expression. My eyes were glued to my cousin and the creatures from Krull.

One of the pointy-headed beings broke away from the uniform circle and approached Earl, seeming to glide rather than walk as he moved.

"Are you here to join us, brother?" it said in a deep, almost mechanical baritone.

"Uh, sure," Earl said.

"Excellent. Follow me."

"All-righty then," Earl said. Then he did something that stunned me. He looked back in our direction and winked.

My jaw fell open. I stood and stared, momentarily paralyzed with fear, as my brave, sweet, stupid, idiotic cousin followed the creature away from us and toward the other side of the bonfire.

"I have to keep an eye on him," I whispered, edging by Grayson, who was peeking out from behind a small cypress tree.

"Right. But stay out of view," he said, following behind me.

"What are we going to do if this goes south?" I asked, crouched over, pushing my way around a palmetto bush.

"I'm working on it," Grayson said. "I hadn't expected so many aliens to come out of that little ship. We're going to have to see how this plays out."

"There he is!" I gasped, freezing in my tracks.

Earl was by the fire, kneeling in front of an alien in a golden robe.

"That must be their leader," Grayson whispered.

We watched from the bushes as the white-robed alien that had made first contact with Earl nudged my cousin with its saber and said something I couldn't hear.

Earl stuck out his tongue.

My heart sunk.

Oh, God, Earl! This is no time to be a smartass!

I pulled out my Glock. Grayson grabbed my arm.

"Wait, Drex," he whispered in my ear. "We don't have a chance against this many of them."

My body went limp. Grayson was right. There was nothing I could do but watch in horror as the strange figure Grayson called the leader reached a spindly arm toward my cousin. Unlike the others, the leader was thin and bronze-colored—almost as shiny as the golden robe it wore. The being placed something on Earl's tongue, then tilted its head skyward and let out an unearthly wail—like a yodeler being stuck with a cattle prod.

Suddenly, all the other aliens echoed the leader's strange call—including Earl! Their haunting shrieks set every hair on my body on end.

I held my breath, expecting to see a light sabre come down on Earl's neck, and his head go rolling off into the fire.

But that didn't happen.

Instead, Earl was given a white robe. Then he jauntily joined a group of aliens who were forming a line at the end of a strip of glowing-hot coals.

"Yugan duit, yugan duit!" the creatures began to chant.

One stripped off its robe and made a mad dash across the glowing coals.

My gut fell four inches. Beneath its robe, the alien was wearing overalls. The only thing "out of this world" had been my imagination.

"Yugan duit," morphed into "You can do it!" as more and more of them stripped off their robes and ran through the hot coals.

I blew out a sigh. These were no alien creatures—not unless Krull was inhabited entirely by middle-aged, flabby white guys.

"What the—?" I muttered to Grayson. But then I spotted Earl in the coal-trotting conga-line and clammed up.

It was his turn to run the gauntlet.

I held my breath, anticipating disaster.

But, to my surprise, like a trooper, Earl high-tailed it through the path of red embers, hooting and hollering the whole way. At the end of his brief, hot-footed journey, he was given back his robe, along with a few hearty claps on the back by his fellow compadres.

As the next guy in line stumbled across the hot coals, Earl put his robe back on and meandered to the edge of the clearing. By some miracle, he managed to choose a spot within earshot of where Grayson and I were hunched over, hiding in the palmetto bushes.

"Psst! Over here," Grayson said.

Earl's head turned sideways. "Where you at?"

"Over here," I said.

"Oh!" Earl fumbled into the woods beside us, a goofy smile on his face, like he'd just come from a spa that offered happy endings or something.

"Boy, howdy," he said. "I gotta tell ya, that was outta this world!" He stuck his arms out like Frankenstein and smiled admiringly at the robe's sleeves, as if they were magic. "Bobbie, look at what them nice ol' aliens done give me!"

Grayson shone a small penlight on Earl, then zeroed in on the robe's chest pocket.

"Hmm," Grayson said. "This is worse than I thought."

I shook my head, finding that hard to believe. "Worse than your lamebrain idea this was an alien invasion from Krull?" I hissed. "Gimme a break!"

"See for yourself," Grayson said, turning Earl around to face me.

"See what?" I grumbled.

Grayson shone the penlight past Earl's shoulder and lit up the robe's pocket. In dark-green embroidery, a three-letter insignia stood out from the white terrycloth.

I blanched. "You've got to be kidding me!"

"Unfortunately not," Grayson said. "It appears these men have fallen victim to their own innate fears, egged on by a charismatic leader feeding them false hopes of an unobtainable utopia."

I stared at the three letters stitched on Earl's robe pocket.

KFC

"Dear lord," I said. "Is this some kind of freaky fried-chicken cult?"

"No," Grayson said. "Something even more unappetizing."

I grimaced. "More unappetizing than grown people licking their fingers?"

"Yes. By a factor of at least ten."

I gasped. I glanced back through the bushes at the robed men dancing around the bonfire, then turned back to Grayson. "What do you mean?"

Grayson grabbed my shoulders and stared into my eyes.

"Drex, I believe what we've stumbled on here is the genesis of a newly emerging *network marketing* scheme."

Chapter Twenty-Eight

"Network marketing?" Garth asked, his mouth hanging open like a bucktoothed Venus flytrap.

Still in his ratty flannel bathrobe, he'd waited up for us by the entry gate to his compound, sprawled out in a lawn chair with a Coleman lantern and his wimpy hound-dog Tooth for company. As soon as he'd spotted us, Garth had hit the remote to open the barbed-wire topped gate, and Earl had driven Bessie on through.

We'd all gathered back inside the RV, where I was busy seesawing between kicking myself for being such a fool, and celebrating that I'd escaped the fate of becoming a space alien's exotic, mail-order bride.

"Yes, network marketing," Grayson said, handing Garth the robe Earl had been given. "Take a look for yourself. It's one of those pyramid schemes. I'm sure of it."

Garth's crusty eyes widened. "KFC? I didn't know they were into—"

"Read the small print," I said.

Garth pushed his dark nerd frames up on his nose. "Kristie's Frickin' Crullers?"

"Yes," Grayson said. "Sorry to disappoint you, Operative Garth. But from what I saw, it appears the 'aliens' are actually a group of hapless recruits taking part in team-building exercises for a new line of donut shops."

"But the white robe," Garth said.

"Yeah," I said sourly. "Not exactly the world's most thoroughly thought through marketing strategy. They'll show every chocolate smear and greasy fingerprint stain."

"I kinda like stains," Earl said. "Reminds me a what I ate. You know, like a scrapbook, only of meals."

Garth glanced at Earl, then leaned over and whispered to me. "What did they do to him?"

I sighed and whispered back. "Nothing. Unfortunately, that's Earl in normal mode."

"But that haircut," Garth said. "Did he undergo some kind of horrible initiation?"

I shook my head. "Nope. Self-inflicted."

Earl frowned and ran a hand through his uneven bangs. "What's wrong with my hair?"

"Everything," I said. "I *told* you to quit going to that weird guy hanging around the old FotoHut in the IGA parking lot."

Earl pouted. "But Bubba's the only one who still cuts hair for catfish."

Garth blanched. "Are you saying a *human* did that to him?"

"Ahem," Grayson cleared his throat. "If I could interrupt this little beauty consultation for a moment, I'd like to get back to the issue at hand."

"Donuts?" Earl asked.

Grayson's scholarly expression skipped a beat. "No. I'm referring to the fact that we're back to square one in explaining what's happened to Jimmy and Wade."

"Wade Parker?" Garth asked.

"Maybe," I said. "If he's the cousin of a waitress named Thelma at Juanita's Casa del Tacos."

"Yeah. That's him," Garth said. "That's the friend Jimmy went fishing with. The one he told me he was looking for—right before he started acting all weird himself."

"Like a murderer, you mean?" Grayson asked.

"No!" Garth frowned and pushed his glasses up on his nose. "Are you *sure* those robed guys weren't aliens? What about that weird message Jimmy left? You know, 'Christ. It's Frickin' Krull'?"

Grayson pursed his lips. "As you recall, the message was garbled. I'm afraid we may have misinterpreted Jimmy saying, 'Kristie's Frickin' Crullers.'"

"You *think*?" I said sourly.

"But what about the *portal*?" Garth argued, sounding vaguely disappointed. "And the alien ship you spotted?"

My ears flushed with heat. I glanced over at Grayson, wondering how he was going to explain this one.

Grayson cleared his throat. "Ahem. Well, Operative Garth, after further examination of the scene ..."

In other words, as the three of us scrambled through the woods back toward the monster truck...

"...it became apparent that the phenomenon we interpreted as an intergalactic portal ..."

...the glowing ring of reddish-orange light we saw in the woods...

"...may have actually been the view of a distant illumination source as partially obstructed by a structure of man-made origin."

...was debunked when Earl banged his head on something that rang like a gong. We'd turned around and were surprised to see the distant glow of the robed guys' bonfire outlining the silhouette of an abandoned propane tank like a glowing orange ring.

"So ... there wasn't any spaceship?" Garth asked.

"Nope. Just a rusty ol' gas tank," Earl said.

"But the hieroglyphics you mentioned," Garth argued.

"Graffiti," I said.

"Yep." Earl snickered. "Somebody done wrote, 'Eat a wiener,' on it."

Grayson cleared his throat again. "I believe the correct phrase was, 'Eat *my* wiener.'"

Garth's face collapsed. "But your Medusa-headed monster," he said, turning to me.

I winced. "Turns out, it was the exposed root ball of a pine tree. And the Conehead was just one of those robed guys."

Garth stared at us for a moment, mouth agape, red nose dripping.

I turned to Grayson and shook my head. "Poor guy. How could we have gotten this *sooo* wrong?"

Grayson shrugged. "Actually, what happened here is a rather common occurrence. Eyewitness reports are notoriously unreliable, Drex. Especially under duress. I think what we have here is a case of *weapon focus*."

My nose crinkled. "Weapon focus?"

"Yes. It's a psychological phenomenon in which a witness focuses in on one feature, such as a weapon, causing all other details to become blurred. In your case, Drex, it was obviously your typical hyper-emotional reactivity that caused your memory distortions."

Earl laughed. "So what you're sayin', Mr, G., is that the thought of them fellers in robes bein' aliens scared ol' Bobbie outta her gourd."

"Less eloquent than I would have put it, but yes," Grayson said.

I glared at Earl. "So, then what's *your* excuse, jerk-wad?"

Earl's head tilted sideways. "For seeing Coneheads, you mean?"

"No," I grumbled. "For being out of *your* gourd!"

I turned to Grayson. "You saw aliens, too. Admit it!"

Grayson shrugged. "Like I said. The stress of disturbing situations can make one highly confident of one's visual accuracy, despite facts to the contrary. In actuality, Drex, there is no 'right' or 'wrong' reality. There is only the one we decide to either accept or agree on."

"Yeah, right, Mr. Mumbo-Jumbo," I hissed.

I walked over and grabbed a bag of candy from the kitchen counter. "So, what are we gonna do now with fifty pounds of Reese's Pieces, Einstein?"

Chapter Twenty-Nine

With the threat of alien probes removed from the equation and a bottle of Boone's Farm implanted in my gut, I crashed into bed and slept like a baby. But, unfortunately, my respite from reality wasn't to last.

As it turned out, our troubles were just getting started.

At the break of dawn, I was woken by the sound of someone banging frantically on the side door of the RV.

"Geez. What now?"

I sat up. The throbbing in my head made me wince. I glanced at my phone. It was a few minutes before six a.m.

"Awesome."

I climbed out of bed, leaving Grayson sleeping like a log, and stumbled into the main room of the cabin.

The knock sounded again. I took a covert peek between the blinds. Garth was standing outside the window, his nose and buck teeth glowing in the moonlight like a deranged Rudolph nightmare. I was beginning to think it was the Boone's Farm when he spotted me and began to wave frantically.

"What's wrong?" I groused, yanking open the door.

"Pandora!" he yelled. "Someone broke in and wrecked my place!"

I pictured the inside of the brothers' nasty, hoarder trailer jam-packed with crap. "How can you tell?"

Garth squinted and pushed his glasses up on his nose. "They left the refrigerator door open."

Seriously?

"Could Jimmy have done it?" I asked, contemplating slamming the door in his mullet-topped face.

"No. He's too energy conscious."

A pain shot through my throbbing head. "How about Tooth?"

"No," Garth insisted, shaking his head. "The beer's still in there."

I let that gem of knowledge ping around in my sleepy brain for a moment, then offered one more possible solution. "Raccoons?"

"Not possible. We sealed the roof vent up tight last time that happened."

"Uh-huh," I grunted.

"Pandora, I think the intruder has to be of human or semi-human origin. This kind of damage generally requires opposable thumbs."

He waggled his thumbs at me. I glanced skyward.

Why is this happening to me?

"Can you come take a look?" he asked.

I blew out a sigh. "Okay. Give me a minute to wake Grayson."

I shut the door, turned around, and slammed straight into something hard and dark. I looked up to see Grayson's green eyes staring down at me in the dim light.

"Go back to bed," he said. "I'll take it from here."

"You heard all that?" I asked.

But he didn't answer.

Instead, like a ninja in black, Grayson opened the door and disappeared with Garth into the moonlit junkyard.

Chapter Thirty

By the time the guys returned, I'd showered, dressed, and slurped down two cups of coffee. In other words, I had attained a conversation-capable level of consciousness.

"So, what did you two find out?" I asked, pouring Grayson and Garth cups of coffee as they scooted into the banquette. "Let me guess. Did Bigfoot do it?"

"Not unless he plays the bongos," Grayson said.

"What?" I said, nearly spilling the coffee I was handing the men.

"Nothing's missing except for some food," Garth said. "And my set of bongos."

"Oh." I pivoted back to the kitchen counter to collect the third cup I'd poured for my cousin. "Wait. Where's Earl?"

Garth and Grayson locked eyes, then glanced up at me.

"We haven't see him," Grayson said. "I better go check the truck."

EARL USUALLY SLEPT in the front seat of Bessie. But the big, black monster truck, was empty. Splayed out on the bench seat was Earl's Superman sleeping bag—and most of the clothes he'd had on last night.

It was as if he'd been beamed up from inside his bedroll.

"This doesn't look good," Grayson said.

I winced. "I know. But he's had that Superman bag since he was a kid."

"No. I meant *this*." Grayson reached into the truck and pulled out an empty bag of Reese's Pieces.

"So? I'm not following you," I said.

Grayson reached in and pulled out two more empty candy bags. "How about now?"

WE FOUND EARL HALF naked, sprawled out in a ditch behind Garth's doublewide like ET after a bongo rave.

His belly was swollen like a toad's. His face was red and feverish. And Earl's arms and legs were covered with minor scratches, as if he'd fought off a pack of rabid gerbils.

It took all three of us to get him up out of the ditch and into the RV. We were all huffing and puffing as we laid him out on the broke-back sofa adjacent to the banquette.

"What happened to him?" Garth asked. "You think he has rabies or something?"

"I don't know," Grayson said.

"What about yellow fever?" Garth asked.

Grayson's eyes widened.

I gasped. "You don't really think it's yellow fever, do you?"

"No," Grayson said, his eyes darting around the RV. "I just remembered the yellow oscilloscope. We need to return it. Where is it?"

"How should I know?" I grumbled. "And who cares about that right now? We need—"

"Y ... you lost it?" Garth stammered. "Holy Gorn clubs! We've got to find it! And fast!"

Grayson chewed his bottom lip. "It must've fallen out of my pocket last night."

My nose crinkled. "What's the big deal, guys?"

"We're supposed to have it back by noon," Garth said, his voice rising with panic.

"So?" I glanced down at my cousin. "What about Earl?"

Grayson shook his head. "I'm afraid Garth's right. Finding the oscilloscope takes priority."

"Why?" I demanded.

Grayson's green eyes locked on mine. "You obviously haven't met Sherman's mother."

My mouth fell open "Seriously?"

"I think he's fine for now," Grayson said, laying a hand on Earl's forehead. "His fever's gone. It's most likely he just OD'd on sugar."

Grayson turned to me. "Drex, I want you to come with me to search for the scope. Garth, you stay here and keep an eye on Earl. Make sure he drinks plenty of water—and don't let him have any more Reese's Pieces."

Garth pushed his glasses up on his red nose. "I'm on it, Mr. Gray."

"Ugh. *Fine*," I grumbled, grabbing my purse. I knew there was no point in arguing with Grayson when he was in "mission mode." I grabbed the keys from his hand. "This had better not take long. And *I'm* driving."

"I agree to your terms," Grayson said, making me blanch.

"Uh ... good," I said. "Then let's get this over with."

I tramped out of the RV and over to Earl's truck. I stepped up on the running board and flung open the door, then pushed the Superman sleeping bag over toward the middle of the bench seat.

As Grayson and I heaved ourselves inside, I noticed a piece of paper laid up on the dashboard. I grabbed it and read the odd words scrawled on it with a thick, black marker.

"Stay Away," I said.

"Sorry," Grayson said. "I didn't have a chance to shower this morning."

"No." I handed him the note. "That's what this note says. What's that supposed to mean?"

Grayson read the two-word message and rubbed his chin. "Hmm. It's possible that your cousin's been deemed unsuitable, based on the recruiting standards of the Kristie's Frickin' Cruller organization."

I grimaced. "Geez. You think they ran his credit?"

"Uncertain," Grayson said. "But this development certainly thickens the plot."

"How so?"

"Whoever wrote this warning obviously knows who Earl is—and where he's staying."

Grayson turned and locked eyes with me. "It appears, Drex, that things have just gotten personal."

Chapter Thirty-One

In the stark light of day, the swampy trail in the woods that had led us to believe in portals and space aliens now appeared mundane—and our intergalactic theories embarrassingly preposterous.

As I stared at the graffiti-covered propane tank and the washed-out root ball of a pine tree beside it, I shook my head in amazement at my mind's silly machinations.

Spaceships and aliens. What the hell had I been thinking?

"Hurry up," I called to Grayson. "I want to get back and check on Earl."

He was a few paces behind me, rifling through the palmettos and weeds along the trail, searching for the lost oscilloscope.

"Just one more place to look," Grayson said as he reached the top of the ridge where I stood. Then he hiked past me toward the clearing where the bonfire had been last night.

I stomped sullenly after him to the edge of the clearing.

"I think we were over there," I said, spotting a trail of trampled plants in the thicket surrounding the clearing. I headed down it, with Grayson following a few yards behind me. Or so I thought ...

"Ah, there it is!" I heard him say.

I whipped back around. Grayson was in the clearing near the fire pit. I tromped back toward him.

"I just looked over there," I called out. "How'd I miss it?"

As I approached, Grayson bent down and grabbed up the yellow gizmo. "Intriguing."

"Yeah. It's truly fascinating that *you* found it," I said. "Now let's get the hell out of here!"

"No," Grayson said. "I meant *this.*"

He shoved the o-scope at my face. The needle was jumping like a kangaroo in a bouncy house.

My lip snarled. "What does that mean?"

Grayson grinned. "It means that just because something *looks* like it could be a portal doesn't mean it *isn't.*"

Oh, crap.

Grayson slipped his backpack from his shoulders and handed it to me.

"Here," he said. "Hold my gear."

AFTER FIFTEEN MINUTES of swatting mosquitos and watching Grayson fiddle with his equipment like a mad scientist, I was jonesing for a Tootsie Pop and a can of *Off!*

"Are you almost done?" I asked, watching him aim the o-scope at some contraption he'd set up on a tripod. He'd positioned the tripod in the center of the black circle where the bonfire had raged last night.

"You know, Grayson, for someone measuring the speed of light, you sure do move slow."

"Precision is critical," he said, his eyes never leaving the device. "Ah. There."

I perked up. "You're done?"

"Yes." Grayson studied the o-scope. "Interesting. The device recorded a discrepancy of six percent."

"That's impressive," I said, trying to sound like I knew what the hell was going on. "What exactly does that mean?"

Grayson glanced up at me. "It means that from where you currently stand, time appears to be moving slower than from where I stand."

I certainly couldn't argue with that.

"Great," I said. "So, can we go now?"

Grayson looked back down at the o-scope and shook his head. A dimple formed a divot in his cheek.

"This discrepancy in the speed of light is impressive," he said. "It indeed opens up the theoretical possibility for unexplained phenomena."

I grimaced. "You mean, like, a *time portal*?"

Grayson looked up and grinned. "Given the data, we can't rule it out."

Chapter Thirty-Two

"*That's* the one," Grayson said as I maneuvered Bessie down the narrow, rural road. He pointed at a prim and proper trailer home surrounded by a yard full of colorful whirly-gigs. "Stop here."

I shifted the monster truck into park. Grayson rolled down the passenger window and slipped the yellow oscilloscope into a battered mailbox shaped like the head of a deformed manatee.

"Okay," he said, slamming shut the unfortunate sea cow's mouth. "Let her rip."

"Ugh," I said. "Do I *have* to?"

Grayson turned and stared at me. "It's imperative."

I rolled my eyes and began mashing the truck's horn, honking out what Grayson called, "the secret code." I glared past Grayson at a family of pink pigs with whirligig wings as I tapped out, *Shave and a Haircut, Two Bits.*

Curtains moved in the front window of the trailer. The face of what I took to be a French bulldog appeared. A meaty hand rose beside the round, jowly face and shot us a thumb's up, then disappeared behind a drape of flowery chintz.

My upper lip hooked skyward.

"Sherman?" I asked.

Grayson shook his head. "His mother."

Grayson blew out a breath as if a giant weight had been lifted from him. "The o-scope's back home in one piece," he muttered, sinking into the seat. "Thank God."

This from a man who chased down Mothman and Bigfoot?

I smirked inside.

I guess nobody ever truly resolves their mommy issues.

I opened my mouth to ask Grayson what Sherman's mother had done to put the fear of God into him, but decided to spare myself the idiotic details. Given we'd already discovered a clandestine donut cult, Earl half-dead in a ditch, and a rip in the time-space continuum, I'd experienced enough weirdness for one twenty-four hour period.

WHEN WE ARRIVED BACK at Garth's, no one answered the intercom button at the security gate.

"Hmm," Grayson said, rubbing his chin. "We can't call Garth on his cellphone. It's still with Jimmy, wherever *he* is."

I bit my bottom lip. "You really think it's possible Jimmy could've been abducted, or swallowed up by that hole-in-time thingy?"

Grayson glanced at me, his left eyebrow an inch higher than his right. "Of course, Drex. Why else would we be here?"

I turned away and stared through the windshield at the mountains of garbage heaped high in Garth's redneck prepper compound. "Good point." I reached over and mashed the intercom button again. No reply.

"We could try calling Earl," Grayson said. "But he may not answer in his current state."

"I've got an idea," I said.

"What?"

I placed a palm on the steering wheel and began tooting out a rousing round of *Shave and a Haircut, Two Bits.*

Garth came flying out of the RV like he'd just kicked a wasp nest.

"Ha!" I said. "It worked!"

I laughed triumphantly—until I saw Garth's face.

"Hurry!" the little mullet-head hollered as he skidded to a stop by the gate. He slammed a fist on the control board. The gate began to open.

"What's happened?" I yelled, rolling down the window. "Is Earl okay?"

"I don't know," Garth gasped, out of breath. "He woke up and went berserk!"

Chapter Thirty-Three

A fter screeching through the gate of the compound, I slammed Bessie into park. Grayson and I jumped out of the monster truck and ran with Garth toward the RV.

"What do you mean, Earl's gone berserk?" I asked, the back of Garth's greasy mullet flapping like a dog's ear as he ran along beside me.

"I don't know," he gasped. "He just woke up and started eating everything he could get his hands on!"

My mind screeched to a halt.

Wait a minute. That's not so unusual...

But Earl playing the bongos was.

I burst into the RV. My cousin was passed out on the couch, his belly the size of a washtub. Every single kitchen cabinet and drawer was wide open. Even the stove was ajar.

My eyes darted to the family-sized bag of Reese's Pieces on the counter. It was empty.

"Good grief, Garth!" I yelled. "How many of those did he eat?"

He winced. "All of them."

I glanced around at the carnage. "Geez! I haven't seen Earl this out of control since he discovered Pamela Anderson was real!"

"Did he say anything while he was conscious?" Grayson asked.

Garth shook his head. "Nothing intelligible."

"Of course not," I said. "But did he make words? Form sentences?"

"No. Just grunts. Then he started rampaging through the kitchen. What's happening to him?"

"Uncertain," Grayson said. "We should move him to the bedroom."

"Aw, geez, Grayson," I said. "You really think that's a good idea? He already broke my sofa bed."

Grayson shot me a look. "I'm aware of that."

"Don't let him ruin the bed, too," I pleaded. "Where will we sleep?"

"We'll worry about that later," Grayson said. "But if Earl wakes up and starts rampaging again, we need to be able to contain him. Now help me lift him into the back bedroom."

The three of us each grabbed a leg or an arm, but in his current unconscious state, Earl flopped and wallowed around like a king-size waterbed mattress. We couldn't budge him. During the struggle, the sofa caved in. Lying prone on his back, Earl sunk down between the sagging couch cushions like some sad, redneck stiff in a makeshift coffin.

"It appears we'll have to leave him on the couch for now," Grayson said, sweating from exertion. He dropped Earl's leg like a slab of ham, picked up his laptop, and scooted into the banquette.

"What are you doing?" I asked.

"Researching Earl's symptoms," he said. "I'll take the animal scratches. You take excessive overeating."

I scowled. "Why'd you give *me* overeating? Are you implying—?"

"Uh, excuse me Pandora and Mr. Gray," Garth interrupted.

I looked over to see him staring at Earl. "Do you think this is what happened to Jimmy, too?"

"Uncertain," Grayson said. "But we're going to find out."

"That's right," I said, not totally convinced. I struggled for words to comfort Garth, but just then, my cellphone pinged.

I fished it from my pocket and read the text message on the display. Despite the sweat on my forehead, chills went up my spine.

I saw you last night. STAY AWAY!

Chapter Thirty-Four

"I think we can rule out rabies and cat-scratch fever," Grayson said, looking up from his laptop.

"Yeah," I said. "I don't think diseases send threatening text messages."

"What are you talking about?" Grayson asked.

I read the text message on my phone again, then handed it to Grayson.

I saw you last night. STAY AWAY!

"Hmm. Whoever it is must be affiliated with KFC."

"Uh ... I wouldn't use that acronym in public," I said. "Besides, it could just be a crank text."

"Unlikely," Grayson said, looking up from my phone. "No one else knew about what we were up to last night."

"Uh ... that's not entirely true," Garth said, and cleared his throat.

I shot him a death stare. "You didn't say anything to your ham radio dweebs, did you?"

"Uh ... I only mentioned it to Sherman."

My molars collided. "*Why?*"

Garth shriveled. He turned to Grayson. "I *had* to. You know, to get the oscilloscope."

"And how did Sherman get my *number?*" I asked, snatching my phone from Grayson.

Garth winced. "Uh ... It might've been part of the barter."

"Super," I said. "That means any crackpot on your prepper list could've sent me this text." I tossed my phone onto the table. Earl let out a moan.

I cringed and locked eyes with Grayson. "I really think we need a doctor."

"I'm a homeopathic physician, remember?" Grayson said.

I frowned. "I mean a *real* doctor."

Grayson stood and raised himself to his full six feet, two inches. "I think I know what's wrong with him."

"What?" I asked.

"I think Earl's suffering from hypoactive delirium."

My nose crinkled. "Hyperactive what?"

"Hypoactive delirium," Grayson repeated. "It's when internalized visions and confusion cause a patient to become withdrawn and incommunicative."

"How'd he get it?" Garth asked, glancing fearfully at Earl in his sofa-coffin. "Is it contagious?"

"No," Grayson said. "Usually, HD is brought on by psychological trauma. But a severe allergic reaction might also trigger it."

"Well, he did think he was going to make first contact with aliens last night," I said. "Could that've done it?"

"Doubtful," Grayson said. "Given Earl's outstanding ability to maintain high levels of alpha waves, I don't believe fear was a factor for him." He tapped a spidery finger on his chin. "There must be an underlying environmental cause."

"Wait!" I said. "Earl ran through those hot coals last night. Maybe he burned his feet and has an infection!"

"Good thinking," Grayson said. "Pull his feet out and let's check." He glanced at me.

I turned and glared at Garth until he shriveled.

"I'll do it," Garth muttered.

He padded over to the broken sofa-bed, where Earl lay wedged inside it like a giant white grub in a plaid-upholstered cocoon. Garth winced, closed his eyes, and tugged out one of Earl's size 13 clodhoppers.

"Appears normal," Grayson said. "Let's see the other one."

Garth bent over the end of the sofa and yanked on Earl's other leg. Ultimately, the bottoms of both feet turned out to be as pink and smooth as bubblegum.

"Hmm," Grayson said, examining Earl's legs. "None of the scratches look infected either. Perhaps we'd better just let him sleep it off."

AFTER LISTENING TO Earl snore until late afternoon, worry got the better of me. "Grayson, what if he doesn't sleep it off?"

"I'm sure he will," Grayson said. "Since he appears otherwise healthy, Earl's delirium must've been brought on by something he ingested. All that candy, most likely."

"Oh my word," I said, slapping my forehead. "I almost forgot. Those Cruller people! The skinny one in the golden robe ... he put something on Earl's tongue!"

"What did it look like?" Garth asked.

"I didn't get a good look at it," I said. "I think it was round."

"A donut hole?" Garth asked.

"Highly doubtful," Grayson said.

I frowned at Grayson. "Why not? Another case of your stupid 'weapon focus'?"

"No," Grayson said. "Crullers don't have holes."

A pain shot through my temple, amplified by the ring of Grayson's cellphone.

He glanced at his phone's display. "I better take this."

Grayson stepped out of the RV and returned less than a minute later, smiling. "Good news, troops. Help is on the way."

"You called a doctor?" I asked.

"No. That was the Uber Eats driver. He's at the gate with my tacos."

LIKE A JELLYFISH, EARL had no discernable brain, but was somehow able to time his hatching to coincide with a good feeding opportunity.

As soon as Garth, Grayson and I sat down to eat, Earl began to stir inside his sofa-bed sarcophagus.

"I told you it would work," Grayson said, then shoved half a taco into his mouth.

"Right," I said sourly. "Ordering tacos was all about Earl."

"Margldisalable," Earl grunted from inside the couch cushions.

I glanced over just in time to see a Frankenstein arm emerge from the sunken sofa frame.

Then another.

Suddenly, Earl's head popped up from between the cushions and turned slowly to face us.

The three of us stared, tacos frozen in midair, as Earl slowly hauled himself out of the broken-down couch.

"Earl?" I asked, dropping my taco. "Are you all right?"

Earl's glazed eyes were pointed in my direction, but they didn't focus on me. Instead, Earl let out an ungodly wail, then stomped clumsily toward the RV door like a zombie in Fruit-of-the-Loom tighty-whities.

"Earl!" I hollered. "Stop!"

He didn't respond, but kept clomping toward the door.

"We need to stop him," I said, trying to scramble out of the booth. But Grayson wrapped his arms around me and held me back.

"Let him go," he whispered in my ear. "We're going to follow him."

Chapter Thirty-Five

Grayson shifted the RV into second gear and we stared through the windshield into the dark, butt-end of Earl's monster truck as it crept down the road, lights off, at the dust-bunny-stirring rate of eight miles an hour.

Garth was on his knees on the floorboard between Grayson and me, hands clasped as if praying for a healing. I hoped he was. Earl was caught up in a strange, zombie-like stupor—and yet somehow managed to get behind the wheel of Bessie and was now weaving the huge truck back and forth across lanes like he'd polished off a fifth of Johnnie Walker.

"Do you really think we should we let him drive in this state?" I asked.

"The roads are empty this time of night," Garth said. "Besides, haven't you seen the folks driving around here? This *is* Central Florida, you know."

"Even if Earl crashed, he's not going fast enough to cause much damage," Grayson said, glancing down at the speedometer. "At his current speed, the only thing in danger of being run over would be a blind, geriatric gopher."

Grayson was probably right. Still, I chewed my lip and held onto the door handle as we tailgated six feet behind Earl's truck. He drove slowly and determinedly along the narrow asphalt lane, the tractor tires pinging like pinballs between the centerline reflectors and the rumble strips lining the road's edge.

Suddenly, Earl's brake lights flashed.

"Aha!" Grayson exclaimed. "Just as I suspected. He's returning to the scene of the crime."

"What crime?" I asked.

"Look over there." Grayson pointed out the windshield toward an all-too-familiar glow emanating from the woods.

I bit my bottom lip. "Crap. Not the KFC again. What do we do now?"

But I already knew the answer.

Follow Earl.

Like a mummy who forgot his wrapping, my cousin had climbed out of Bessie and was slowly tramping across the muddy clearing on the side of the road, straight toward the woods where we'd been last night. His tighty-whities glowed like a bobbing beacon in the moonlight.

"Let me grab my galoshes from the back of the truck," I said, flinging open the RV door.

"Good thinking," Grayson said. "We've got time, given his sluggish rate of ambulation."

We donned our rubber boots while Garth kept an eye on Earl.

"He just went into the woods right over there," Garth said. "By that big cypress tree."

"Good," Grayson said. "Stay here and keep watch over the vehicles."

"Roger that," Garth said, looking pensive, but relieved.

"He's moving faster than we thought," I said, and took off toward the cypress tree.

I could hear Grayson sloshing in the ankle-deep muck a few paces behind me. As I reached the rough, red trunk of the cypress, a pointy branch scratched my arm. I wasn't falling for another stupid Medusa tree alien, so I swatted at it angrily.

"Ouch!" a voice said.

Cold adrenaline shot through my spine.

I jumped and pivoted toward the voice. But before I could reach my Glock, a hand grabbed my arm.

"I told you to stay away," a voice hissed—from beneath the hood of a white, terrycloth robe.

Chapter Thirty-Six

"Let go of me!" I screamed at the jerk who'd grabbed my wrist. I tried to knee him in the groin, but the white robe he was wearing made it hard to locate my target.

"Don't struggle," the man said, tightening his grip on my arm.

He reached across me, trying to grab my other wrist.

"Forget you!" I yelled, and reared back and kneed him in the gut.

The creep grunted, let go of me, and stumbled backward, crashing into the cypress tree.

Suddenly freed from his grasp, I lost my balance and went tumbling to the ground. But what I landed on didn't feel like dirt.

It was Earl, lying prone in the mud.

"What did you do to him?" I yelled, struggling to grab my Glock as the man in the robe came boomeranging back toward me.

"Freeze!" another voice sounded.

My attacker stopped dead in his tracks.

"Hold it right there," Grayson said.

Dressed in black from head to toe, Grayson looked like a shadow come to life as he stepped out of the underbrush and into the scant moonlight. I spotted the glint of his Ruger against the robed-guy's ribs.

"Don't shoot!" the man said. "It's *me*."

"Me *who*?" I grunted.

"Jimmy Wells! Garth's brother!"

"Geez!" I gasped. "What are you doing here? And what did you do to Earl?"

"There's no time to explain," Jimmy said, pulling down his hoodie so we could see his face. "Help me. We need to get Earl out of here *now*, before it's too late!"

Chapter Thirty Seven

"What did you do to him?" I asked Jimmy again, my hand on Earl's chest. "He's still breathing, thank God!"

"Nothing," Jimmy said. "I only knocked him down, just to disorient him for a minute until you two could get here."

"Oh," I said, and slapped Earl gently on his cheeks, trying to rouse him. "Sorry about kicking you in the gut. I didn't realize it was you. You've put on a few pounds since I saw you last."

"Don't worry. It didn't hurt much," Jimmy said, then rubbed his massive belly.

A branch snapped in the forest nearby. Silently, we all exchanged glances. Jimmy's head jerked in the direction of the noise. His eyes narrowed. "Look," he whispered, "like I said, I'll explain later. But we need to get out of here, and *fast*."

"Okay," Grayson said. "Help me get Earl to his feet."

"No time for that," Jimmy said, his eyes growing wilder.

"We can't just leave him here!" I hissed.

"No," Jimmy said. "Stand aside. I'll get him up."

I shook my head. "How?"

"With this. Now step aside."

The young cop knelt beside Earl and held up a small orb. "Hey, buddy," he said, slapping Earl's face a bit harder than I had. "You looking for this?"

Earl's eyes fluttered open. He grunted, then began flailing his arms and legs like a turtle trying to turn itself over.

"Grab him," Grayson said. "Or he'll head off into the woods."

"No he won't," Jimmy said. "Let him be. He'll follow me." He turned back to face Earl. "Right, buddy?"

Jimmy got off his knees. Earl scrambled to his feet.

"It's right here," Jimmy said, holding up the orb. "Come and get it!"

Jimmy took off toward the RV. Earl fumbled at first, then found his bearings and stumbled after Jimmy like an inebriated hippo.

"Wow," I said, sloshing through the swampy muck with Grayson. "That was weird."

"I agree," Grayson said. "Jimmy runs surprisingly fast for a fat man."

WHEN WE ARRIVED BACK at the RV, Jimmy was dancing around beside it, playing keep-away with Earl.

"Hurry!" Jimmy yelled as Grayson and I sprinted toward him. "We've only got a few seconds before he goes nuts! You still have that monster trap in the back bedroom of this RV, right?"

"Yes," Grayson said.

"Good." Jimmy gasped, huffing from exertion. "We need to get Earl in there. Now!"

Garth flung open the side door to the RV. "Jimmy! It's you!"

"Yes, it's me. Now step aside, little brother. You've got company!"

Jimmy ran past Garth and into the RV. Earl bumbled behind him like a muddy Frankenstein. I ran up to the door and looked inside, stunned to see Jimmy take the round object in his hand and fling it down the hallway toward the bedroom. Earl scrambled past him down the hall like a rabid dog after a filet mignon.

"Hurry! Lock him in!" Jimmy yelled at me.

"Why?" I asked. "I don't understand."

"I'll explain once we've got him secured," he yelled back. "Come on! He'll realize he's been duped any second."

I eyed Jimmy skeptically. "I don't think you know Earl like I do."

"No, I don't," Jimmy said. "But I know the craving."

My gut flopped. "The *craving*?"

"Yes. Now lock him up in there—before it's too late!"

Chapter Thirty-Eight

Grayson checked the eight locks sealing Earl into the back bedroom monster trap, then shot Jimmy a thumb's up. "Well, we won't have to worry about your cousin wandering off to a buffet again any time soon. Thanks again for your help getting him to go in there."

"Glad to be of service," Jimmy said. He peeked nervously out the blinds. "But I think we should get a move on, just in case we were followed."

"Good thinking," Grayson said, and walked to the driver's cab.

Jimmy and I followed him, vying for the empty passenger seat. I won. I flopped into my chair and celebrated with a Tootsie Pop. Jimmy stood in the gangway between us like a bodyguard, holding onto the back of both seats.

Grayson cranked the engine and eased the RV off the muddy shoulder of the road.

"Thanks for talking Garth into following us back with Earl's truck," Jimmy said. "I need to talk to you two—alone."

"It was the logical thing to do," Grayson said, slowly driving past Bessie. He gave a quick wave to Garth, who was waiting diligently behind the wheel like a wormy NASCAR reject. "After all, it really *is* vital to our ongoing investigation."

"What is?" I asked. "Getting Bessie back to the compound?"

"No," Grayson said. "Keeping whatever's going on here with Earl and the Cruller Clan under wraps. Don't get me wrong, Jimmy. Your brother Garth is a worthy operative. But the man can't keep his mouth shut to save his soul."

I couldn't argue with that.

"That's exactly why I didn't tell him about my undercover operation," Jimmy said.

I nearly swallowed my tonsils. "Wait. You've been working *undercover?*"

I hadn't raised my voice from surprise, but in order to be heard over the din. Suddenly realizing he was trapped in the back bedroom, Earl began banging on the door and hollering like an astraphobic hound-dog in a raging thunderstorm.

"Uh ... yeah," Jimmy said. "Not officially, though." He sighed and shook his head. "I thought I could handle this alone. But now I know I'm in over my head. I could really use your help."

"So exactly what do you think is going on?" Grayson asked.

Jimmy shook his jowly head. "I'm not sure. But whatever it is, it's not normal. I'd been trying to keep Garth out of it. But I realized a couple of days ago that I needed backup. That's why I sent Garth the messages. I figured he would call you guys."

"He did," I said. "But your messages to him were pretty much incoherent."

"I know," Jimmy said. "That was by design. I was trying to be vague. I wanted Garth to know I was okay, but I couldn't let him know what I was up to."

"Why not?" I asked.

"My investigation would've been blown in two minutes. You know how he is. He'd have gabbed every bit of information I shared with him to his ham radio buddies. There'd have been a pile of guys tramping around the park before I could finish taking a shower."

My eyes met Grayson's. "That's a very reasonable assumption."

"I wanted to meet with you," Jimmy said. "Try to explain things. But when I saw Earl stumble into the Cruller Crew meeting last night, I knew you all had already discovered their secret meeting place. I left a note on Earl's dash, trying to warn you to keep clear of them."

"You're Mr. STAY AWAY," I said.

"Yes. When I didn't hear back from Garth, I started texting *you* instead."

"I don't get it," I said. "You want us to help, but you don't want us to investigate the Cruller Club?"

"Right," Jimmy said. "I mean, I want you to, but not yet. You see, I wanted to document the participants first. Tonight, I was planning on videoing the meeting and capturing the faces of the guys under the robes."

"Why?" I asked.

"As evidence gathering for my investigation," Jimmy said. Then he hung his head. "And to prove I'm not crazy. I mean, how can you describe what's going on out there without sounding like a lunatic?"

"Fair enough," Grayson said, nodding his head. "But no worries there. We believe you. We were with Earl last night. We saw the ceremonies ourselves."

"Thank goodness!" Jimmy sighed with relief.

"Wait a minute," I said, elbowing the young cop. "How'd you get my phone number?"

"From Garth's phone. I found it in my gym bag. Just in time, too."

"Why's that?" I asked.

Jimmy chewed his lip. "Well, at first, I'd thought this was a simple case of a bunch of rowdy redneck entrepreneurs just letting off steam. But now ... let's just say that whatever's going on out there, there's a lot more to it than that. I'm quite certain of it."

"Intriguing," Grayson said. "By the way, have you got any idea what might've happened to Wade?"

"Yes," Jimmy said.

His voice cracked and he let out a small wail. Then he hung his head and whispered, "I killed him."

Chapter Thirty-Nine

I f Jimmy was a murderer, he was certainly an extremely repentant one.

He cried all the way to the compound.

After Garth lead us inside and closed the gate, Grayson parked the RV while I settled a sobbing Jimmy into the banquette booth. Then Grayson scooted in opposite him while I put a pot of coffee on to boil.

"Tell us everything," Grayson said, softly coaxing the distraught, rather portly young cop. "Start from the beginning."

Jimmy lifted his double-chinned head from the table and sniffed. "It all began last weekend, when I went out to the Hi-Ho with Wade," he said, his face ashen. "We were out night fishing for catfish when we spotted something glowing in the woods. That's how we stumbled onto this meeting thing—or whatever it is."

I handed the poor guy a cup of coffee and slid into the banquette next to Grayson. That put me directly across from Garth, who had his arm laid across his brother's shoulders.

We didn't want the tattle-tale there, but we had no choice. Garth had been so thrilled to discover his brother was alive and well that once we got back to their prepper compound, he'd latched onto Jimmy and wouldn't let go.

I studied the red-nosed, *Wayne's World* wannabe and wondered if he'd have given his brother the same love and attention if he knew Jimmy had just confessed to murder.

I turned my gaze to Jimmy and shook my head. I'd have bet money that he was no killer. But then again, I knew all too well that people could harbor surprisingly dark secrets. After all, my cousin Earl was a closet Methodist.

"What happened then?" Grayson asked.

"Wade and I saw the glow in the forest and went to check it out," Jimmy said, the three of us hanging on his every word. "That's when we discovered a bunch of guys in robes dancing around a bonfire. We were getting ready to leave when one of them spotted us—and invited me and Wade to join them."

"Who invited you?" I asked.

"I dunno. Just a random guy from the crowd, as far as I could tell," Jimmy said. "I didn't realize what we'd gotten into until I saw the initials on his robe. KFC." Jimmy hung his head a bit. "I thought it was the, you know. But as it turned out, KFC stands for Kristie's Frickin' Crullers."

"We know," Grayson said with a quick nod. "Don't beat yourself up over it. It's a common mistake."

I shot Grayson a look, then smiled sympathetically at Jimmy. "It's okay. We're with you so far. Go on."

"Uh ... okay," Jimmy said. "Anyway, Wade and me were outnumbered. So I whispered for him to just to play along. So that's what we did."

"Then what happened," Grayson asked.

"The guy led us over to a dark-tanned woman wearing a gold robe."

"That was a *woman*?" I asked.

"Yeah. She told us to kneel down and stick out our tongues. She dropped something into our mouths and told us to eat it. I pretended to, but spit mine into my palm when no one was looking. But before I could tell Wade not to swallow it, he'd already gulped it down."

Jimmy's voice cracked. A tear ran down his cheek. "After that, we danced around the fire with the guys, trying to fit in, you know. A while later, the group broke up. Wade and I went back to my truck, laughing at what a bunch of crazy weirdos those guys were."

Jimmy looked up, then directly into my eyes. He shook his head. "Everything seemed okay. Like it was just a random, crazy night to remember. Wade got in my truck with me. I drove him back to Juanita's restaurant and dropped him off at the parking lot. I went home. And that's—" Jimmy's voice cracked. "That's the last time I saw or heard from him."

Jimmy collapsed onto the table, his head resting atop his crossed arms. "I should've warned him," he mumbled, rolling his head left and right. "It's all my fault! I killed Wade!"

"It wasn't your fault," Garth said, leaning over and hugging his brother.

Grayson cleared his throat. "Until proven otherwise, Jimmy, there's no evidence Wade is actually dead."

Jimmy burst into tears. "Then where is he?"

I placed a hand on Jimmy's. "What Grayson means is, you're not responsible for whatever's happened to Wade."

Grayson's eyebrow formed a flat line. "That's not what I said at all. I meant—"

I stomped Grayson's foot under the table, then whispered softly to Jimmy, "Continue with your story. We need to know all the facts we can if we're going to figure out what's really going on here."

Jimmy raised his head, sniffed, and turned to Garth. "I'm sorry, bro. I didn't want you to get tangled up in this."

"Don't you worry," Garth said. "Like Pandora said, we'll figure this out together."

"If it helps, just think of it like a regular case," I said to Jimmy. "Right now, we're investigating a missing person. That's all. You dropped Wade off Saturday night. Then what?"

Jimmy nodded and straightened his shoulders. "The next morning, Sunday, I called Wade to make sure he was all right. He didn't answer his cellphone. That wasn't like him at all. So I went back to Juanita's restaurant. His truck was still in the lot. That surprised me pretty good."

"What did you do then?" Grayson asked.

"Well, I checked inside the restaurant. He wasn't there. So I went into the park. I thought I'd find him hurt or snake bit on one of the trails in the Hi-Ho. I spent the whole day walking trails out there, but I couldn't find a footprint, a cigarette butt, *nothing*. It's like he vanished without a trace."

Grayson glanced over at me. "Sounds familiar."

Chapter Forty

Jimmy sat back in the banquette and shook his head. He'd confessed to being the last one to see his friend Wade, but from what I could tell, Jimmy very much hoped to see his friend again—alive and kicking.

"I think we can guess why you didn't call the cops about Wade going missing," Grayson said.

"What good would it do?" Jimmy said. "I knew even if I filed a missing person report, the other cops wouldn't take it seriously. At least not for another couple of days, anyway. If Wade was out there hurt in the woods, I knew I might be his only hope to make it out alive."

"So *that's* where you've been all this time," Garth said.

"Yeah. I walked the Hi-Ho trails till sunset on Sunday. Then, as I was getting ready to head home for the night, I thought about those guys dancing around the fire in robes. I started wondering if *they* had something to do with Wade going missing.

"Either way, I couldn't leave Wade alone out there. So I called in sick Monday, then asked for the rest of the week off on vacation. I've been camping out in the Hi-Ho—I mean Edward Medard Park—ever since."

"What've you been doing with your time?" I asked.

"Walking the trails by day. Watching the Cruller meetings by night. I've been lurking in the bushes, trying to make out what's going on. But I bring the robe with me that they gave us. And I even sent away for a sword—you know, so I'd fit in better—in case I needed to infiltrate the meetings. I wanted to see if Wade came back or was being held against his will. But I haven't seen him since."

"Wade's been gone five days now," I said. "Isn't it time you requested backup from the other cops on the force?"

Jimmy winced. "I'm trying to lay low. I'm worried they'll book me for Wade's murder. Thanks to that alien invasion thing last summer, most of the guys already think I'm a loose cannon." Jimmy locked eyes with me. "You remember what happened."

I grimaced. "Uh, yeah."

Jimmy sighed and stared at the table. "You know, I still find tinfoil hats in my chair at work sometimes."

"Alien invasion was a perfectly plausible explanation at the time," Grayson said, then sniffed. "But let's get back to the investigation at hand. What evidence have you gathered so far from your undercover operation?"

A tight smile edged the corners of Jimmy's plump cheeks. "Not a lot. I think the woman in the gold robe is the head of the organization."

"Did you get a good look at her?" Grayson asked.

Jimmy nodded. "Yeah. She's young. Maybe thirty, tops. Blonde. Nice-looking face. Pouty lips. Skinny body. Kind of big-bosomed. For some reason, she seems to have some kind of hold on these guys."

"Gee," I said. "Imagine that."

Jimmy locked eyes with me. "No. It's more than *that*, Ms. Drex."

"What kind of control are you talking about?" Grayson asked.

Jimmy's eyes darted down to the table. "It's hard to say. She seems to have some kind of ... I dunno ... *mind control*."

I shook my head. "What reason would a woman like her have for wanting to control a bunch of pasty, old white guys?"

Jimmy shrugged. "I don't know. But she calls herself Queen Kristie."

"Pshaw!" I laughed. "*Queen* Kristie?"

"Hmm," Grayson said, rubbing his chin. "Then this woman definitely sees herself as an authority figure. Perhaps even as superior to her subjects."

I snorted. "A bunch of desperate, overweight, middle-aged hillbillies? Hard not to."

"But that's just it," Jimmy said. "They weren't overweight. I mean, not at first. And a lot of them drive *cars*."

"As opposed to what?" I said. "Spaceships?"

"No," Jimmy said. "*Trucks*. These guys park their vehicles along the side roads inside Hi-Ho. There's only a handful of four-by-fours in the bunch. Some of the license plates are even from outside Polk County. I ran the plates on a few, looking to see if they were relatives of Wade's or something. One belongs to a mayor. Another's a high-school principal. One's a fry cook at Wendy's."

I blew out a breath. "Apparently, this cruller queen's lust for cash knows no boundaries. She must not realize the school system pays squat. That fry cook probably has more in his wallet that the principal."

Jimmy shook his head. "I don't think her primary motive is money."

I blanched. After all, Florida was still technically *America*.

"If not money, then what?" I asked.

Suddenly, from the back room, Earl let out a groan that reverberated down the hallway.

Grayson pursed his lips. "Whatever the Queen's personal motivation is will have to wait. The more pressing question for now is *how* she's accomplishing mind control over the men."

"I think I know," Jimmy said. "I believe there's something in the round wafer thing she makes the guys eat at the beginning of each meeting. I've noticed the more times each man attends, the crazier—and fatter—each gets. When I saw Earl this evening, I could tell he'd already eaten at least one. Am I right?"

I glanced down the hallway and bit my lip. "Yes. You're right, Jimmy. I saw Earl eat it."

Jimmy blew out a breath. "I *knew* it. That's why I knocked him down. If he'd gotten ahold of another one, it might've been game over for him."

"But ... you *gave* him another one, didn't you?" I asked.

"No," Jimmy said. "I only pretended to throw it into the bedroom." He pulled the small, round, doughy object from his shirt pocket and held it up for us to examine.

"What *is* that?" I asked.

"I don't know," Grayson said, studying it with a magnifying glass.

I sneered at it. "You think it's laced with some kind of drug?"

"Indubitably," Grayson said. He pulled a baggie out of his pocket. "Drop that in here, Jimmy. I want to test it."

"For drugs?" Jimmy asked. "What kind do you suspect?"

Grayson chewed his lip. "Perhaps *performance* enhancers."

"Ugh!" I groaned. "Men will do anything to—"

"I meant *sales* performance enhancers," Grayson said. "From what you and I observed ourselves, the meetings appear to include some kind of team building exercises, do they not?"

"Maybe," I said.

"Oh!" Garth said. "I know! Maybe the drugs are *mood* enhancers—and the meetings are pep rallies. You know. To get the guys all jacked up to sell more crullers."

Jimmy shook his head. "I think there's more to it than that. Or, should I say, *less* to it."

My nose crinkled. "What do you mean?"

Jimmy clicked the display on his cellphone. "If this is only about selling Kristie's Frickin' Crullers, the company itself doesn't appear to be doing much to build any kind of retail presence."

"Intriguing," Grayson said. "Go on."

"Okay. At the end of each meeting, Queen Kristie hands each guy a bag of donuts. But as far as I can tell, there aren't any retail shops in town. No online delivery ones, either. In fact, I haven't seen a single sign of Kristie's Frickin' Crullers outside of these bizarre nighttime bonfire meetings."

"That's odd." Grayson said, tapping on his computer keyboard. "You're right, Jimmy. There's not a single mention of Kristie's Frickin' Crullers on the web."

My nose crinkled. "What does *that* mean?"

Grayson closed his laptop with a snap. "It means that Kristie's Frickin' Crullers is either a front for something else, or whoever's running it is keeping the operation top secret until it's ready to be rolled out."

"Whatever it is, it's big," Jimmy said. "I heard Queen Kristie tell one of her minions that her plan was going to change the world as we know it."

"Indeed." Grayson's eyebrow went up like Spock's. "I've heard those exact words before. But not to worry, my friends. No matter how well-funded or charismatic the leader, not every plan works out as intended."

My lip snarled. "Grayson, are you comparing Queen Kristie to *Hitler*?"

"No," he said. "Steve Jobs. Remember the Segway?"

I sighed, shook my head, and turned to Jimmy. "Not to be rude or anything, but I couldn't help but notice you've put on a few pounds yourself. How many of those queen's Quaaludes have *you* eaten?"

"None," Jimmy said, his body stiffening. "I swear!"

"Well, kudos to *you*, then," Grayson said. "You certainly take your role seriously. Not everyone could gain that much weight so quickly for an undercover role."

"Uh ... I didn't," Jimmy said.

Then he dug his fingers into his neck behind his ears and pulled off his double chin.

Chapter Forty-One

"**A**ack!" I screeched, as a pork-chop sized hunk of Jimmy's neck fell off. I scrambled out of the banquette like my hair was on fire. "He's turning into ... into *one of them*!"

"Relax!" Jimmy said, peeling off his double chin like it was a neck brace. "It's foam rubber. I'm wearing a fat suit."

My jaw hit the floor. "But .... Why?"

"Ha!" Grayson said, and pounded his fist once on the table. "I *knew* you ran too fast for a fat man!"

"Don't worry, Ms. Drex! It's part of my undercover disguise," Jimmy said. "Like I told you, I noticed all the guys in the Cruller clan were getting fat. So I had Sherman's mom make me up. She's a master of disguise, you know."

"Uh ... yeah," I said. "I saw her human bulldog mask."

The guys all stared at me, not uttering a word.

I grimaced. "That was no mask, was it?"

Jimmy pursed his lips and shook his head. Then he held up his fake chin. "Anyway, I wore this to fit in. Once I noticed everyone ballooning up, I thought I'd better follow suit."

Grayson laughed. "*Follow* suit, *fat* suit. I get it."

Garth grabbed the rubber chin and shot me a buck-toothed grin. "Like I said before, Pandora. You can get anything on Amazon."

Still reeling slightly, I shot Jimmy a weak smile. "Uh, sure. It makes perfect sense now. So Jimmy, you've actually been attending these bonfire meetings?"

Jimmy nodded. "A couple."

"Well, what have you learned?" I asked.

"Not a whole lot. At the beginning, the guys line up and eat the wafer thing. Then they stand around while Queen Kristie talks. I've tried to listen to what she's saying, but I can't seem to retain anything. I just zone out, nod and smile."

My brow furrowed. I glanced over at Grayson. "You think she might be hypnotizing them?"

"Unlikely," he said. "From what I've observed, that's what normally happens to a man when a woman speaks." Grayson winked at Jimmy. "Son, that's your survival instinct kicking in."

I smiled tersely and kicked Grayson's shin under the table. "Jimmy dear, before you uh ... *tune out*, have you been able to remember anything Queen Cruller's said?"

He shook his head, his now slim, pinkish neck looking like a plucked turkey neck compared to his still fat foam-rubber body.

"Nothing that makes sense, Ms. Drex. From what I could gather, it's mostly sales mumbo jumbo. Percentages, infestation rates, that kind of stuff."

I nearly swallowed my tonsils. "*Infestation* rates?"

Jimmy bit his lip. "Uh ... she might've said *penetration* rates."

Garth snickered.

I grimaced.

Geez. Which is worse?

"What else happens during the meetings?" Grayson asked. "Concentrate. *Any* detail may prove significant."

Jimmy thought for a moment, then spoke, looking at the ceiling as if recalling the scene play by play.

"At the end of each meeting, Queen Kristie draws her sword and points it to the sky. She stomps her feet. Then she lets out a weird yell."

"I think we've heard that," Grayson said. "Like someone throttling a yodeler?"

"Yes!" Jimmy said. "I call it the Cruller Holler."

"What happens next?" I asked.

"The men holler back. Queen Kristie lowers her sword, and all the men follow her lead, like they're her soldiers or something. From what I can tell, that concludes the official part of her meeting. Afterward, the guys either run through hot coals or disperse back to their vehicles."

Grayson rubbed his chin. "So this actually *could* simply be some kind of 'pep rally,' just as Garth said."

Garth beamed with buck-toothed pride.

"Maybe," I said. "But a pep-rally for what? She could be building a sales team or an army of soldiers. We need to find out more about this Queen Kristie chick."

"Absolutely," Grayson agreed. He turned to Jimmy. "Have you tried tailing her?"

Garth snickered. I rolled my eyes.

"Yeah, I've tried," Jimmy said. "But so far, I haven't been able to see where Queen Kristie goes after the meetings. I've followed her down Whirlwind Trail twice, but it's like she disappears into thin air."

"Maybe she just takes off her robe and turns sideways," I said sourly. "The woman's a donut pusher and she's as thin as a stick. Something isn't right about that. As my grandma Selma always said, never trust a skinny cook."

"Don't hate her because she's beautiful," Jimmy said.

"Beautiful?" I hissed. "I got a quick look at her when Earl went up to Miss Queenie's 'throne' to eat that damned wafer thing. If you ask me, there was something oddly inhuman about her face. You know. Like a Kardashian."

"Hmm," Grayson said. "This information could change everything." His glowing green eyes locked onto Jimmy, who was tugging at the torn neck of fat suit as if it were itchy. "You said the first time you were offered a wafer, you put it in your mouth."

"*She* did," Jimmy said. "But I didn't swallow."

Grayson's eyes narrowed. "Why not?"

Jimmy leaned back in the booth. "I was suspicious."

"That it was part of a cult initiation?" Grayson asked.

"No," Jimmy said. "Because crullers don't have holes."

"Yes!" Grayson pounded his fist on the table again. "My thoughts exactly! Excellent deductive reasoning, Jimmy."

You've got to be kidding me...

"So," Grayson said, leaning over the table toward fake-fat Jimmy. "Did you note any effects from your brief oral contact with the suspicious donut hole?"

"Actually, now that you mention it, yes," Jimmy said. "I felt ... a jolt of euphoria. I immediately thought the wafer might contain Ecstasy or LSD or something. So I spit it out and slipped it into my pocket. Then I started to feel anxious."

"That's understandable," I said, "considering you were surrounded by weirdos in robes, dancing around a damned bonfire."

"Yeah," Jimmy said. "But what I felt was more than just anxiety. It was ... I dunno ... a hollow, *unsatisfied* feeling."

"Are you saying you felt *hungry*?" I asked.

Jimmy chewed his lip. "Yeah. Sort of. But it was a strange kind of hunger. I'd call it more of a *craving*. When I got home, no matter what I ate, I didn't feel satisfied. Like when you eat something sweet, then you eat something salty to balance it out. You know what I mean?"

I glanced away. "I have no idea what you're talking about."

Jimmy sighed. "Well, anyway, it was *that* kind of feeling—only on steroids."

"What did you do to satiate this feeling?" Grayson asked.

Jimmy looked down at the table. "It was pretty overwhelming. I didn't feel like I could fight it. So I took a sleeping pill to knock myself out, and slept the whole night. When I woke up, I felt okay."

"So you slept off the effects," Grayson said. "How long did it take?"

"I woke up at close to noon," Jimmy said. "So, I guess twelve hours?"

"And that was from just a taste," I said. "Earl ate the whole thing."

"So did Wade," Jimmy said. "And now he's missing. Like I said, I think there's a lot more going on here than a bunch of country folks on a sales jamboree."

All of a suddenly, an unearthly howl reverberated from the back bedroom.

Jimmy winced. "Whatever's going on here, Earl's got it bad. He just let out one hell of a Cruller Holler."

Chapter Forty-Two

Earl let out another horrible holler and began banging on the door to the back bedroom.

I winced. "What's going to happen to him?"

"I don't know," Jimmy said. "But if you don't keep him caged up in there, he could disappear like Wade did."

"From the sound of it, he's going to have to detox," Grayson said.

"I agree," I said. "How long will that take?"

"Uncertain," Grayson said. "Perhaps a day. Maybe more, depending on his metabolism."

"He sounds terrible," Jimmy said. "Are you sure he only ate one of those donut-hole things?"

"No," I said. "But, I mean, where else could he have gotten ahold of any?"

"Wait," Garth said, his eyes growing large. He elbowed his brother. "That bag of those crullers you brought home—"

Jimmy blanched. "You got my message not to eat them, didn't you?"

Garth pushed his glasses up on his nose. "*That's* what your weird message was about?"

"Yes," Jimmy said, grabbing his brother by the shoulders. "I said, 'Whatever you do, don't eat them.'" He glanced up at me. "You got the text, right? Please! Tell me you didn't eat them!"

"I didn't," Garth said, wiping his nose on his sleeve. "This rotten cold's ruined my appetite for sweets."

"Neither did we," I said.

"Thank God," Jimmy said, then blew out a breath. "We need to destroy those things before they fall into the wrong hands."

Earl hollered again like a goat with a yodeling problem.

Garth gasped and shook his head. "If I'm right about this, I think we're too late for that."

GARTH WAS RIGHT. WE found the empty donut bag in the ditch, right where we'd found Earl lying about like a hobo gambler who'd just lost his last game of strip poker.

"It's official," Jimmy said, holding up the mangled paper bag. "Your cousin Earl ate them all."

"Good grief," I said, horror filling my gut. "Earl doesn't have enough spare brain cells to survive this!"

"What are we gonna do?" Garth asked, chewing on a fingernail.

Grayson shook his head. "His detoxification could take weeks. Or he may never return to normal."

"Even if he did," I said, shaking my head, "how would we ever be able to tell?"

JIMMY CAME OUT OF THE restroom carrying thirty pounds of foam rubber in a giant Walmart bag. In his deflated clothes, and with patches of foam on his face, he looked like the sole survivor of a post-apocalyptic Weight Watchers marathon.

I poured him a cup of coffee. "How'd you know where we would be tonight, Jimmy?"

"After I saw Earl stumble into the meeting the night before last, I knew you were in town," Jimmy said. "I figured you'd come in through the swamp from the main road. I found your tire tracks and waited to see if you showed up."

"Why didn't you just call us?" I asked.

"I should have. But I wanted to keep Garth out of this, and I wanted to protect you guys from whatever's going on out there. But as soon as I spotted Earl, I knew he had the craving. I was too late."

"I'm curious," Grayson said. "If what's happening to Earl is also happening to all those other men, why hasn't anyone else reported it?"

"I think I've got this one," I said, raising my index finger. "Let's see. A bunch of middle-aged men overeating, ignoring their spouses, grunting like wild boars, and gallivanting at night with no good explanation when they get home. Gee. I haven't got a clue why their wives would think something odd is afoot."

Grayson and Jimmy exchanged glances, then shrugged.

Suddenly, something scratched at the side door and whined.

"That must be Garth," Jimmy said. "He's back from feeding Tooth."

Suddenly, the side door to the RV flung open. In the doorframe, a pair of yellow eyes and fangs greeted us.

"Tooth!" Jimmy said, calling to the massive black hound.

The dog jumped inside and leapt up in the booth with Jimmy.

"How are you, boy?" Jimmy asked, rubbing the slobbering hound's ears. He glanced up at his brother. "Tooth looks skinny. Have you been feeding him?"

"Of course," Garth said. "But apparently not enough."

"Why?" Jimmy asked. "Did he get into the garbage again?"

Garth shook his head. "No. Earl beat him to it. But he snuck out of the gate this evening. I think he ate a roadkill possum."

"You *think* he did?" Jimmy grimaced and wiped his slobbery face with a sleeve.

"Pretty sure. You saved me the tail, didn't you boy?" Garth said, patted the dog's massive head.

The dog licked Garth's face, then lunged for the wafer in the baggie on the table. Grayson snatched it away in the nick of time.

"Not today, Doggie Wonder. I need to analyze this," Grayson said, tucking the baggie into his shirt pocket. He turned to Jimmy. "Tell me. Besides the craving to eat more donuts, have you noted any other side-effects among the Cruller clan?"

All of a sudden, from the backroom came an unearthly banging.

"Let me outta here!" Earl yelled. "I gotta use the toilet! Bad!"

"Uh ...," Jimmy grunted. "Just *that* one."

Chapter Forty-Three

E arl banged and kicked on the dead-bolted steel door like a mule trying to shake a mountain lion. His frantic, noisy efforts had the whole RV rocking and rolling.

"Geez! What are we gonna do?" I yelled to Grayson over the din. "Earl's gotta use the bathroom, bad. Are we gonna let him out or not?"

"It depends," Grayson said, shifting his gaze to Jimmy. "What kind of behavior should we expect from him if we do?"

Jimmy shook his head. "I really couldn't say for sure. But from what I've seen, the men who go to those meetings aren't dangerous. They're more ... I don't know. *Confused*, I guess."

"Confused?" Grayson asked. "You're going to have to do better than that if Earl's going to get to use the privy."

Jimmy shrugged. "I dunno. They seem to be able to function well enough to drive, but they're disoriented somehow. Zonked out. And the next evening, when they come back to the meetings, they look grumpy."

My nose crinkled. "*Grumpy?*"

"You know," Jimmy said. "Irritable. Grouchy. Out of sorts."

I frowned. "I don't know what you're talking about."

"Grumpy angry, or grumpy desperate?" Grayson asked.

"Desperate," Jimmy said. "It's like all they want to do is get back to the meeting."

"Hmm," Grayson said. "Peer pressure has been proven to be a formidable social force. In one study—"

"Wait," I said, smiling slyly. "I think I know what's going on here."

"Voodoo mind control?" Garth asked.

I glanced across the room at the mullet-headed nerd. He was still standing by the side door, his face so hopeful at the prospect of voodoo that I hated to burst his geeky bubble. Still, it had to be done.

"No, Garth," I said. "But close. I was thinking more along the lines of *addiction*. Grayson, you really should test that sample for drugs as soon as possible."

Jimmy's face lit up. "That *must* be it. What else would drive grown men to walk on hot coals? Or dance around with swords like pagan weirdos?"

Garth gasped. "Maybe it's a Comic-Con convention!"

All of a sudden, an audible hissing noise sounded, like air escaping a balloon. I thought maybe Garth's brain had sprung a leak. But then a horrible stench filled the air.

"Ugh!" I groaned. My eyes began to burn. "Who did that?"

"Let me outta here!" Earl hollered from down the hall.

I turned to Grayson. "Well? What are we gonna do? We're out of time. Are we freeing Earl to use the toilet, or turning your bedroom into a rolling redneck outhouse?"

Grayson sniffed the air. "My olfactory receptors indicate your point may already indeed be moot."

"Don't do it," Jimmy said, climbing out of the banquette. He sprinted to the hallway entry that led to the bedroom. Then he braced both arms against the sides of the doorframe, blocking our access to it.

"It's still night out," Jimmy said. "If you let Earl out now, he'll be desperate to get back to the meeting. He'll be like a homing pigeon."

"A *three-hundred pound* homing pigeon," Garth added.

"If it *is* drugs and he ate all four crullers, he'll be unstoppable," Jimmy said.

"We could dart him," Garth said. "You know, like they do on *Mutual of Omaha's Wild Kingdom*?"

I opened my mouth to speak and nearly gagged. The disgusting smell was getting worse, not better. "Couldn't we at least let Earl get to the bathroom?"

"No," Grayson said, grabbing his laptop. "Apparently, he's had a mega-dose. Jimmy's right. He'll be as unstoppable as a drunken linebacker." Grayson's fingers flew as he tapped on the computer keyboard.

"What are you doing?" I asked. "Looking up drug side effects?"

"No," Grayson answered, his eyes glued to the keyboard. "I'm ordering a new mattress."

Chapter Forty-Four

The initial round of smelly, eye-burning gas had subsided somewhat. We'd all survived the blast. It was nearing 2 a.m., and it appeared our battle with Earl was turning into an all-nighter.

For the last half hour, I'd been dropping hints for Garth and Jimmy to go back to their trailer, but they weren't biting. Dead tired, I wanted to lay down so badly that even the broken-down sofa-bed coffin was starting to look good.

"Come on, Grayson, can't we call it a night?" I begged.

"Sorry, Drex. But until we're able to analyze the contents of that contaminated cruller hole Earl ate, we can't be sure of what we're dealing with. The only thing for certain is that something is warping and twisting the minds of those men, turning them into festering mush. Does anyone have any other ideas besides drugs?"

"How about stupidity?" I said, my face hot with anger. "There seems to be a lot of *that* going around."

"No, it can't be stupidity," Grayson said matter-of-factly. "It's not transferrable, as far as I'm aware."

"How about greed?" Jimmy asked.

Grayson's eyebrows crunched. "Hmm. Love of money has been known to make people do foolish things. But as you pointed out before, there's no evidence of selling behavior on anyone's part—either retail or wholesale."

"Then it must be drugs," Garth said. "It's the only thing that makes sense."

"Bbblllbbrrt," someone said.

We turned and stared. The odd sound had come from Tooth—but not from his mouth.

The same, horrible stench as before poisoned the air.

Grayson grimaced as if in pain and yelled, "That's it!"

"Sorry, Mr. Gray," Garth said, grabbing Tooth's collar.

I waved a hand in front of my face. "Dear lord, Garth! Open the door and let that dog out of here!"

"No," Grayson said, wiping his eyes. He nodding toward the dog. "What I mean is, *that's* it! Tooth has the answer!"

"What?" I said, pinching my nose closed. "Are you saying Earl and the other guys are being driven crazy by noxious dog farts?"

"Not exactly," Grayson said. "It's not the farts *themselves*, you see. It's what's *causing* the farts."

"A dead possum?" Garth asked.

Grayson jumped to his feet. "No! Come on, people. Put on your thinking caps!"

I stared at Grayson. "Can I opt for a gas mask instead?"

Grayson shook his head. "Look. I'll give you a hint. It starts with a B."

"Bologna?" Jimmy asked.

Grayson shook his head.

"Beanie wienie?" Garth asked.

"Nope," Grayson said. "Try again."

"Barbeque?" I asked, my mind numb from lack of sleep.

"No, no, no," Grayson said, reaching down to pet Tooth's head.

"Bbblllbbrrt," Tooth repeated.

Grayson laughed. "Exactly, my canine friend!"

He looked up at us, his green eyes twinkling like Jack Nicholson in *The Shining*. "*Bacteria, people. It's bacteria!*"

Chapter Forty-Five

Of all of Grayson's lame-brained ideas, this one had to be the absolute lamest.

Bacteria was driving these guys crazy?

I got up and sprinted to the side door of the RV and gulped in a lungful of flatulent-free air. Then I turned back to Grayson, who had sat back down in the banquette.

"Let me get this right," I said. "You think *bacteria* is turning those robed rednecks into Pillsbury dough zombies?"

"Yes," Grayson said. "You appear shocked. I'm curious. Why would that surprise you?"

I sucked in another breath of outside air and turned to face him. "Why *wouldn't* it?"

Grayson studied me from his perch at the banquette, while Garth, Jimmy and I studied him as if we were the hapless, doomed crew aboard *The Ship of Fools*.

Maybe we were.

Grayson seemed to sense we were about to mutiny. He raised his arms and said, "Gather round and let me explain."

"Yes, please do," I muttered, then reluctantly scooted my ass into the booth.

"You see, the human body consists of roughly thirty trillion cells," Grayson said, spreading his fingers like two fans. "But our intestines are home to over forty *trillion* bacteria, give or take a recent defecation."

I closed my eyes, not at all sure I wanted to know where this conversation was leading.

"Let me demonstrate," he said.

Dear lord, no!

My eyes flew open. Grayson scooted out of the booth and placed both spidery hands across his stomach.

"You're not gonna—" I gasped.

"Please! Hold all questions to the end," Grayson said, then began rubbing his belly. "Now, my fellow associates, it's not widely known, but up to a trillion bacteria reside in each gram of intestinal content. That means the major component of feces is *bacteria*."

"Ugh!" I groaned. "We get it, okay? Poop is full of bacteria. Is there a point to all this?"

Grayson's eyebrow rose like Spock's. "I thought I just made it." He glanced at me, then at the two brothers, who appeared as confounded as I was.

Grayson's Spock eyebrow collapsed. "Don't you see? Cellularly speaking, we're actually *more bacteria than human*."

My lips curled downward in disgust.

Well, there goes kissing anyone—ever again.

"Is that for real?" Garth asked, his eyes two bloodshot boiled eggs behind the thick lenses of his horn-rimmed glasses.

"Absolutely," Grayson said. He patted his belly. "On any given day, each of us is carrying around up to four and a half pounds of bacteria in our digestive tracts."

"Whoa!" Garth said. "That's like—sixteen Big Macs!"

"I said no disruptions," Grayson said. "Now, most of our gut bacteria belong to thirty or forty species, but there can be up to a thousand different kinds inside us, each struggling to survive within our individual microbiomes."

"Microbiomes?" I sneered. "You make it sound like our guts are bacterial *Thunderdomes*."

"An excellent analogy," Grayson said, "because what goes on in our guts is truly a matter of life or death."

"Phew," Jimmy said, pushing Tooth away. "It sure *smells* that way."

"Yeah," Garth said, crinkling his red nose. "How could Tina Turner stand it?"

I shook my head.

If I had her money, I'd be sooo outta here...

Grayson's brow furrowed. "I think you're missing the point here, men. You see, when it comes down to it, our gut is actually *key* to our body's survival. It's constantly sending messages to the brain that are critical to our ongoing health."

"Really?" Jimmy asked, looking down at his stomach.

"Yes," Grayson said. "If our stomach is empty, our brain needs to know that—so we don't starve. On the other hand, if we eat something poisonous or rotten, the brain needs to know that, too—so it can make arrangements to rid itself of anything threatening to our well-being."

"Yay," I said dully. "Our guts are important. But Grayson, what has any of this got to do with the way Earl's been acting?"

"I'm getting to that." Grayson lowered his hands. "I never told you this, but back in my research days, I was involved in studies related to the brain-gut-enteric microbiota axis."

My weary brain skipped like a needle on a record. "The *what*?"

Grayson sighed. "For you laymen, it's the study of how gut bacteria influence psychology and behavior. During our clinical trials, we discovered that bacteria in the intestines can activate stress circuits by directly stimulating the vagus nerve."

I ground my teeth. Forget that stupid vagus nerve thing. Grayson was on my *last* nerve.

I curled my fist and started counting down from thirty. Grayson had half a minute to make his point, or I was gonna knock him unconscious and make a dive for the sofa-bed coffin.

"Like I said, when necessary, the gut can communicate directly with the brain," Grayson prattled on. "If you've ever eaten a bad burrito, you know what I mean."

"Ooooh," Garth said. "Point taken, Mr. Gray!"

"So our gut talks to our brain?" Jimmy asked.

"Yes. Through the enteric nervous system," Grayson said. "Our gut has over two-hundred million nerves in it. That's about as many as in a dog's cerebral cortex. Looking at it another way, our gut is about as smart as the average dog."

Garth grinned. "You mean my poop shoot is as smart as Tooth here?" He patted the dog's massive, dumb-looking head.

"Yes," Grayson said. "In fact, some call the gut 'the second brain.'"

Garth grinned. "Cool!"

"It kind of *is*, isn't it," Grayson said, a dimple forming on his right cheek. "Actually, the enteric nervous system in our gut could be considered the *original* brain. It developed when we were basic organisms—mere primitive digestive tubes, if you will."

"You mean like Earl is now?" I grumbled. "I hope there's some point to this biology lesson, Mr. Professor. We need to do something about Earl, and soon."

"Patience, Grasshopper," Grayson said, making my fist curl tighter.

"Now, here's my point." Grayson said, directing his gaze my way. "Besides regulating bowel flow, there's good evidence that our bacterial ecosystem—the microbiome I mentioned earlier—*can influence how we think and feel*. In other words, bacteria can moderate both our brain *and* our behavior."

I sat up, my anger evaporating. "Seriously?" I asked. "How does *that* work?"

Grayson shrugged. "No one knows for sure."

"Great," I grumbled, collapsing back into the booth. "We sat through all of that malarkey just so you can tell us there's nothing we can do about it?"

"I didn't say *that*," Grayson said.

"Then there *is* something we can do?" Jimmy asked.

"Perhaps," Grayson said. "As it turned out, during experiments with both mice and human subjects, we found we could improve their anxiety levels, obsessive-compulsive disorders, and even memories simply by giving them probiotics."

I winced. "Probiotics?" I asked, not sure if I'd heard that right.

Grayson's green eyes twinkled. "Yes! By increasing our subjects' *good* bacteria, we were able to reduce their undesirable mental symptoms. So, extrapolating from that evidence, it seems plausible to postulate that *bad* bacteria could have been the cause of some of those undesirable symptoms in the first place."

My jaw dropped. "Are you saying Earl's under the influence of *bad bacteria*?"

Grayson gave a quick nod. "Yes. I believe so."

I frowned. "But if that were *true*, wouldn't we *all* be acting the same way he is?"

"We would indeed—if we'd all eaten one of these babies," Grayson said, holding up the baggie with the donut hole.

"You think that thing's full of bad bacteria?" Jimmy asked.

"Not only *bad*," Grayson said, "but from a whole other *galactic neighborhood*."

Chapter Forty-Six

I waved goodnight to Garth and Jimmy, then closed the RV door and looked over at Grayson and shook my head.

"I'm sorry, but intergalactic gangster bacteria taking over our thoughts and actions? That's just too out there to believe."

Grayson looked up from his laptop and shrugged. "Believe it or don't—at your own peril. But the truth is, it's already happened."

I gasped. "It has?"

"Sure. Every year Earth's bombarded by thousands of tons of asteroid dust. We touch it. Eat it. Breathe it in. Given those facts, microbial colonization by a more aggressive extraterrestrial species seems more than possible. It's *inevitable*."

I cringed and slid into the banquette opposite him. "Are you saying we're *doomed*?"

"That's one way to look at it. But in reality, like I said earlier, we've already been colonized by thousands of different types of bacteria. They're such a part of us now that humans can be categorized into three separate enterotypes."

"Enterotypes?"

Grayson nodded. "They're like blood types, but instead of human cells, they refer to the types of bacteria inhabiting our microbiomes. What's fascinating about that is the distribution doesn't appear to be related to geography, sex, or race."

"Seriously?" I said. "How is that possible?"

Grayson shrugged. "It's a mystery. Perhaps we're actually nothing more than advanced biological hosts for microbes."

I frowned. "What do you mean?"

"There are a thousand times more bacteria in us than there are stars in our galaxy. And hundreds of times more bacteria in our bodies than actual human cells. One could argue the idea that our own consciousness is merely a passenger inside a bacterial bus."

My lip snarled. "How romantic."

Grayson laughed. "On the bright side, if we ever do get superseded by bacteria, we probably won't be aware of it. We'll simply become the hapless hosts of the invaders, shuffling along, doing their bidding, totally unaware of what we've lost in the exchange."

I locked eyes with Grayson. "You mean like Earl ... and those other guys."

Grayson sighed. "Perhaps."

"But you said there's a chance probiotics could cure him."

"Not necessarily *cure*. But perhaps lessen the symptoms."

I straightened my sagging shoulders. "I want a *cure*."

Grayson rubbed his chin. "To do *that*, we'd have to rid Earl's body of all the bacteria in it."

I perked up a bit—a feat considering how beat I was. I grabbed Grayson's hand. "How can we *do* that?"

Grayson studied me for a moment. "I think I know a way. Look, why don't you stretch out on that side of the banquette and try and get some rest."

"What are you gonna do?"

Grayson smiled tiredly. "I'm going to order some stuff on Amazon."

Chapter Forty-Seven

I woke up with a crick in my neck and second thoughts running through my mind.

Bacterial mind control? Seriously?

The only thing that made sense was the pot of coffee on the stove and the note Grayson had left next to it.

In the shower. Keep eye out for Amazon delivery.

I poured myself a cup and flopped back into the banquette that had been my beddy-bye for the night. Considering some of the dives we'd stayed at over the past eight months, the old vinyl booth wasn't all that bad.

And then I realized Grayson wasn't singing. The shower was running, but his mouth wasn't.

Then I remembered Earl was in the back bedroom. He probably didn't want to wake him. I tiptoed down the hall and pressed my ear against the door. Earl was snoring faintly.

Maybe he was going to be all right after all.

I smiled and tiptoed back past the bathroom. Just as I reached the main cabin, someone banged on the side door. I sprinted over to it and yanked it open.

"Mornin', Miss Pandora!" Garth said.

"Shh!" I hissed, raising my finger to my lips. "Earl's sleeping."

Suddenly, from the back bedroom, Earl bellowed out the now familiar "Cruller Holler."

Garth winced. "Sorry about that."

"Never mind. Y'all come on in."

"Maybe these'll make up for it," Jimmy said, and handed me a bag.

"Donuts?" I asked. "Seriously?"

I WAS FINISHING OFF my second with Garth and Jimmy when Grayson graced us with his presence. Somehow, he managed to look neat as a pin. I couldn't say the same for me. Running on two cups of coffee and four hours sleep, I looked like I'd just finished the night shift at a Waffle House.

"Gentlemen," Grayson said, tipping his fedora at us as he passed the banquette and made a beeline for the coffee.

"Uh, Grayson, we were just going over what we discussed last night," I said.

"Oh, good," he said, glancing at his phone. "The probiotics and the enema kit should arrive sometime before ten o'clock."

"Enema kit?" Jimmy asked.

"Grayson thinks the fastest way to get Earl better is to remove all the bacteria in his gut."

"About that," Jimmy said. "Me and my brother still have a few questions."

Grayson poised his coffee cup mid-sip. "Such as?"

"Ahem ... No disrespect or anything, but Garth and I are still not completely convinced some little bacteria can be responsible for making these guys act so weird."

"Totally understandable," Grayson said. "The fact is, no one knows with any certainty what kind of influence bacteria has on our behavior, how we react, or who we even are."

"Right, but—"

Grayson sidled into the banquette next to Jimmy. "I, for one, am both amazed and amused at the idea that humans, as intelligent and advanced as we consider ourselves to be, are at least partially under the control of single-celled lifeforms."

I glanced around at the men around me—a crazy-eyed disbarred physicist, a bucktoothed doomsday prepper, and a conspiracy-nut cop who last night peeled himself out of a fat suit.

"Maybe *you* are," I muttered.

"Believe what you will," Grayson said. "But we would all do well to remember that our bacterial brethren predate us by *billions* of years, and are likely to outlive our species by billions more."

"What if you're right," Jimmy said. "Let's say bacteria *is* what's driving Earl and those other guys nuts. How do you explain how they got so *fat* so quickly?"

"Elementary," Grayson said. "Yeast is a form of bacteria. The byproduct of yeast's digestion of sugars is *gas*."

"Like Tooth with the possum stink?" Garth asked.

Grayson gave a quick nod. "Precisely. And it's this exact type of 'bacterial flatulence,' if you will, that causes bread dough to rise."

Grayson glanced over at me. "Ironically, Drex, it appears your satirical description of these men being 'Pillsbury Dough Zombies' is both colorful *and* relatively *accurate*—despite its being arrived at based on mere anecdotal evidence."

My eyes narrowed. "Was that a compliment or an insult?"

A dimple formed in Grayson's chin. "Who says it can't be both?"

Wait a minute. If we're mostly bacteria, and bacteria produce farts ... dear lord! Are we nothing more than the hapless pawns of parasitic gas bags?

I'd suspected as much for years.

"Uh ... excuse me," Jimmy said. "If I understand you right, Mr. Gray, you're saying bad bacteria got inside Earl through the donuts, right?"

"Precisely," Grayson answered. "And it's currently driving his thought processes and behaviors."

"And the solution is to remove it?" Jimmy asked.

"Via enema." Grayson said. "Then we'll recreate a healthy microbiome by reintroduced probiotics afterward."

I blanched, envisioned the three of them hogtying Earl, then ... ugh!

Garth's bottom jaw dropped loose. "Uh..."

Jimmy grimaced. "Sorry, Mr. Gray. But there's no way we could wrestle him down for that."

"I've got a better idea," I said.

"Thank God!" Garth said.

All three men turned their attention my way. "What do you propose?" Grayson asked.

"Uh ...," I stammered. "I propose we send a message up Earl's Las Vegas nerve thing using an artificial chemical stimulant."

Grayson eyed me curiously. "I'm not following."

I smirked.

Ha! I finally got one over on him! Score!

I stuck my nose haughtily in the air. "Well, if I *must* explain, I'm talking about giving Earl the old X-Lax/chocolate switcheroo."

"Of course!" Garth said, reaching over to give me a high five. "That would do it!"

"What?" Grayson asked.

"We're gonna give him a chocolate bar," Garth said. "Only the 'chocolate' ain't chocolate."

Grayson's eyebrows inched closer together.

"It's a *laxative*," Jimmy said.

"Oh." Grayson rubbed his chin. "I supposed that could work." He grabbed his laptop. "Garth, quick. What's your address here?"

I smirked. "Ordering Ex-Lax on line?"

"No," Grayson said, tapping away at his keyboard. "I'm putting a rush delivery on that new mattress."

Chapter Forty-Eight

Grayson was right about one thing.

What goes in, must come out.

Luckily, as it turned out, there was no need for Grayson to order the Ex-Lax online. Jimmy and Garth had a stockpile of it in their prepper pantry. Apparently, freeze-dried survivalist meals could really clog one's pipes.

After Jimmy climbed up on the roof of the RV and dropped the clandestine "chocolate" through the air vent above the back bedroom, the brothers retreated back to their trailer, leaving Grayson and me behind to "face the music."

It didn't take long for us to realize Earl had taken the bait.

From the symphony of sounds and smells emanating from the locked-down monster trap bedroom, I knew without a doubt that Grayson and I were going to require alternative sleeping quarters for the night, whether we ever let Earl out of there or not.

Grayson put a stethoscope against the bolted steel door and listened. "Hmm. From the sound of it, it appears the interstitial cells of Cajal have given up."

My eyebrows met. "Is that the name of the alien species of bacteria that's got a hold of him?"

"What?" Grayson asked.

"Those Cajal things! Were they what was on that donut hole thing Earl ate?"

"Oh." Grayson's shoulders straightened. "No. Testing of the cruller fragment isn't yet conclusive. I need to give the cultures a bit more time to grow."

"So what are those intergalactic Jihad cells you were talking about?"

Grayson dropped the stethoscope, letting it hang loosely around his neck. "The interstitial cells of Cajal?"

"Yeah."

"They're actually quite terrestrial, Drex. They're the cells responsible for intestinal activity. They're inside each of us, acting as the 'pacemakers of the bowels,' if you will."

Earl let out a wail. Either that, or the world's longest fart in c-sharp.

I cringed and glanced at the bedroom door. "Thanks for the biology lesson, Professor Grayson. But if you think I'm cleaning up that mess in there, you're gonna need your *own* pacemaker."

Grayson looked down his nose at me. "May I remind you, Drex, giving him Ex-Lax was *your* idea."

"Yeah. But locking him in the bedroom without a pot to piss in was *your* idea."

Grayson pursed his lips. "True. But we couldn't chance letting him out. It seems unlikely he'd be able to control his urges. There's nothing more addictive than the white stuff."

I blanched. "Cocaine? I thought you said your test results on the donut hole weren't conclusive!"

"Not completely, no," Grayson said. "But the white stuff to which I refer isn't cocaine. It's *sugar*."

My mouth dropped open. "You think Earl's gone nuts over *sugar*?"

"No. It's only the catalyst," Grayson said.

"Huh?"

Grayson locked eyes with me. "Drex, if the bacteria infesting the donut wafer sample follow the traits of most known harmful bacteria, *sugar* is their food of choice."

I blanched. "Sugar?"

"Yes."

I swallowed hard, unable to fathom what Grayson was saying. "Okay. Let's say sugar *is* this alien bacteria's food of choice. How does that translate into Earl becoming a flatulent lunatic?"

"The bacteria are in control of his actions now," Grayson said. "And what they need to replicate is more sugar. So they're compelling Earl to go out and find it."

"Like some kind of zombie? I'm sorry, but I just can't wrap my head around that."

"My theory is not without precedent," Grayson said. "Take the case of *Toxoplasma gondii.*"

I closed my eyes. "Do I have to?"

"I thought you wanted an explanation—"

Earl let out another wail. My eyes flew open.

I grabbed Grayson's hand. "I *do* want an explanation, Grayson. Please. Go on."

"*Toxoplasma gondii* is a parasite that prefers to live in the guts of cats. The best way to arrive in a feline colon is to be eaten by the cat. So, what does it do?"

My nose crinkled. "Climb into a box of Meow Mix?"

Grayson's cheek dimpled. "Close. It gets inside of mice and messes with their minds."

"What?"

"It's true. The parasite lives in cats' guts and is expelled in their feces. In lab experiments, it's been proven that mice who ingest this infected cat feces lose their fear of cats. Some mice even become sexually attracted to felines."

I blanched. "So, you're saying this plastic Gandhi parasite *knows* what it's doing?"

Grayson shrugged. "Single-cell sapience. What other explanation is there? Survival of the species is prime directive number one, Drex. And now, here we are, standing on the edge of a new frontier."

"New frontier?"

"Yes. A microbial one. We are the new cats, Drex. And this new bacteria is making humans crave sugary foods—to suit their ultimate survival needs."

"Oh, come on, Grayson. Any reasonable person can control themselves and not eat a stupid donut!"

His left eyebrow arched. "Are you sure about that?"

"Absolutely!"

"Okay. Let's put your conviction to the test."

"Huh? How?"

Grayson reached into his pocket and pulled out something near and dear to my heart.

"Roberta Drex, I hold in my hand your very last Tootsie Pop."

Uh-oh.

I straightened my shoulders. "Yeah. So?"

"If you can control yourself and not eat this blue-raspberry lump of caramelized sugar for twenty-four hours, *I'll* clean up the bedroom after Earl gets out."

I grinned and reached for the Tootsie Pop. He pulled it away.

"But if you *can't*," Grayson said, "*you* have to do the dirty work."

"Ha!" I laughed confidently. "Deal!"

Grayson's cheek dimpled. "I suggest you order yourself a bucket and some rubber gloves. I'm wagering that, given the sugar-loving bacteria you've been cultivating in your gut all these years, you won't last a whole day without one."

I sneered. "You're on, professor nerd man!"

"Excellent."

Grayson turned and walked into the main cabin. He pulled open a kitchen drawer by the stove. "I'll put the Tootsie Pop right here for safekeeping."

"Fine," I said defiantly. "Suits me."

Grayson stuck the Tootsie Pop deep into the drawer behind the rubber tray holding the forks and spoons. He glanced at his cellphone. "It's now seven minutes past noon. If the sucker's still there at 12:07 tomorrow, you win. If not, you've got an unenviable date with Mr. Clean."

"Or *you* do," I quipped confidently.

But as I watched Grayson shut the drawer, I began to feel an itchy paranoia.

My gut gurgled.

All of a sudden, there was nothing in the entire universe I wanted more than that damned blue-raspberry Tootsie Pop.

Chapter Forty-Nine

After another hour of monitoring my bacteria-ridden cousin flailing and moaning in the back bedroom, Earl suddenly stopped pounding on the door. His wails ceased, and he became eerily silent.

I peeled my ear from the bedroom door and went and got Grayson. He leaned in and placed his stethoscope cup to the steel panel.

"Is he dead?" I asked.

Grayson let the stethoscope drop. "Not unless the dead snore."

"He's sleeping!" I whispered with relief. "Is that a good sign?"

"I don't know." Grayson pulled the stethoscope from his ears. "Earl's either eliminated the enemy within, or it has eliminated him."

My mouth fell open and my gut dropped four inches. "Be honest with me, Grayson. Do you really think bacteria has taken over Earl?"

He pursed his lips. "Unfortunately, that's the working theory."

I glanced worriedly at the door. "So, what do we do now?"

"Fill him with bacteria again. But this time, the good guys."

"Probiotics?" I asked.

"Yes. But we need an inducement."

"Inducement?"

"Yes. Something to make him take the capsules."

I followed Grayson back to the kitchen. He reached into the refrigerator and pulled out his favorite snack.

"This ought to help," he said, holding up a quart-sized tub of plain yogurt.

"Seriously?" I asked. "You're the only person I know who would consider plain yogurt an '*inducement*.'"

Grayson stared at me. "I eat it all the time—for my health."

My nose crinkled. "I thought you just kept that stuff around because you knew I wouldn't touch it."

"It's full of natural probiotics," Grayson said, looking slightly offended. "But I plan on adding some of these, to boost the dosage."

Grayson picked up a bottle of probiotic capsules from the counter and shook it.

"Seriously?" I said. "You think a tub of sour milk and some bacteria pills are gonna cure Earl?"

"According to the studies I told you about, it's indeed possible," Grayson said, pulling the lid off the yogurt.

He opened the probiotics and started cutting into the capsules, then pouring the powder into the tub of flabby, white yogurt. "These little guys should help balance out Earl's moods."

I blew out a breath. "I sure hope this dumb plan works."

"We need to replenish his microbiome," Grayson said, glancing down his nose at me. "It's been shown that lab mice void of gut bacteria act brashly and take a lot of risks."

"Act brashly?" I said sourly. "How does a *mouse* act *brashly*?"

Grayson grabbed a spoon and stirred the yogurt. "That's not the point, Drex."

"So what *is* the point?"

"When bacteria were introduced into mice missing gut flora, the aggressive ones become calmer—and the calmer ones become more aggressive. Therefore, one could infer that *bacteria* play a vital role *in our moods*."

I crossed my arms.

Then I must be completely infested with pisstoffagus femalopilus.

Grayson turned and headed down the hallway, the tub of yogurt in his hand and me on his heels.

"Hold this," he said, handing me the yogurt.

I took it, then watched in silent horror as Grayson knelt down and began unlocking the eight deadbolts securing the monster trap.

"Wait!" I said. "What kind of mood do you think this probiotic concoction will put Earl in?"

Grayson cracked open the door and slipped the yogurt inside. Then he quickly closed the door and began securing the deadbolts.

"That remains to be seen," he said, sliding the last lock closed. He turned to face me. "Let's hope it'll be a good one."

Chapter Fifty

With Earl tucked away in the back bedroom, hopefully eating copious amounts of probiotic-spiked yogurt, it was time to call a powwow with Garth and Jimmy to plot our next move.

Earl's unfortunate "mood swings" had rendered the RV unfit for human inhalation. So the four of us opted to move our discussion outside, to the wooden deck tacked onto the front of the Wells' boys' trailer home.

"Okay, let's review what we know for certain," Grayson said.

I stifled a snicker. Grayson was perched on the edge of a broken-down beach chair, pointing a stick he'd picked up in the yard toward a cardboard box that once contained a fifty-gallon water heater. Topped with that vintage black fedora of his, he looked like a contestant on *Pimp My Junkyard*.

"Garth, my drawing instrument, please," Grayson said.

Garth leaned over and handed him a charcoal briquette. Not missing a beat, Grayson skewered the pointy end of his stick into the charcoal, then scrawled the letters Q and K on an area of the box devoid of printing.

"So," Grayson said. "We have an entity calling herself Queen Kristie, correct?"

"Yes," the men said.

Grayson glanced over at me.

"Uh ... sure," I said, then settled into my faded-yellow-and-orange Flintstone car that was missing its roof. My gut gurgled. Apparently, my bacteria was finding this all very amusing.

"The Queen, as we'll refer to her for purposes of this meeting," Grayson continued, "is running some kind of scheme she calls Kristie's Frickin' Crullers."

"That's right," Garth said, then scooted the patched inner-tube he was riding a foot closer to Grayson's cardboard lectern.

Grayson turned to Jimmy, who was straddling a rusty Schwinn bike with a ripped banana seat. "You agree this could be a network marketing scheme, correct?"

"Maybe," Jimmy said. "But with Wade missing, and given what's happened to Earl, it seems to me there's something a lot more sinister going on here."

Garth slapped the side of his inner-tube. "She and her bacteria bandits are trying to take over the world!"

"Right," Grayson said calmly. "But let's not get ahead of ourselves. Right now, we're sticking to the absolute facts at hand."

I snorted.

Grayson turned to me. "Drex, do you see something we're missing?"

Besides chromosomes, you mean?

"Uh ... sure," I said.

I sat up. My knee accidentally tooted the little orange Flintstone horn. "Come on, Grayson! Why would an alien come all the way from outer space to Earth to peddle donuts?"

"That's exactly what this meeting is about," Grayson said. "We all agree with Jimmy. There's got to be much more to her plan than that."

"You mean like franchising?" Garth asked.

Grayson shook his head. "No. More than that."

"Enslaving the entire human race?" Jimmy asked.

Grayson sniffed. "Closer."

My molars pressed down at five-hundred pounds of pressure per square inch. "We're all tired of playing your guessing game. If you know something, say it!"

"Fine," Grayson said, directing his attention to Garth and Jimmy. "As I told Drex earlier, there's a bacteria in cat feces that attracts rats."

"Oh!" Garth blurted. "Did you know that the pearl fish lives its entire adult life inside a sea cucumber's butthole?"

I shot the bucktoothed inner-tube pirate a look that could've popped his galleon. "What on *Earth* would compel you to say something like that?"

Garth shriveled and drew his arms into the tube. "Sorry, Pandora. I thought we were exchanging weird facts. Me and my friends do that sometimes."

I turned to Grayson, growing more irritable by the second. "For the love of God, not the cat crap story again. Is there some point to it that applies here?"

"Of course," Grayson said defensively.

"Then spare the guys the details and *make* it." I scowled and checked my watch. Damn. It was quarter to three. Tootsie-Pop time. My sugar bacteria were growing restless.

"Fine," Grayson said. "I'll make it brief. The universe adores a symbiotic survival mechanism."

"Huh?" Garth asked.

Grayson shot me an *I told you so* smirk.

"Ugh," I grunted. "Fine. Tell them whatever it takes to make that make sense."

Grayson's cheek dimpled. "As I explained to Drex before lunch, *Toxoplasma gondii*—the bacteria in the cat feces—makes itself alluring to rats, so cats can catch them easier."

"Why would it do that?" Jimmy asked.

"To ensure its own survival, and that of its host," Grayson said. "When the cat gets fed, the bacteria get fed. Both species benefit from the relationship. That's *symbiosis*. In extreme cases, some species become so dependent on each other, they can't survive without each other."

"Like the pearl butthole fish?" Garth asked, then glanced over at me warily.

"Yes," Grayson said. "Exactly like that."

I scooted my Flintstone car closer to Grayson. "Are you saying this Queen Kristie woman *needs* the bacteria she's peddling in the donuts in order to survive?"

Grayson shrugged. "Perhaps. Or it could be as with *Toxoplasma gondii*. The Queen needs what the bacteria *is attracting*."

My gut dropped four inches. "*We're* the rats?"

Grayson smirked. "Quite possibly."

"Come on!"

I scrambled out of the plastic Flintstone mobile. Grayson scooted his lawn chair out of kicking range of my boots.

"Hear me out, Drex," he said.

I folded my arms across my chest. "You have thirty seconds to make your point, or I'm outta here."

Grayson's eyebrow arched. "Fine."

He stabbed the stick at the QK scrawled on the box. "What if Queen Kristie's ultimate plan is to infest the human race with sugar-loving bacteria that fatten us up?"

My jaw fell open.

Garth raised his hand. "Why would she do that, Mr. Gray?"

"To turn us into toro," Grayson said.

Jimmy's head cocked. "Lawnmowers?"

"No," Grayson said. "Tuna belly."

The brothers stared at him blankly.

I shifted to one foot. "Fifteen seconds," I said. "Get to the point!"

"*Sushi*, people!" Grayson said. "Don't you see? *Toro* is the soft, fat belly muscle. It's considered the best part of the tuna. Desirable, sushi-grade specimens can go for over $400 a pound."

"Wait," Jimmy said. "You think they're going to soften us up and *eat* us?"

Grayson's cheek dimpled. "Bingo! Hand that man a prize!"

Or maybe a pair of chopsticks...

Chapter Fifty-One

"We're gonna to be turned into food for space aliens?" Garth gasped, jumping up and squirming out of his patched inner-tube like a mullet-topped worm from the middle of a charred donut.

"That's ridiculous," I said, stomping my foot. "Even if it were true, why in the world would aliens choose *Polk County of all places* to begin an invasion?"

Grayson teetered on the edge of his battered lawn chair and chewed his lip. "Perhaps Queen Kristie is using this as a test market. That could explain Wade's disappearance. Perhaps he was Experiment Number One."

My mind went to the mystery folder I'd scoured the RV for when Grayson wasn't looking.

Experiment #5

My gut flopped.

Is Grayson *testing humans for some devious plan of his own?*

Am I *Experiment #5?*

Stunned, I blinked blankly as Garth pushed his glasses up on his nose and said, "Of course, Mr. Gray! That could explain the use of KFC, too."

"Absolutely," Grayson said. "The aliens are working from an outdated guide to intergalactic cultures—one before KFC became so popular."

"Exactly!" Garth said. "It all fits perfectly now!"

My molars pressed together hard enough to crack granite. Was Grayson an alien himself? No more dancing around the subject. I wanted to know. *Now.*

I glared at Grayson. "How do you know so much about alien guidebooks and stuff?"

"Simple," he said. "I have a subscription to *The UFO Enquirer.*"

"So do I," Garth said. "They had a whole section on alien travel guides in last month's issue."

I let out a long, slow breath. "Fine. Let's say Queen Kristie doesn't read magazines, and she's fattening us up for a bacteria-infested barbeque. Where's she getting all this bacteria?"

"Excellent question," Grayson said. "As you all know by now, bacteria need hosts. Queen Kristie herself could be a fruiting body."

My lip snarled. "Fruiting body?"

"Yes. An incubator, if you will."

I grimaced. "You're not suggesting this woman is some sort of intergalactic bacteria factory, are you?"

Grayson tapped his stick in his palm like a pointer. "Do you have another explanation for why she appears to be able to stay slim despite dispensing a veritable sea of donuts?"

My gut flopped.

Geez. Maybe he's right.

Grayson smirked. His green eyes glowed with scientific fervor. "Think of it! Queen Kristie could be a sapient form of extraterrestrial microbiome, designed solely for the remote manufacture and distribution of alien bacteria in the most insidious way possible!"

I winced. "Through mind control?"

"No," Grayson said. "Free samples."

Jimmy and Garth gasped. "Diabolical!"

"Indeed," Grayson sighed and nodded. "It's something the ordinary man is incapable of resisting."

My nose crinkled. "But this bacterial bimbo's too skinny to be eating these guys herself. What's in it for her?"

Grayson gazed up at the heavens. "If the fractal nature of the universe is correct, patterns repeat themselves in perpetuity. It's highly unlikely that life originated here on Earth. So who's to say profit and greed have solely Earthly origins, either?"

I cringed. "Are you saying she's a profiteer? That *humans* are a cheap and easy source of intergalactic protein?"

"Why not?" Grayson said. "We multiply like rabbits, and we'll eat darn near anything."

We all stared silently at the ominous QK scrawled on the old water-heater carton.

There was no arguing with the naked truth—no matter how preposterous or flabby or middle-aged it was.

Chapter Fifty-Two

"Mr. Gray," Jimmy said, dismounting his rusty Schwinn bicycle and laying it down on the deck. "What's your take on how this whole alien-bacteria infestation scheme works?"

Grayson studied the charcoal-stained end of his pointing stick for a moment, then glanced up at the sky. "As far as I can tell, once a victim ingests one or two free donut samples, the partaker becomes an unwitting host."

"An unwitting host?" Jimmy asked. "You mean like Earl?"

"He said unwitting, not witless," I muttered.

Grayson shot me some side-eye, then nodded at Jimmy. "The alien bacteria disorient the host, causing brain fog, as we've witnessed with Earl. You said you've seen similar behavior with the other men participating in Queen Kristie's rituals, correct?"

"Yeah," Jimmy said. "But what happens next? Is that her end game—harvesting these guys' fat stomachs and taking off for Krull?"

Grayson pursed his lips. "Perhaps. But I think Queen Kristie may have even *bigger* plans in store."

"Bigger?" I asked. "Like what?"

Grayson locked his green eyes on me. "Global infestation."

I nearly swallowed my tonsils. "*What*?"

"Consider this, if you will," Grayson said. "These infected men leave the meetings unaware they're hosting the alien bacteria, right?"

My nose crinkled. "Uh ... okay."

"So then, no longer in their right minds, the infected men go about spreading the bacteria to the population, unaware they're mindless pawns in a microscopic alien game of chess."

Jimmy shook his head. "I don't understand. How can the infected ones spread it to others?"

"Oh!" Garth grunted. "Through sex?"

I snorted. "If so, *you've* got nothing to worry about."

What am I saying? Neither do I!

"No," Grayson said. "Through *feces*. Weren't you listening when I said it's comprised mostly of bacteria?"

I grimaced. "Gross! Are you saying they make people eat their poop?"

"No," Grayson said, staring at me like I was nuts. "How could you even think such a disgusting thing? I meant that, with every flush, Queen Kristie and her infected troops will be infecting the water supply via their raw sewage."

I winced. "Oh."

"Wouldn't water treatment plants stop that?" Jimmy asked.

"Hey bro," Garth said, "if an alligator can survive in a sewer, why not this alien bacteria stuff?"

"Both of you bring up good points," Grayson said, tapping the bottom of his stick on the deck like a cane. "Perhaps water treatment *will* stop the bacteria. Perhaps *not*. We're in uncharted territory, here. But one thing's for sure. We need to stop Queen Kristie now, before her bacterial brew has a chance to spread."

"How do you propose we do that?" Jimmy asked.

"The only way possible," Grayson said. He leaned over and jabbed his stick at the QK scrawled on the water heater box. "We need to give that parasitic princess the royal flush."

"The royal flush? I asked. "What are you talking about?"

"This." Grayson turned and stabbed his stick through the QK on the water-heater box, then pulled it out and pointed to the ragged hole in the cardboard. "I'm talking about sending Queen Kristie back through the same space hole she dropped out of."

"Space hole?" Garth asked.

"The *wormhole*," Grayson said. "We need to find the portal she rode in on and send her packing back through it!"

"Argh!" I groaned. "Not that whole portal-wormhole crap again!"

"It's not crap," Grayson said, straightening his shoulders. "Unless, of course, you think Einstein was full of crap."

I opened my mouth to protest, but Grayson beat me to it.

"Wait," he said, arguing with himself. "Einstein was human, so I suppose he *was* full of crap, intestinally speaking, of course." Grayson glanced back over at me. "But that's beside the point. What I'm talking about is his *postulate*."

"Einstein's prostate?" Garth asked. "I don't get it."

"No. *Postulate*," Grayson said. "Einstein's belief that the Theory of Relativity allows for shortcuts across the Time/Space Continuum."

"Huh?" the three of us grunted simultaneously.

"Drex, don't you remember?" he asked, then flung his stick into the junkyard. "The discrepancy in time I found with the oscilloscope yesterday. It's the fingerprint of a *real* Einstein-Rosen Bridge. Right *here* in Polk County! Somewhere in the Hi-Ho there's a wormhole connecting it to the planet Krull!"

"Cool!" Garth said, bobbing his head.

My face collapsed. I shook my head. "Let me get this straight, Grayson. You think this Queen Kristie chick came through an interstellar wormhole just so she could dance around a bonfire in the middle of nowhere with some random fat guys?"

"Don't be ridiculous," Grayson said. "Her actions aren't random. Though I must confess I'm beginning to doubt the validity of the KFC connection." Grayson rubbed his chin. "There's *got* to be another reason."

"Maybe she chose Florida because she thought she could do her bidding unnoticed," Garth offered. "We are kinda a mecca for strange down here."

I sighed. "That makes as much sense as anything I've heard today."

"Hmm," Grayson said. "Garth, you could be on to something with the Florida angle. The tropical climate here could replicate her home planet. Bacteria generally prefer warm, moist places to colonize."

A sharp pain stabbed me between the eyes. "Enough, already!" I blurted. "Let's say you're right, Grayson—about everything. Florida is this blonde bimbo's new nirvana and fat guys are her bread and butter. *What do you propose we do about it?*"

"I thought I just explained that," Grayson said. "We send Queen Kristie back to Krull using the same wormhole she rode in on."

"Krull?" Jimmy said. "I thought that was just a made-up movie planet."

"No," Garth said, elbowing his brother. "Think about it. Krull. *Crullers?* A coincidence? I don't think so."

I'D EXCUSED MYSELF from Grayson's *Lord of the Flies* porch meeting on the premise of needing an aspirin. It hadn't been a complete lie. My headache had been real enough. But when I'd checked on Earl, I'd gotten some immediate relief. The tub of yogurt Grayson had left just inside the bedroom door was missing—and I could hear Earl softly snoring again. Hopefully, the probiotics were working their magic.

I was also pleasantly surprised to find that, in my absence, Grayson had ordered food delivered. He and the guys were busy munching on tacos at the picnic table he'd set up nearby the RV.

What I *wasn't* so happy about was the conversation going on over the crunch of crispy taco shells.

"First off, we need to find the wormhole's location," Grayson said, biting into a taco. "Then we've got to figure out how to make it open on command."

Right. Should we try "abracadabra" or "open sesame?"

"Good idea," Garth said, picking tomato slices out of his taco.

I sat down next to Jimmy and eyed the heap of wrapped tacos in the center of the table. "Correct me if I'm wrong, but wouldn't it be easier to just make our own wormhole to send Queen Bimbo back where she came from?"

Grayson snorted. "Don't be ridiculous."

I rubbed my forehead. My headache was attempting an encore performance. "Excuse me, but how is *that* ridiculous?"

Garth snickered. "Pandora, to create a wormhole we'd need the energy of like, fifty-thousand hydrogen bombs."

"Exactly," Grayson said, pointing at me with his taco. "And *that's* just to create an opening the size of a molecule."

I shook my head and grabbed a taco. "How do you guys know this weird stuff?" Then I glanced at Garth. "Never mind. I forgot. You speak Klingon."

"Hey," Garth said. "It comes in handy sometimes."

"Yeah," I said, unwrapping my taco. "I bet the chicks really dig it."

"The right ones do," he said, then flung a tomato wedge onto the ground.

While the guys chewed thoughtfully on their tortillas, I took a slurp of Dr Pepper and a snarky thought hit me.

"Hey! I know," I said. "Why don't you guys just *rent* a wormhole? You know. Look in the yellow pages under portal letting?"

"They do that?" Garth asked.

"I wish," Grayson said. "Unfortunately, our only viable option is to locate the existing wormhole and figure out how to make it open at our will."

I laughed. "Here's another idea. Why don't you just follow Queen Bimbo around and see where she beams up from?"

"I've tried that," Jimmy said. "I haven't been able to catch her actually using a portal, but I know she leaves the meetings by way of Whirlwind Trail."

"That must be the general vicinity of the portal," Grayson said. "Excellent. We'll go there again tonight and attempt to nail down the location more precisely."

I blew out a sigh. "Okay. Say you find this wormhole, Grayson. What then? You gonna push Queen Cruller in and slam the door? I mean, what's to keep her from coming right back out again?"

"Hmm," Grayson said, wiping salsa from his lips. "I guess we'll have to cross that Einstein-Rosen Bridge when we come to it."

I nearly dropped my taco.

How could this possibly *get any more absurd?*

"Oh, by the way," Grayson said, taking a slurp of Dr Pepper. "I've come up with a name for our mission. I'm calling it, 'Operation Mercy Flush.'"

And there it is.

Chapter Fifty-Three

"Why, why, *why*?" Grayson muttered as we left the picnic table and walked back to the RV.

I shrugged. "I ask myself the same thing *all* the time, Grayson. *Why* did I leave Point Paradise? *Why* did I think I wanted to be a private eye? *Why* did I just spend the afternoon with a bunch of nerds, discussing how to send Malibu Bimbo back through a wormhole?"

And, most of all, why *do I still find you attractive when you're such a complete and utter weirdo?*

Grayson eyed me sideways as he opened the RV door. "What I *meant* was, you were right to question the *mission*, Drex. Why *now*? Why *Wade*? Why *this* park in the middle of nowhere?"

"Oh," I said, shriveling inside. "Uh ... I better go check on Earl."

I'D RETREATED TO THE underbelly of the smelly RV, hoping to avoid Grayson after our spat. But it hadn't worked. After listening in on Earl through the bedroom door, I turned to find him standing right behind me.

"How's the patient?" he asked.

"Still snoring," I said, and handed him his stethoscope. I looked up and offered him a weak smile, worried he'd been offended by me questioning well ...*everything*.

"Good. Let him sleep," he replied.

Grayson's tone sounded normal, as if my confession had meant nothing to him. Maybe it hadn't. Maybe Grayson really *didn't* care one way or the other how I felt about the mission *or* about him.

"Hopefully he'll be back to himself in the morning." Grayson said, opening the window above the banquette to let in some fresh air. "There's got to be something I'm missing."

That's an understatement if I've ever heard one.

I decided to let our disagreement go. I perked up and played along. "What do you mean, something's missing?"

"Portals require massive amounts of energy to work. That's why Paulides believes location is so important. His map shows that nearly every one of the park disappearances he's investigated occurred in an area where quartz boulders and mountains were present."

"Oh, yeah," I said, wincing against the odor. I cracked open the side door. "You said quartz is a natural conductor, right?"

"Yes." Grayson walked over to the kitchen window. "And as such, it can also *store* energy. That's why Paulides' crew was able to pick up evidence of energy fluctuations around the sites of some of the vanishings."

"I remember that," I said. "He thought those fluctuations could be the potential fingerprints of portals, right? Tears in time and space?"

Grayson's cheek dimpled. "Correct."

I shook my head. "But like you said, Florida doesn't have any quartz. So how can it be the site of a portal?"

"That's what I'm trying to figure out."

Grayson turned toward the kitchen sink. Suddenly, he slammed his fist down on the counter. "Dammit, Drex!" he yelled, spinning around to face me. "I thought I told you to clean those test tubes."

I scowled at the dirty vials I'd left in the windowsill for two days. "I'm not your *maid*, you know!"

"I know that!" Grayson's shoulders slumped. "Sorry, but this case has me stumped. I really hoped I could count on you."

He turned around and picked a test tube out of the rack. "I didn't think it was such an unreasonable request. You simply take the cap off like this, then put it under the tap—"

"I know how to wash a damned test tube!" I yelled. "I'm not an imbecile!"

Grayson turned and held up a dirty test tube for my inspection. "Then why haven't you—"

"Because Earl's pee is in them!" I bellowed.

Grayson froze. His mouth fell open.

"That's it," he muttered.

My heart pinged.

Crap! Has Grayson finally had enough of me?

"Look," I said. "I'm sorry. I'll clean the stupid ... I mean, I'll wash the test tubes, okay?"

"No." Grayson said, shaking his head. "That's *it*."

I cringed. "I'm *fired*?"

"What?" Grayson asked. His eyes shifted from the test tube to me. "No, Drex. Pee."

My eyebrows rose an inch. "You want me to *pee* for you? Sorry, but I don't play that—"

"No!" Grayson yelled. "*Pee*. That's the answer!"

"Great," I said, smiling weakly.

The answer to what?

Chapter Fifty-Four

Despite the lingering outhouse aroma, Grayson had seated himself at the banquette. Hunched over a microscope, he was examining the contents of one of the dirty test tubes I'd been too lazy to wash.

As I tried to sneak out the door, he looked up from the scope. "It all makes sense to me now."

I turned around. "Well, that makes one of us."

"Here. Have a look."

Grayson scooted over and patted the seat beside him. I slid into the booth next to him and cautiously placed an eye on the microscope viewfinder. A weird, black, honeycomb-like mesh came into focus.

"What *is* that?" I asked.

"Black phosphorous," Grayson said. "Preserved by Earl's urine and crystalized by the sun." He shook his head and laughed. "I probably wouldn't have figured it out without you two."

I peered back into the microscope at the odd, interlocking cell-like structures. "Figured out what?"

"Everything," Grayson said. "Including why Queen Kristie picked an abandoned phosphate mining area to set up her scheme of taking over the world. And where she's getting the energy for her portal."

"Whoa, there Grayson," I said, glancing up from the microscope. "I'm gonna need you to back up and start from the beginning on this one."

"Of course." Grayson smiled, leaned back, and interlaced his fingers behind his head. "Once upon a time, back in 1669, a German physician named Hennig Brand boiled, filtered and processed about sixty bucketsful of urine."

"Whoa!" I said, grimacing with disgust. "Uh ... you don't have to go *that* far back. And seriously, what was this guy hoping to discover boiling buckets of piss?"

"Phosphorus, Drex. That's how it was first isolated as an element." Grayson licked his lips. "You know, I'm suddenly thirsty for a beer."

I laughed and shook my head. "Only *you*, Grayson. Stay there. I'll get you one."

I scooted out of the booth and fished around the tiny, nearly empty fridge. I reached into the back and pulled out the last Corona and a Dr Pepper. I handed the beer to Grayson. "So this Brand guy discovered black phosphorous?"

"No," Grayson said, taking the beer. "He discovered *white* phosphorous. That's the most common kind. Nowadays, it's primarily obtained from phosphate rock. Florida and North Carolina are loaded with it."

I cracked open the Dr Pepper. "So, how many kinds of phosphorous are there?"

"Three." Grayson cracked open the beer. "There's white, which is poisonous and highly combustible when in contact with air. Then there's red phosphorous, which is made by heating white phosphorus to 482 degrees, or by exposing it to sunlight. In that form, it's not poisonous and a lot less dangerous."

I shook my head in wonder at Grayson's encyclopedic knowledge. Too bad he was missing a few vital pages.

"So, what's it used for?" I asked, then took a slug of my soda.

"Red phosphorous?" Grayson asked. "Mostly for safety matches, fireworks and smoke bombs."

"Huh," I grunted. "All that strip mining for a something as trivial as fireworks shows? Hardly seems worth it."

"For phosphorous alone, maybe not. But it's the byproduct—phosphoric acid—that's the big money maker. It's used commercially in all kinds of things."

"Like what?"

"Fertilizers. Cleaning detergents. Florescent light bulbs. TVs." He tipped his beer in an air toast. "Even that soft drink you're chugging."

I grimaced. "Ugh! Seriously?"

"Seriously."

I set my soda on the table and took another peek through the microscope lens. "What about this stuff? Black phosphorous. What's it used for?"

"Until recently, pretty much nothing."

I looked up from the microscope. "I feel a big 'but' coming on."

Grayson's cheek dimpled. "Your instincts are correct, cadet. Hold out your hand."

I showed Grayson my palm. He opened a test tube and poured some black powder into it.

"Touch it," he said.

I rubbed my index finger in it. The black powder felt flat and grainy, like the stuff in the center of pencils.

"Feels like graphite, doesn't it?" Grayson asked.

I nodded. "Yeah."

"A few years ago, black phosphorous was considered useless. But that thin, flaky structure you feel is now being used to create nanosheets for use in nanoelectronics."

"Uh, okay," I said. "But what's any of this got to do with wormholes and portals and pee?"

"Oh, my," Grayson said, then laughed.

I gave him half a smile for that one.

"Well, you see, Drex, pee is actually the answer to black phosphorous' future. Researchers found that black phosphorous became more resilient when in contact with ammonia, probably because ammonia donates electrons that neutralize holes in the black phosphorous' molecular structure, making it more stable for use in nanotechnologies."

"How did they discover that?" I asked.

"Don't ask."

"Fine." I smirked. "Okay. So, how do intergalactic portals fit in this story?"

"I'm getting there," Grayson said. "You see, unlike white or red phosphorous, *black* phosphorous is thermodynamically stable at room temperature and pressure."

I pretended like I got that. "Yeah? So—"

"And, here's the kicker," Grayson said.

He leaned toward me until our faces were inches from each other. He locked his mesmerizing green eyes on my dull brown ones and said, "Even though black phosphorous contains no metal, *it conducts electricity.*"

I gasped. "Are you saying this black stuff in my hand is the energy source for Malibu Bimbo's portal?"

Grayson's cheek dimpled. "And I was beginning to think you were just a pretty face."

Chapter Fifty-Five

By the grace of God, I'd convinced Grayson to leave the stinking outhouse on wheels and continue our discussion at the picnic table. Garth and Jimmy had joined us there. We were attempting another brainstorming session. The only thing we needed now was a pair of fully-functioning brains.

"Good news, men," Grayson said. "Drex and I have determined the portal's energy source."

Grayson passed around the test tube containing black phosphorous. "Now we need to find the wormhole's location. We're in agreement with Jimmy. Our best bet is to surveil Queen Kristie and catch her in the act."

"Of eating donuts?" Garth asked.

"No," Grayson said. "Of activating the portal. We need to study her actions. Learn her habits."

"Her habits?" I asked.

"Yes," Grayson said. "I believe that, as a fruiting body, bacteria could be determining the timing of Queen Kristie's Earthly comings and goings."

"You think Queen Kristie's under the same bacterial mind control as her followers?" Garth asked.

"Hmm." Grayson rubbed his chin. "I hadn't considered that. What I meant was the alien bacteria Queen Kristie's using could be following an extraterrestrial circadian rhythm."

"Huh?" Garth asked, saving me the effort.

"A circadian rhythm is a natural, internal process," Grayson said. "It regulates the sleep-wake cycle. On Earth, it repeats roughly every 24 hours."

I rolled my eyes at Grayson's latest tangent. "What's Queen Bimbo's beauty-sleep ritual got to do with anything?"

"Circadian rhythms have been widely observed in plants, animals, fungi, and cyanobacteria," Grayson said. "Therefore, it's logical to infer that Queen Bim—I mean Queen *Kristie's* activities could be driven by the circadian rhythms of her internal bacteria's life cycle."

I snorted. "Yeah. Either that or she uses a watch."

Jimmy winced. "Well, Mr. Gray, I *have* noticed she always starts the meetings at 7:15 on the dot, and ends them at 8:30."

"Right," Grayson said. "That means either the alien bacteria reach critical mass an hour or so after ingestion, or Queen Kristie is only able to maintain portal stability for that long."

I rolled my eyes. "Or maybe she just wants to get home in time to watch *The Bachelor*."

"Excellent work, everyone," Grayson said, ignoring my remark. "Tonight, we'll follow Queen Kristie, find the location of the portal, then figure out how to jump-start the wormhole ourselves."

"Sure. Sounds simple enough," I quipped.

"I'm glad you think so," Grayson said. "We leave at quarter to seven. I suggest we all wear either camo or black."

I smirked. "You make it sound like we're heading off to battle, Grayson."

Grayson shot me a serious look. "Perhaps we are."

He turned to Garth and Jimmy. "This may be our last stand, gentlemen. But Drex, you shouldn't have anything to worry about. It appears Queen Kristie is only interested in taking *men's* lives—as is the custom during wartime."

"Wartime?" I said.

"That's not true," Jimmy said.

I breathed a sigh of relief. "War is a pretty strong word, Grayson."

"Oh, the whole *war* thing could be right," Jimmy said. "But not the men-only thing."

"What do you mean?" I asked.

Jimmy pursed his lips. "I just got off the phone with Thelma over at Juanita's restaurant. Apparently, Wade's girlfriend Connie has gone missing, too."

Chapter Fifty-Six

Before Jimmy had dropped the bombshell that Wade's girlfriend Connie had also gone missing, I'd comforted myself with the idea that only humans of the male persuasion were dumb enough to fall for Queen Bimbo's blonde, big-bosomed, bacteria-laden charms.

But with that myth now busted, I felt a growing paranoia that, as a female, I also was in real danger.

I glanced up at Grayson, Garth and Jimmy, all crammed into the bench seat of Earl's monster truck. Dressed in black, camo and flannel, they appeared ready to foolishly face whatever fickle fate awaited them.

My mind flitted back to Earl, battling for his life in the back of Grayson's RV. If my cousin had known we were getting ready to face down Queen Cruller without him, he'd have rolled over in his filthy mattress.

"Come on, let's go," Grayson said. "Get in."

Jimmy offered me a hand up.

I hesitated.

If three's a crowd, then four's a feel-up.

"Thanks," I said. "But I think I'll ride in the back."

I SAT ON THE TOOLBOX in the back bed of Bessie and peered into the rear window at the men sitting solemnly with their weapons of war in their hands. As far as I could tell, they were all electronic.

"Turn here," I heard Jimmy say.

I braced for the curve, then bounced like a toad in a sack as Grayson maneuvered the monster truck off the main road and down a dirt lane mired with potholes.

As we rode along, I was surprised to see an odd assortment of vehicles parked on the side of the dirt road. Grayson pulled the truck into a space between a Lincoln Town Car and an eight-seater golf cart sporting a festive trimming of gold-tassel fringe.

"Let's roll," Grayson said, shifting into park. The engine cut off and everyone piled out.

Grayson ambled over to a ragged-out pickup truck and peered into the passenger window. "Intriguing. It appears the men's addiction has escalated. There's evidence here of habitation."

I let out a sarcastic laugh. "Yeah. Or these losers could just be living in their cars because their wives threw them out."

"That's a point we'll have to ponder later," Grayson said. "Right now, we've got bigger fish to fry."

He nodded toward the woods. Just above the treetops, I spotted an all-too-familiar, faint, orange glow.

"Destiny awaits," he said. "And it's born of fire."

I sighed.

Super. I only hope we don't all go up in smoke.

WE'D BEEN HUNKERED in the bushes beside the clearing for the better part of an hour. But so far, the only thing we'd managed to infiltrate was a motherlode of mosquitos. Just my luck, the three geeks surrounding me had brought every stupid contraption known to man—except for mosquito repellent.

Over by the bonfire, Queen Kristie was up to her usual feminine wiles, charming fat guys in robes with her donuts and her doodads.

Grayson's eyes were glued to a pair of binoculars, trying to read her lips. "It's no use," he said, lowering his spyware. "I can't hear what Queen Kristie is saying. Jimmy, we're going to need you to sneak into the meeting."

"I can't," he said, swatting at a mosquito.

"Why not?" Grayson asked. "You brought the robe, didn't you?"

"Yeah. But Tooth ate my fat suit." He nodded toward the circle of men in robes. "Look at those guys. They're huge! I can't blend in anymore."

Grayson frowned. "You're right. You'll stick out like a toothpick in a sausage factory."

"Ward!" Garth said.

"What? Where?" Jimmy grabbed his brother by the shoulders. "Point him out to me!"

"Uh ... sorry," Garth said. "I meant WWARD. What would Amazing Randi do?"

I blew out a sigh.

He'd kick all your rotten heads in, that's what he'd do!

"I know," I quipped. "Why don't we all just go home, and come back after we've gained three hundred pounds?"

"Three hundred pounds," Grayson muttered. His eyebrow shot up like Spock's. "Earl!"

"Of course," Jimmy said. "He could get in there unnoticed! And, bless his heart, that man can do the Cruller Holler like nobody's business!"

"Then it's settled," Grayson said. His glowing green eyes zeroed in on me. "Bobbie, you've got to talk Earl into it."

Chapter Fifty-Seven

Mercifully, I'd had overnight to figure out how to communicate with my incoherent cousin in a language he'd understand. Unmercifully, I'd had to spend that same overnight curled up in the front seat of Earl's monster truck—wrapped up inside his Superman sleeping bag.

I woke up and rubbed my sore neck. Then I peeled out of the bedroll, climbed down out of Bessie, and went in search of a hot cup of java.

Little did I realize that there wasn't enough coffee in the world to prepare me for the task I was about to face

I'D DECIDED ON A POP Tart—hooked to a fishing line.

Slowly and silently, I'd slid open the eight deadbolts securing Earl within the monster trap. Then I'd cracked open the door and slid the Pop Tart in sideways.

The bait set, I'd pulled the door nearly shut, tiptoed down the hallway, then pulled the line taut.

It didn't take long for me to see the bobber move.

"He's taking the bait," I whispered to Grayson. He was standing out of sight, holding a fishing net—just in case.

"I'm ready," he said. "Just give the signal if you need me."

"Okay."

We'd already worked out what that the signal would be—me screaming my bloody head off.

Suddenly, the line jerked out of my hands. The door squeaked open, revealing Earl standing in his underwear, munching on the toaster pastry, looking like a Kewpie doll that had miraculously survived a poop-factory explosion.

He spotted me and stopped chewing.

Time stopped for a moment as Earl and I stood frozen, checking each other out.

"Earl?" I said tentatively.

"Bobbie? What happened?"

I smiled. "It's a long story. But the good news is, there's more Pop Tarts where that one came from. And there's clothes in the bathroom. Go get a shower, and I'll explain everything.

WHEN EARL EMERGED FROM the bathroom, he looked normal. But I could tell there was still something off about him.

"We got any more of those donuts?" he asked.

Uh-oh.

I glanced out the window. Grayson was just pulling away in Bessie. I'd told him everything was fine. Why the hell did he choose that moment to finally trust me?

"Nope, fresh out," I said, forcing a smile at my big, hungry bear of a cousin. "But we've got Pop Tarts."

I reached for the box. "I'll put some in the toaster for you."

"No," Earl said. "I like 'em raw."

Good. Because I just remembered where Grayson is going—to get a new toaster to replace the one I'd busted.

"Sure. Knock yourself out," I said, and handed him the box.

Earl pulled out a foil pouch and tried to take a bite of it.

I winced. "Um ... you gotta unwrap it first, Earl."

"Oh, yeah."

"Sit down. I'll get you some coffee."

Earl settled into the banquette. I handed him a mug, but remained standing. The way his body was wedged into the booth, I figured that, if I needed to, I could make a run for the door before he could get free from it.

"So, how you feeling?" I asked.

Earl's eyes spun in his tired face. "Wrung out like a week-old wash rag. And so hungry I could eat a broccoli sandwich—without cheese."

I smiled. "That's pretty hungry."

His face grew blank. "But I'd rather have me a donut."

"Uh ... right. You mentioned that. Here, have another Pop Tart."

I gave Earl another open pouch of pastries. While he munched them, I broached the subject of our mission, trying to ascertain if he was up to the challenge.

"Earl, do you remember the mission we're on?"

"Mission," Earl said, a flicker of recognition dancing in his eyes. "We're lookin' for worm buttholes, right?"

"Uh, sure. Cosmic ones."

Earl stared up at the ceiling. "You know what, Bobbie? I was thinkin'. What if the Earth is like our old fillin' station back home?"

"What do you mean?"

"You know. What if we was the last stop for a fill up until you got to the other side of the Milky Way?"

"Well, that's an interesting—"

"I sure could use me a donut."

I stared at my cousin. His face was blank again.

Crap. Maybe Grayson's right. Bacteria may be the only thing driving his thought processes.

As far as I could tell, Earl was in no shape to be crashing a party, much less a crazy intergalactic donut convention. I gave up on that idea and concentrated on part two of my mission—collecting a saliva sample.

According to Grayson, I needed Earl to lick or drool on something that wouldn't absorb his saliva.

I walked over to the kitchen drawer and pulled out the Tootsie Pop Grayson had stashed there. I glanced at the clock. It was quarter to nine.

Nearly three hours to go to win my bet with Grayson. I closed my eyes and pictured Earl how he looked as he'd emerged from the back bedroom. I didn't even want to *think* about the rest of the room. I didn't want to lose that bet.

I winced and unwrapped the sucker.

Just one lick. Who would know?

My fingers began to tremble. I raised the Tootsie Pop toward my lips ...

"I want a donut," Earl said, his breath on my neck.

"Wha?" I whirled around to find him standing mere inches from me.

"Here," I said, shoving the sucker at him. "Have a Tootsie Pop. You'll feel better."

Earl grabbed it from my hand and crunched it between his massive molars. Then he yanked the mangled paper stick from between his lips.

"I'll take that," I said, grabbing it and dropping it in a baggie.

"I wanna donut," Earl repeated. "I wanna donut!"

"Sure," I said. "You wait here. I'll go get you one."

Then I snuck out of the RV and locked my poor cousin inside. Again.

Chapter Fifty-Eight

When Grayson returned, Earl was still rampaging around in the RV. I had no idea what my poor cousin was doing in there, but it was obvious he was no happy camper.

"Hmm," Grayson said, watching the RV shudder from the pounding Earl was giving it from inside. "I suppose this means I'll be unable to ascertain whether you passed our little Tootsie Pop challenge."

"Really?" I said. "*That's* what concerns you about this scenario?" I put my hands on my hips and struck a defiant pose. Then remembered I had nothing to be defiant about.

"Oh. By the way, mission accomplished," I said, reaching into my shirt pocket. I pulled out the baggie containing the lollipop stick and dangled it in front of Grayson's nose.

He smirked. "So you succumbed to the whims of your bacterial brethren, I see."

"No!" I said. "*Earl* did. He ate the pop. You'll find it's *his* saliva on the stick."

"Really?" Grayson's eyebrow rose in surprise. "You better hope so. Otherwise, the bucket and hair net I just bought have *your* name on them."

"I'M IMPRESSED, DREX," Grayson said from his perch on the picnic bench. He held up a rainbow-colored test strip panel. "You were telling the truth. The saliva on the Tootsie Pop stick matches Earl. He's a secretor. You're not."

My nose crinkled. I didn't know what being a secretor meant, but as long as I wasn't one, I didn't care.

"Told you," I said. "Were you able to isolate any alien bacteria?"

"No." Grayson closed the test kit. "*That's* going to take some serious lab work."

I smirked. "Speaking of serious work, get ready to join the bucket brigade, Bozo." I grabbed a marker and started writing Grayson's name on the shiny new pail he'd bought at Walmart. "Ha!" I laughed. "Who's the sucker now?"

"In the spirit of good sportsmanship, I bought you this," Grayson said, handing me a Walmart bag.

I peeked inside. It was loaded with Tootsie Pops. I felt like a turd.

"You shouldn't have," I said.

His cheek dimpled. "I know. But I'm a sucker for a gal with sweet gut bacteria."

I nearly blushed. For Grayson, that was tantamount to a marriage proposal.

"Uh, Grayson, I hate to spoil this Hallmark moment, but I've got some bad news. Earl's way too out of it to be of any use infiltrating Queen Quaalude's Cruller meeting. What are we gonna do?"

"I'm not sure." Grayson rubbed his chin. "I suppose we could ask Sherman—but he has to be home by eight-thirty."

Seriously?

"Uh ... yeah," I said. "I don't think his mother would let him go, anyway."

Grayson sighed. "You're probably right. But no matter. If we can locate the portal today, infiltrating the meeting will be a moot point."

He stood up and waved for me to join him. I didn't move.

"Come on, Drex. Let's go."

My nose crinkled. "Where?"

"To locate the portal—or did I not just say that?"

Chapter Fifty-Nine

By this time, it wasn't hard to find Whirlwind Trail—or the clearing. We just followed the trampled trail left by my galoshes and Grayson's and Earl's muddy clodhoppers.

"Spooky," Garth said.

He was right. Without Queen Kristie and her Cruller Crew dancing around in it, the clearing felt oddly abandoned. That didn't stop Grayson from marching right into the middle of it.

"It was right about here that I set up the time dilation experiment," Grayson said, standing at the edge of the burned-out bonfire. "This area showed a six-percent discrepancy in the speed of light."

"Whoa," Garth said. "That's heavy-duty."

"What exactly does that mean?" Jimmy asked.

"According to Einstein, it means anything is theoretically possible—including portals leading to other dimensions." Grayson placed his hands on his hips. "Now, where are you, you sneaky little devil?"

"Um, Mr. Gray," Jimmy said. "Not to rain on your parade or anything, but if there's a time portal around here, why don't the robed guys get sucked up into it?"

"Yeah," Garth said. "Why don't *we* get sucked up?"

"It could be any number of reasons," Grayson said. "But I believe Queen Kristie has control of it somehow. Perhaps she's waiting for the men to ripen before she plucks them and takes them back to Krull."

"Ripen?" I asked, my nose crinkling.

"As we all noted last night, the men have obtained impressive girths," Grayson said. "Human toro-belly could be quite the delicacy on the intergalactic black market. If so, don't forget that Queen Kristie's getting paid by the pound."

"I bet that's why she gave them the robes," Jimmy said. "She didn't want them to realize they don't fit into their clothes anymore."

"That doesn't appear to stop some people," I muttered. "I've seen things at Walmart I'll never be able to un-see."

"True dat," Garth said, then wiped his nose on his sleeve.

"Speaking of fat, does anyone smell bacon?" Jimmy asked.

"I don't," I said. "But then again, my nose may be broken from having to smell Earl in the RV."

"Now that you mention it, I do," Grayson said, sniffing the air.

Jimmy walked over by Grayson and sniffed. Then he toed at the ashes of the bonfire—and kicked out what looked like a human arm bone.

"Huh," Grayson said. "My money was on raw flesh. I hadn't thought of intergalactic barbeque."

"Good grief!" I shouted. "If Queen Bimbo's barbequing these guys, who's to say we won't be next?"

"We *will* be—*humanity* will be—if we don't stop her," Grayson said.

We all stared at the cracked bone lying amid the ashes. A deepening dread made my gut gurgle.

"Think, troops," Grayson said. "We need to find that portal and shut Queen Bimbo's butcher shop down tonight—before anyone else ends up dead."

I chewed my lip. "Uh ... Grayson, would it help to go back and borrow Sherman's o-scope thing again?"

"Sure it would help," he said, exchanging grimaces with Garth. "But I think we men concur, given his mother, it's not worth the risk."

Chapter Sixty

I stared at the three men as they poked around Queen Kristie's Kannibal Kampfire.

Great. Humanity's at stake, and our only line of defense are three doofuses who're afraid of a little old lady who looks like a bulldog.

Boy, has she got them trained.

I blinked. Then stared.

Wait. Maybe that's it!

"Uh, Grayson," I said. "Do you think maybe Queen Kristie isn't having these guys do team-building exercises, but instead is *training* them?"

The guys all stopped poking around and stared up at me.

"Training them for what?" Jimmy asked. "Size XXXL sweatpants?"

"No," I said. "To *trust* her."

The three of them simultaneously gasped.

"Trust a *woman*?" Garth asked. "That's not possible, is it?"

My last nerve gave out. "Excuse me, twerp! You believe in *Klingons* but not—"

Hold on! You're better than this, Bobbie!

I shut my own mouth, closed my eyes, took a deep breath, and started again.

"Look. Queen Kristie's training the guys to walk on coals, right?" I asked.

The guys nodded.

"So, what if those are just the baby steps?" I said. "What if her ultimate goal is to desensitize them to fire? You know, reduce their fear of flames."

"To what end?" Grayson asked.

"So they'll follow her orders," I said. "What if these guys are gradually being brainwashed into demonstrating their ultimate proof of loyalty—by running into the bonfire at her command?"

"That would explain the charred bones," Jimmy said. "I just found another one."

"But what's the point of it all," Grayson asked. "Other than to watch the men suffer? Which, I've heard, is a favorite pastime of women throughout the known universe."

I ignored his remark. "What if the bonfire wasn't just a bonfire? What if it was also *the opening of the portal you've been searching for?*"

Grayson's jaw dropped. "Of course! What better place to hide a portal's opening than where no one in their right mind would dare to tread!"

"Exactly," I said.

Grayson shook his head. "Ingenious. Having them run across hot coals as the baby steps to the ultimate leap of faith."

"And this may just be the latest batch," I said.

"What do you mean?" Grayson asked.

"This could've been going on a long time. Think about it. The Native Americans named this Whirlwind Trail. What does it look like when someone's sucked up into a portal?"

Grayson locked his green eyes on me. "Like they went up in a whirlwind."

Chapter Sixty-One

We returned to the compound to find a box leaning up against the chain-link gate. Garth hopped out of the back of Bessie and dragged it out of the way, then hit the secret code to open the chain-link barricade.

"Uh, some help over here?" Garth called out as Grayson parked the truck. I climbed out and saw the little nerd trying to pull the two-foot square, six-foot long box up the driveway.

"What's in there?" I asked.

"I dunno," Garth said. "It's for Commander Grayson."

I rolled my eyes. "You don't have to call him that."

"No," Garth said. "That's what's written on the Amazon shipping label." He turned to Grayson, who was walking up to join us. "Is it some kind of secret weapon? A missile, maybe?"

"No," Grayson said. "It's my new mattress." He picked up the box like it was full of feathers, settled it on his right shoulder, then marched toward the picnic table.

Garth and I scrambled after him.

"Now that we've located the portal, we need to figure out how to seal it shut for good," Grayson said, laying the box on the picnic table. "Any ideas?"

"Uh ... none off the top of my head," I said.

Grayson took out a pocketknife and slit the box open. The mattress burst out of the box like a busted roll of Pillsbury biscuit dough. It unfurled and sucked in air until it flattened out and had completely covered the table top.

"That's it!" Grayson gasped. "What we need is the rapid expansion in volume associated with an extremely vigorous outward release of energy."

"Huh?" I grunted.

He grinned. "We need to blow the portal up!"

I SENSED SERIOUS TROUBLE ahead.

Grayson had set up his whiteboard and filled it from top to bottom with the kind of math formulas that caused common men to lapse into drooling brain comas.

"Uh ... what's going on here?" I asked, not really wanting to know.

Grayson grinned. "This is a diagram on how we're going to obtain enough red phosphorous to blow up the portal."

"Oh," I said. "Didn't you say red phosphorous the stuff they use in fireworks?"

"Correct," Grayson said. "But I figure we'll need a few tons of it."

"How are you going to come up with that much of the stuff? Order it on Amazon?"

Grayson shook his head. "No. I looked. They don't have it in stock. We're going to have to make our own by heating common white phosphorous to 482 degrees."

"With what?" I quipped. "A flame thrower?"

"Oh!" Garth said, raising his hand. "We've got a couple of those!"

"Excellent," Grayson said.

"But Mr. Gray," Garth said, "Isn't white phosphorous poisonous and highly combustible when in contact with air?"

"I sure hope so," Grayson said. "Because I'm counting on it."

"Uh ... Grayson," I said, raising my hand. "I just want to put in my bid for *not* being the one who has to strike the match on this fiasco."

"No need. We'll be using the built-up static-electric charge of the black phosphorous as a detonator."

"Oh, sure," I said. "Makes perfect sense to me."

Not.

Grayson rubbed his hands together. "Okay, troops. Now all we need is a covert vehicle to transport ourselves and our supplies to the portal site."

"Well, you can forget the RV," I said. "It'd never make it. Besides, Earl's still locked in there."

"What about Earl's monster truck?" Jimmy asked.

"No," Grayson said. "We can't risk explosion blowback through the windows. We need something with an enclosed passenger capsule. Something impenetrable that can make it through swampy terrain and up sandy ridges."

The brothers exchanged glances. Then they nodded and shook hands.

Jimmy locked eyes with Grayson. "I think we've got just the vehicle. Follow me!"

WE FOLLOWED JIMMY AND Garth along a narrow, weedy trail behind their trailer that wove its way around various heaps of rusting junk. Finally, we arrived at a large, aluminum shed. Jimmy opened the padlock on the door and raised the hangar door.

My mouth fell open.

"Pandora and Mr. Gray, meet Bimbo!" Garth said proudly.

"Bimbo?" I asked, staring at the strange vehicle that looked like the bastard child of a weekend bender between a jeep, a jet, and a WWII tank.

"BIMBO stands for Biological Impact Mobile Bug-Out," Jimmy said. "We built it ourselves. You know, for the end of the world."

Bug-out was right. The contraption looked like a sheet-metal beetle on tank treads.

"We modeled it after the most indestructible organism on the planet," Jimmy said.

Grayson's brow furrowed. "Tardigrades?"

Jimmy shook his head. "No. *Cockroaches.* They've been around since the dinosaurs. They've survived everything from extinction events to nuclear blasts."

"Intriguing," Grayson said, walking around BIMBO as if performing a military inspection. "I see it's equipped with tank treads for all-terrain travel."

"Yes sir," Jimmy said. "Steel plated with chain-link traction!"

"Armor-plated passenger transport?" Grayson asked.

"Complete with aeration fan and a week's water supply!"

Grayson nodded. "Periscope?"

"Dual action, with night-vision capabilities!"

"Cargo space?" Grayson asked.

"No," Garth said. "Car go *road.* But it can really burn up the asphalt, can't it Jimmy!"

Chapter Sixty-Two

The sun was hanging low in the sky. I wondered if I'd see another sunset. Soon, I'd be climbing into a giant cockroach packed with a ton of highly combustible materials and three trigger-happy guys toting flame throwers.

I should've eaten that damned Tootsie Pop.

I needed to say goodbye to Earl, just in case this was, you know, the last time I'd ever see him.

I picked up Grayson's pointer stick and walked over to the dilapidated old RV. I tapped the charcoal-stained end on the window above the banquette.

The blinds moved. Eyes peeked out between them.

"Hey, Earl," I called out.

He yanked up the blinds and stared at me through the window. Even though the pane was open, the window frame was too small to allow Earl's girth to escape from between it.

"Lemme out," he said.

"I can't. We locked you in there for your own good."

"I'm starvin'," he said.

"No you're not. Listen, Grayson says we've gotta destroy Queen Kristie's portal. From the sound of it, it's gonna be pretty dangerous."

Earl frowned and placed his open palm against the pane. "Don't go, Bobbie. Don't leave me here."

"You'll be okay. I hid a door key inside there, Earl. Just keep looking."

"Why'd you hide it?"

"So you couldn't follow us. You're not in your right mind for a mission right now. I hope getting rid of Queen Bimbo will also get rid of your brain fog."

"But I don't feel foggy. Just hungry." Earl shot me a puppy-dog pout. "I sure could use a donut, you know?"

My heart pinged.

I know, buddy. I know.

"Listen, Earl. If I don't come back, I want you to know I put the keys to Bessie under her front wheel."

Earl frowned. "What do you mean, if you don't come back?"

"I gotta go." I turned to leave.

"Don't leave, Bobbie!" Earl called after me. "Don't go!"

I stopped in my tracks.

Maybe Earl is over his infestation. Maybe he really is cured.

I started to take a step to turn around.

Earl let loose a bellow.

A horrible, blood-curdling, Cruller Holler.

I wiped a tear from my cheek, set my jaw to lockdown, and marched toward my date with destiny.

I FOUND THE GUYS SWARMED together, eating leftover tacos off the hood of the giant, brown cockroach.

John Keel was right. Who says the Universal mind has to be sane?

"All right," I said. "Let's get this roach-coach rolling! It's time to kill two bimbos with one stone."

Grayson poised mid-bite. "This isn't a *suicide* mission, Drex."

I shot him some side-eye. "Ha ha. I meant the *blonde* bimbo queen and this stupid machine," I said, kicking the cockroach's tank treads.

"Biological Impact Mobile Bug-Out," Garth said, patting its fender.

"Whatever," I said, hitching up my camo sweatpants. "Come on, guys. Let's roll."

Chapter Sixty-Three

When I saw the familiar, faint orange glow emanating from above the forest, my Rambo-like bravado evaporated. Panic shot through me like motor oil through a busted carburetor. My knees started knocking—which was hard to hide, considering I was sitting on Grayson's lap.

BIMBO had only been designed to hold two nerds. Yet there we were, four idiots crammed inside the already tight passenger cabin.

Jimmy was seated at the vehicle's bizarre control panel, which had more indicators on it than a nuclear power plant. Grayson had shotgun position beside him, with me perched on his knobby knees. Garth, odd man out, had been relegated to standing in the space between us, his head sticking out the round opening in the ceiling we'd all squeezed in through, his mullet flapping in the breeze like a hound-dog's ears.

And flap it did. True to its reputation, BIMBO really *could* haul ass—on the asphalt, at least. It didn't take long until I sighted the glow in the woods—even before lookout Garth had—thanks to BIMBO's handy, night-vision periscope.

"We're here," I said, squeezing the words from my suddenly tight lungs.

"Before we go into battle, I'd like to say a few words," Grayson said, his breath hot on my neck. "Troops, as we face our enemy, our best weapon against fear is the ability to choose one thought over another."

"Huh?" I grunted, squirming in his lap.

"The human mind can only focus on one thing at a time," Grayson continued. "I want everyone to assuage their fears by focusing on their safe places. Got it?"

Jimmy shifted to a lower gear and nodded. "I'm there, Mr. Gray."

"Me, too," Garth said, forming an okay sign with his thumb and forefinger.

As for me, I envisioned curling up in my Grandma Selma's lap. I tugged my imaginary blanket over my head, closed my eyes and nodded. "I'm there."

"Good," Grayson said. "Now tell me. What are your safe places?"

"Inside BIMBO," Jimmy said with a shrug. "She's indestructible."

"Me, too," Garth said.

"And you?" Grayson asked me.

"Uh ... in a lap," I squeaked.

He locked eyes with me and smiled. "Excellent."

Then, to my shock, Grayson squeezed my thigh. Before I could react, he turned to Jimmy and said, "Okay, troops. It's time for BIM-BO to kick some butt."

"Yes, sir!" Jimmy said. He turned the giant cockroach toward the glow in the woods, deep into the swampy, hilly terrain of the Hi-Ho.

Riding off-road inside BIMBO was like taking a spin inside a clothes dryer, except the sheets and towels had been replaced with knees and elbows. By the time Garth called out that he could see the old propane tank on the top of the ridge, I was pretty sure I'd already suffered a concussion and a black eye.

"Hold up," Grayson said to Jimmy. "Take her slow and easy from here on out."

"Will do." Jimmy shifted into low gear and aimed the cockroach toward the hill.

Slowly, like a tortoise digging a nest to lay its eggs, BIMBO climbed the sandy ridge. I could tell we'd reached the top when the gravity inside the cockpit leveled out, and my back was no longer glued to Grayson's chest.

"Good work," Grayson said. Then he tapped the back of Garth's knee with two knuckles, making the nerd's leg buckle.

The buck-toothed geek popped his mullet head back down into the guts of the roach's cabin. "What's up?" he asked.

"Let me have a look," Grayson said.

The two exchanged places—only Garth was the one who sat on *my* lap.

"Just as I suspected," Grayson said, surveying the scene with night-vision goggles. "It's business as usual for Kristie's Frickin' Crullers."

"What's the game plan?" I asked.

Grayson tucked his head back into the passenger cabin. "We'll lay low here for a bit and wait for an opening. I don't want to run over anyone with BIMBO. Not if we can help it, that is."

"Why can't we just wait till the meeting's over, and blow up the bonfire when everyone's gone?" I asked.

"Because everyone could be *literally* gone before that," Grayson said. "This could be the night Queen Kristie chooses to harvest them as Krull Krispies with her portal of doom."

I chewed my lip. "But what if she really *is* just a dingbat pushing a new donut chain?"

"The time for that discussion is over," Grayson said. "We've opened this can of worms. It's time to lie in it."

Chapter Sixty-Four

Despite all odds in the known universe, Grayson had been right. It did *indeed* appear to be D-Day for the donut dingdongs.

As we peered from the ridge with periscopes, night-vision goggles, and thick, nerdy glasses, we watched silently as Queen Kristie organized her robed minions and had them add a new section to the path of hot coals—one that connected directly to the blazing fire pit.

"Looks like somebody's in for a robe awakening," Grayson said, peering through his goggles. "I wonder how much she spent on those things."

"We're staring down the sphincter of some intergalactic butthole, and *that's* what you're worried about?" I said, grabbing his goggles. I took a look for myself and gasped.

"Oh my lord," I said. "I think she's getting ready to send the first batch into the rotisserie."

"All right, troops," Grayson said. "Battle stations!"

We all crammed into the cockroach mobile, arms and elbows hanging up on each other like a barrel of monkeys. Once we'd all claimed our own body parts, Grayson said, "Gentlemen, start your engines."

"Yes, sir!" Jimmy barked. He turned the key. BIMBO didn't budge.

"Huh," Grayson grunted. "Try again."

Jimmy turned the key again. It broke off in the ignition. "Uh ... looks like we're going to have to go to auxiliary power, Mr. Gray."

"Excellent," Grayson nodded. "Make it so."

Jimmy grimaced. "Uh ... that means we have to get out and push, sir."

Suddenly, an unearthly wail pierced the air. Queen Kristie had just given the Cruller Holler. A moment later, it was echoed by the horde of robed fat guys.

"Hurry," Jimmy said, pushing Garth through the opening in the ceiling. "The meeting's finishing. She'll be sending them down the coal paths next!"

Jimmy disappeared out the hole behind Garth.

"You next," Grayson said.

I nodded, then scrambled up the ceiling hatch, Grayson pushing my butt-cheeks from behind. As my head popped out, I saw Garth and Jimmy staring at the woods—in the opposite direction of Queen Bimbo and her bonfire of doom.

"I thought we were gonna push," I called out to them. They didn't react.

Then I saw what they were staring at.

Beams of light were barreling through the woods, heading right for us.

"Move it, Drex!" Grayson yelled from below, pushing on my butt again.

I unfroze and scurried out of the hatch. I crawled over the cockroach's back and jumped onto the ground. Then I sidled up next to Garth.

"What are all those lights?" I asked.

Garth whispered, "The mothership."

"UNBELIEVABLE!" GRAYSON shouted.

I turned to see his head and elbows protruding from BIMBO's ceiling like a hatching larvae. He aimed his night-vision goggles at the light beams heading toward us from the woods.

"What is it?" I cried out.

"I don't believe it," he said, lowering his goggles. "It's my RV!"

I gasped. "Earl must've hotwired it!"

Or he found the key I hid for him.

Grayson piled out and scrambled over the giant cockroach. I grabbed his goggles and had a look myself.

"Dear lord!" I cried. "Is Earl wearing a Star Wars bedspread?"

Grayson grabbed the goggles back. "I bought it online as surprise for you."

I grabbed the goggles again. "You really don't know *anything* about women, do you?"

"In my own defense, who *does*?" he yelled, giving up trying to command the goggles.

"Ugh!" I grunted, then lifted the goggles to my eyes and stared as Earl barreled up the ridge in the ratty old RV.

"What's he doing?" Garth asked.

"Is he coming to help?" Jimmy asked.

"Obviously," Grayson said. "The question is, *who* is he coming to help? Us or Queen Kristie?"

THE RV CAME TO A SCREECHING halt at the top of the ridge. We couldn't tell if it was intentional, or it was because the middle had bottomed out and left the RV stranded with both front and rear tires spinning in the air.

Earl rolled down the window and waved.

"Howdy, fellers," he said, as if he'd just dropped by for a beer.

"What are you doing?" I yelled.

"Helpin' y'all get rid a that Kristie critter," he said, fiddling with his Star Wars toga. "Now, what can I do to be of service?"

"BIMBO's dead," Jimmy said. "I say let's transfer her payload to the RV."

We all looked over at Grayson. He nodded. "Make it so."

"NOW, YOU UNDERSTAND the plan, right?" I asked.

Earl grinned. "I'll get her aimed right, then bail out. And if'n it don't work out, just remember, I had me a big ol' time workin' with y'all." Earl winked at me. "Anyways, Bobbie, it's *you* what's got the brightest future. Now, y'all gonna give me a push, or what?"

"Good luck, Earl," I said, and kissed him on the cheek.

Goodbyes exchanged, the four of us lined up and pushed up on the back end of the RV, trying to raise it enough to let the front tires find traction.

The RV's tires spun.

The front-end fell forward.

As soon as the tires met sand, Earl let out a Cruller Holler and stomped on the gas. He and that old motorhome went barreling down the ridge, making a beeline for the bonfire.

"Poor, heroic, *stupid* Earl!" I wailed, watching the RV rambling down the ridge like it was being chased by revenuers. "I don't understand. How does he have the guts to be so brave?"

Grayson touched my hand. "Probiotics have been shown to lower our reactions to threatening images."

I jerked my hand away and turned to stare at him. "Oh. My. God. Is *that* why you eat yogurt?"

He shrugged. "Perhaps."

My mouth fell open. "That means ... all this time you've been *cheating* on that damned EEG machine!"

Grayson's eyebrow rose. "I wouldn't call it *cheating*. You could eat yogurt, too."

"Not on your life!" I hissed. "And while we're spouting our true confessions, tell me *this*. If you could have a new mattress delivered overnight, why couldn't you have ordered me a new sofa-bed by now?"

Grayson winced. "I had my reasons."

"There he goes!" Jimmy yelled.

I gasped and turned back just in time to see the old RV ramble into the clearing. It raced toward the bonfire—the men in robes scrambling around like fat, white mice.

Then a flash of bluish-white light akin to a nuclear blast went off.

I felt a breeze against my cheek, but I didn't hear a thing.

Instead, I saw a speck of something silver heading toward me.

Then the world went black.

Chapter Sixty-Five

I *was swimming in a sea of Reese's Pieces.*
My mouth tasted like a rainbow of dead goldfish.
I needed some mouthwash, bad.
I reached for the Tootsie Pop sticking out of the kitchen drawer.
But when I tried to peel the wrapper off, the paper read Dum-Dum.

I AWOKE TO FIND MYSELF lying in an unfamiliar bed—in an unfamiliar room. Everything was so ... *white*. And peaceful. And quiet.

Either I'd died, or my last assignment with Grayson had finally ended with me in a psych ward.

I sucked in what felt like my first breath in ages. The place smelled like plastic. And disinfectant. And ....

Fritos?

Slowly, I turned my thumping head to the left. My cousin Earl was passed out on a vinyl recliner beside me. Atop his potbelly, a family-size bag of corn chips rose and fell in rhythm with his breathing.

"Earl?"

My voice sounded strange—like it was underwater. A twinge of concern upped the volume in my throbbing head.

"Earl?"

Earl snorted himself awake, then glanced over at me.

His eyes nearly doubled. He shot up out of his chair as if it were an ejector seat. Fritos flew everywhere.

"Bobbie!" he shouted. "You're awake!"

"You've got a real knack for the obvious," I cracked.

My words echoed weirdly inside my skull. Déjà vu washed over me. I felt as if I'd been here before—done all this before...

"What happened?" I croaked. "Where am I?"

"In the hospital," Earl said. "Don't you remember?"

"I think so," I said. "There was that guy at the mall—the one in hot-pants..."

Earl eyed me sympathetically, but cautiously, as if I might be contagious. "Uh...yeah. That's right, Bobbie."

I tried to sit up, but the IV tube in my arm had me partially pinned down. "Tell me straight," I said. "How bad off am I?"

Earl winced. "The good news is, you'll live. The bad news is, you've got one hell of a Kentucky waterfall."

"What?"

I reached for my forehead. My fingers glided across my bald scalp, stopping at the edges of a big bandage on my forehead. "Argh! Gimme a mirror!"

Earl's lips curled slightly as he handed me the mirror lying on the table beside my hospital bed.

I peered at my reflection. My face went slack. The top of my head all the way to my ears had been shaved bald. I dropped the mirror onto my chest in disgust. "Ugh! Not again!"

Earl gave me a funny look. I recognized it as the same one he used to give Aunt Clara after she got dementia.

"Uh...look, Bobbie," he said. "You been out a good while. But there's somebody here who's been dying to see you. Let me go get him."

"Who is it?"

"Your boyfriend," Earl said, then snickered.

My heart pinged.

Grayson!

"I'll leave you two alone," Earl said, then disappeared out the door.

A moment later, a familiar face peeked inside the doorframe. I recognized the comb-over in an instant.

It was Carl Blanders.

My slimy, cheating ex slunk into the room waving a box of cheap chocolates at me like a booby prize from the state fair.

"I heard you got shot in the head," he said sheepishly. "I came as soon as I could."

I scowled. "Where's Grayson?"

Carl blanched and retracted his box of chocolates. "*Who?*"

"Grayson!" I hissed. "I want to see *Nick Grayson*!"

Carl recovered his smarmy smile and patted my hand. "Oh. Is that your nurse? Are you in pain? Should I call for him?"

I *was* in pain. Agony, actually. And I was beginning to realize it wasn't the kind even morphine could take the edge off of.

"We've all been so worried about you, Bobbie," Carl simpered. He leaned over and kissed my cheek. "You've been in a coma for quite a while, now."

My gut flopped.

There it was. My fate delivered by my mealy-mouthed ex-boyfriend.

I'd been shot in the head at the mall—and I'd suffered severe brain damage.

I wasn't a P.I. intern.

I wasn't chasing monsters with some ridiculous private eye named Nick Grayson.

All of that nonsense had been a dream. The machinations of my mangled cerebral cortex.

I looked into the cheating, hazel eyes of Carl Blanders and felt my heart break.

The Earth was *indeed* a galactic toilet.

And I was just a turd in the frickin' punchbowl.

Chapter Sixty-Six

I checked my fingernails. The grease under them didn't lie.

All the crazy adventures I'd had with Grayson had all been absurdities. Asinine figments of my comatose imagination.

Brain farts.

The reality was, I was just a deadbeat mechanic stuck in the dead-end town of Point Paradise.

Hot tears trickled down both sides of my face. I closed my eyes, wishing my crummy ex Carl would get the hell out of my room and let me die in peace.

"Cheer up," he said, opening the chocolates and helping himself. "I went by your dad's shop to pick up this. I thought it might cheer you up."

I cracked open a tear-filled eye, then wanted to kick myself for falling for his false charms again.

Carl was leering at me with his horse-toothed smile, holding up the baseball cap he'd given me to commemorate our second anniversary of going together.

I vaguely remembered the cap had been signed by some stupid baseball hero of his. It would've made the perfect gift—if I'd happened to have been Carl Blanders.

I'd hated it then. I still hated it now.

"Get out," I said.

"What was that?" he asked. "Oh. I get it. You need to take a leak or something, right?"

"No," I hissed. "I need to get a new life. One without *you* in it."

"But Bobbie, baby—"

"Don't *Bobbie baby* me!" I yelled. "What's the matter? Did Candy finally get wise to your philandering ways? Boo hoo! Now, I said *get out!*"

Carl stared at me, stunned. I'd never shown him that kind of gumption before.

"Uh ... sure," he said. "I don't want to upset you, honey. You had major brain surgery. You're not thinking straight. I'll come back when—"

"No," I screamed. "Get out! And don't ever come back!"

The door to my hospital room flew open. Earl stepped in, his shoulders as broad as a barroom bouncer's. "I believe my cousin just asked you to hit the road," he said.

Carl shook his head. "She's suffering from delirium."

"Well, now, that's nothin' a little Kaopectate can't cure," Earl said, grabbing Carl by the arm. "Now, why don't you mosey on outta here, like Bobbie said."

"Fine," Carl said. "I'll come back later."

"Don't bother!" I yelled.

"Have a nice life," Earl said, then shoved Carl out the door.

He shut it behind him, then turned and smiled at me. "'Bout time you got shed of that rotten ol' rascal, Bobbie."

"I know. Thanks, Earl."

"Just doin' my cousinly duty. You up for another visitor?"

I winced. "Someone else to pour salt in my wounds? No thanks. Not right now. I just want to be alone for a while."

"You sure?"

"Yeah." I felt a crying jag coming on. "I think I need a nap."

"Okie-dokie, then," Earl said. "I'm headin' back to the auto shop."

"Okay. I'll be out of here soon and can help you out."

"Don't you worry about that. You just get well. I been doin' all right without you."

"Oh."

Despite my best efforts, I sobbed. Tears spilled from my eyes.

Earl rushed over to my side. "You okay?" He took off his prized Redman Chewing Tobacco cap. "Here. Lemme leave Old Red here to keep you company."

"Thanks," I said, running my fingers across the tattered old cap. "Do me a favor?"

Earl smiled. "Sure."

"Take that stupid cap Carl left," I said. "It's yours."

Earl's lip snarled. "You sure? I don't want him thinkin' I stole it, now."

"Don't worry. You're no kleptomaniac."

"What's that?" Earl asked.

I sighed. "Just a mental disorder."

"Oh." He winked. "Can you *take something* for it?"

I laughed and swatted him with Old Red. "Sometimes you're not as dumb as you look."

"I appreciate that," Earl said, trying Carl's cap on for size.

He leaned over and took my hand in his bear-sized one. "Listen. I know you got to get better and all, Bobbie. But if it makes you feel any better, we got rid of 'em."

"Carl?" I asked. "I *know*. I just saw you do it. I'm not *that* brain damaged—am I?"

Earl shook his head. "I wasn't talkin' about that butthole Carl. I was talkin' about *them*."

I sighed. "Look, Earl. I'm tired. What do you mean, *them*?"

Earl cocked his head and looked at me funny.

"The *aliens*, Bobbie. Don't you remember?"

"What?"

Suddenly, the door to my room flew open. A doctor in a white lab coat entered, studying my chart.

"I see the patient has finally awakened," he said to Earl.

The doctor's voice sounded vaguely familiar. Then he glanced over at me.

His green eyes twinkled.

"Grayson!" I gasped. "You're *real*!"

He grinned. "As far as you know, yes."

"Woohoo! She knows you!" Earl hollered.

"Of *course* I do," I said, feeling the life rush back into my veins. "What ... what happened?"

Grayson shrugged. "Well, I lost my fedora in the explosion—and my moustache, too."

"W ... what?" I stuttered. "No. I meant—"

"I know what you meant," Grayson said, taking my hand. "Just lay back and relax. I'll explain everything when you're ready."

Chapter Sixty-Seven

I was so overwhelmed with joy to see Grayson that I could barely concentrate on the words tumbling from his clean-shaven lips.

Without his moustache, Grayson looked like Theo James and George Clooney rolled into one dark-haired, mysterious, green-eyed, spider-fingered, hunk-a-palooza.

Mama-mia!

"'Operation Mercy Flush' was a complete success," Grayson said.

I sighed and shook my head.

And there's the ying to his yang.

"It dang sure was!" Earl said. "We done sent Queen Witchy Poo back to whatever spaceworm butthole she crawled out of."

"Wait," I said. "My memory's kind of sketchy. Could you start at the beginning?"

"Uh, sure," Earl said. "You was born a tomboy in the little town a Point Paradise, Florida."

I rolled my eyes. "Not *that* far back."

"Do you remember that I got word on the Mothman scat samples?" Grayson asked.

I shook my head. "No."

He nodded. "I did. The results were inconclusive. The lab required more samples to test."

I smiled. "That's *good*, right?"

"It *would've* been," Grayson said, glancing over at Earl.

"What's the big deal?" I asked. "Just send them the ones in the—"

"I can't," Grayson said. "They were ... uh ... ahem ..."

"I *ate* 'em, okay?" Earl blurted, his face puckering at the thought.

I grimaced. "You *ate* them?"

"Yeah. When you locked me up in that blasted RV when I was all crazy-like." He shuddered. "What'd y'all keep them dookie balls in the fridge for, anyway?"

Grayson shook his head. "It doesn't matter, Drex. The RV was lost during our last mission."

A flash of memory twanged inside my brain. "I think I remember something about that." I raised my hand to my bandaged head. "Is that what happened to me?"

"Yes and no," Grayson said. "During the explosion, you were struck in the head by flying debris. A chrome door-handle, to be exact. We brought you to the hospital unconscious."

"That's how I ended up here," I said. "But ... did the handle stab me in the head or something?"

"Nope. Your skull was too thick for that," Earl said, tapping his knuckles on his shaggy pate. "You and me got Grandma Selma's genes."

"You did sustain a head wound," Grayson said. "But the MRI showed a different complication. It seemed your twin was ready to be born."

"Twin?" I asked. "You mean my—"

"Yes. The vestigial twin lodged inside your brain."

My jaw went slack. "They took it out?"

Grayson nodded.

I sat up in bed. "What did it look like?"

Grayson grinned. "I had a feeling you might want to know. I hope you don't mind, but I had Earl sign a consent form so we could keep it."

"We got it in a jar behind the seat in Bessie," Earl said. "Wanna see it? Gotta warn ya, though. It's darn near as ugly as you are."

I laughed, then locked eyes with Grayson. "Yeah. I wanna see it."

"I'll bring it by later," he said. "But right now, you've got another visitor waiting to see you."

My lip snarled. "Please. Not Carl again."

"Nope," Earl said. "Me and her done run him off."

"Her?" I asked. "Beth-Ann?"

"Who else?" she said, peeking her Goth-painted face in the door.

BETH-ANN WATCHED GRAYSON and Earl leave, then turned to me and giggled.

"Hubba hubba! Is it just me, or did the sexy detectsy just get sexier?"

I smirked. "You noticed."

"Uh ... yeah. Apparently *you* did, too."

I sighed. "Yeah. But Grayson doesn't see me as girlfriend material. I'm nothing but a number to him."

"What are you talking about?"

"I think I'm the one in his folder. You know. *Experiment #5.* I'm like his fifth partner or something. I've seen the way he looks at me. I'm just a lab rat in jeans."

Beth-Ann glanced up at my shaved scalp. "Well, that hair of yours sure isn't helping. I gotta hand it to you, Bobbie. You sure know how to give a hairdresser a challenge."

"I'm hopeless," I said. "But forget about me. Can you do something about Earl's hair? He looks like a Neanderthal Prince Valiant."

Beth-Ann stiffened. "What do you mean?"

"You've seen it. That guy behind the IGA—"

"*I* cut his hair, Bobbie."

I gasped. "*You* did that to him? *Why?*"

Beth-Ann shrugged coyly. "I have my reasons."

"Like *what?*"

"I like him, okay?" she confessed. "I cut Earl's hair like that to keep the other women away."

I stared at her, stunned.

"Don't look at me like that. Pickings are mighty slim in Point Paradise, my dear. Or do I have to remind you about Carl Blanders?"

I winced. "Fine. You can have him. Just don't—you know—treat him bad, okay?"

"I won't," she said, grabbing my hand. "Bobbie, I think I'm in love with him."

I gasped. "Does Earl love you back?"

"I don't know. But he *will*."

I smiled. "How do you know you're in love?"

Beth-Ann shrugged. "I guess because the thought of Earl with anyone else drives me nuts."

I snorted. "That's not love, Beth-Ann. That's obsession."

"What's the difference?"

"About fifteen to life."

We laughed together for a moment, then I asked her a question that'd been plaguing me since I woke up from my coma.

"Beth-Ann. Have you heard anything from my mother—the newly married Mrs. Applewhite?"

My best friend smiled at me softly and shook her head. "Nope. But let's face it, Bobbie. Nobody *ever* resolves their mommy issues."

Chapter Sixty-Eight

I sat up and fussed with the auburn, shoulder-length bob Beth-Ann had given me from her emergency wig box. Lumpy and a bit square after being stretched over my bandages, I feared I looked about as attractive as *ET* had when he'd played dress-up in that little girl's clothes.

Then again, maybe aliens were what floated Grayson's boat ...

A knock sounded on my hospital door. I checked my makeup in the hand mirror, then tucked it up under my left elbow.

"Come in," I said.

Grayson appeared carrying a quart-sized pickle jar.

"Hello there," he said, flashing a fabulous smile.

I couldn't believe he'd been hiding it all this time beneath that horrid moustache burned off in the explosion.

"I want you to meet Innie," he said, and held up the jar for my perusal.

"Innie?" I asked, staring at the blob floating in clear liquid.

"Yes. That's what I named your twin. You know, because it was *in* your brain."

"Oh," I said. "But aren't there *two* things in here?"

"Yes," Grayson said. "My Nubbin's in there with her."

I looked up at him. "I recognize this. I thought you said it was a Nubian fertility statue."

Grayson shrugged. "So, I took a little poetic license."

"But the jar was in the RV—"

"It *was*," Grayson said, cutting me off. "But I took it out when we transferred the phosphorous from BIMBO. It's the only thing I was able to save, I'm afraid."

I thought about all that cash he had stashed inside the RV's paneled walls.

"But ... why Nubbin?" I asked.

"I guess because it's *part* of me, Drex." He locked eyes with me. "Is that creepy?"

I shrugged. "Not as creepy as saving toenail clippings, I guess."

Grayson laughed. "How about this? Is *this* creepy?" He took the jar and twirled it. The two masses inside danced around, then settled against each other. "Look how they fit together."

I gasped. Floating side by side, our vestigial twins looked like a pair of macabre salt and pepper shakers.

"That's uncanny," I said. "What do you think that means?"

"I don't know," Grayson said. "But I'd say the odds of them nesting together like that are astronomical."

I shook my head. Either Grayson and I were destined for each other, or my life was a totally freaky Sci-Fi movie. I mean, identical vestigial twins? Who could make that shit up?

Had we both been infected with the same extraterrestrial spores? Were these things biological alien implants? Were Grayson and I both aliens? Or alien hybrids? I needed something else to think about, and fast! I nearly fainted with relief when Earl poked his head in the door.

"How's it goin'?" my cousin asked.

"Come in," I blurted. "I want to hear about the showdown with Queen Kristie. You bailed out in time, obviously. But is everybody else okay?"

Earl lowered his head. "Sometimes, Bobbie, life just sucks the jelly right outta your donut."

"What?" I asked, my eyes growing wide. "Did something happen to Jimmy and Garth?"

"No," Grayson said. "They're fine."

"Then who?"

"Gizzard," Earl said.

"Oh my word!" I blurted. "Don't tell me you *ate* Gizzard!"

Earl drew back as if I'd stuck him with a cattle prod. "Geez, Bobbie! I'm not an *animal*!"

"Well, technically you *are*," Grayson said. "A mammal, to be specific."

"Guys!" I said. "What happened to Gizzard?"

"I put her out of the RV before I took off to go rescue y'all," Earl said. He cringed. "Then I kinda ran over the terrarium when I was backing out."

I winced. "Oh."

"Hold on," Grayson said. "When we got back to the compound, we found the broken terrarium pieces lying on the driveway," Grayson said. "There was no blood or body parts around. I believe she escaped into the junkyard unharmed."

"What will happen to her now?" I asked.

"She's an anole," Grayson said. "They're natural ecomorphs. She'll be able to adapt to her new environment. After all, she's a native Floridian, just like you two. From what I've seen, you all are one tough bunch."

"Yep. We Floridians know how to survive," Earl said.

I adjusted my wig. "Yes, we most certainly do."

Grayson smiled. "Good. Now, I think we should let you rest up, Drex. You're getting released tomorrow."

"Finally!" I said.

"If you're up for it, I'd like to take you to visit the grave of our fallen comrade."

I gulped. "Who died?"

Chapter Sixty-Nine

As promised, Grayson arrived at my hospital room at 9 a.m. sharp. I figured I'd enjoy one last lie-in before I had to face the reality that I was broke—and so was Grayson. With no funds and no RV, our little enterprise seemed doomed to any further exploration of new life and new civilizations.

"Ready?" Grayson asked, slipping his head inside the door.

"Yes!" I practically yelled. I hopped out off the end of the bed and slipped my feet into my cowboy boots. "Get me out of here before Carl Blanders comes back."

Grayson's lip twitched at the sound of Carl's name. I did a double take.

Could he actually be jealous?

I smirked.

Maybe he's human after all...

"You still haven't told me how things went with Queen Cruller," I said. "Or who died."

"I'm aware of that," Grayson said, picking up my duffle bag. "But I think it's better to wait until you're out of here."

My nose crinkled. "Why? Are you afraid I'll scream or something?"

Grayson headed for the door. "I'll opt for 'or something.'"

"YOUR EYES LOOK RED," Earl said as I walked out to the hospital parking lot with Grayson. "Have you been crying?"

"No," I said. "*Your* eyes look glazed. Have you been eating donuts?"

Earl grimaced. "No way. I've sworn off a them thangs for life."

I glanced over at Bessie and did a double take. She was sporting a brand new periscope sticking up from the ceiling of her cab.

"What did you do to her?" I asked.

Earl grinned. "After I seen that one on that ol' roach mobile, I just had to have me one."

"Incredible," Grayson said, shaking his head. "Earl, did you install that last night?"

"Yeppers."

I laughed. "Grayson, you should be used to this by now."

"Don't worry about it none, Mr. G.," Earl said. "My friend Danny says that sudden exposure to redneck engineering can throw some people into a discombobulated state of consciousness."

I grinned. "And you, my dear cousin Earl, are *definitely* a redneck."

"Thanky," Earl said. "I take that as a compliment."

"A compliment?" Grayson asked.

"Why shore," Earl said. "After all, a redneck is just an entrepreneur with more imagination than money."

I thought of our empty coffers and offered up a bittersweet smile. "I guess that makes us *all* rednecks now. So, where are we going?"

"We're off to the memorial of a beloved colleague," Grayson said. "But first, we have an important stop to make."

Chapter Seventy

We pulled into the parking lot of an old motel.

"The Imperial Motor Court?" I said sourly. "Geez. They should rename this the Royal Flush."

Across the lot, Jimmy and Garth piled out of their 1966 light-blue Chevy pickup and sprinted toward us.

"Hi, Pandora! Earl! Mr. Gray!"

"Hi," I said. "Excuse me, but what the hell are we doing here?"

"Actually, it was Jimmy who found this place," Grayson said.

"By accident," Jimmy said. "I was out on a robbery call when I spotted her."

My nose crinkled. "Wade's missing girlfriend, Connie?"

"No," Jimmy said. "Queen Kristie."

I'D BEEN CHOMPING AT the bit to know what had happened to Queen Kristie, but Grayson had been chomping at the bit for tacos. After a quick vote all around, he and the guys had won. The five of us piled back into our vehicles and traded the Imperial Court Motel for a booth by the window at Juanita's Casa del Tacos.

"So, what the frick and frack happened?" I asked after patiently waiting for Thelma to take the men's orders.

"I was out on a routine robbery call last week," Jimmy said. "Some guy complaining some woman had ripped him off."

"Goody," I deadpanned. "So? *What happened* to Queen Kristie?"

"I'm getting there," Jimmy said. "The guy who got robbed told me the woman who did it was in Room 13 at the Imperial Motor Court. So I walked over, gun drawn. Who comes to the door? Queen Kristie."

"How'd you know it was her?" I asked.

"She was, believe me," Jimmy said, sharing a smirk with the other guys. "She was blonde, tanned, big bosom—"

"Yeah, I get the picture," I said. "But what evidence do you have it was the same woman who was out in the woods running those bonfire meetings?"

"Well, for one thing, she had about a hundred robes in her room," Jimmy said. "She'd stolen from a one-day stint as a maid at the Royal Inn & Day Spa."

"Okay," I said. "But that's hardly conclusive evidence."

"She also had a box of donut holes and a baggie full of ecstasy," Jimmy said.

"Well, okay, but—"

"And the guy whose wallet she stole? She'd told him to call her Queen Kristie."

"Okay, fine," I said. "So, what about Wade?"

"I got a call from him last weekend," Jimmy said. "It seems he and Connie decided to run off and start a new life together in New Jersey."

I glanced over at Grayson. "So much for your 'sucked up into a portal' theory."

He shrugged. "New Jersey. Alpha Centauri. They both have their own unique appeal."

"So this whole thing really *was* just some hot bimbo duping guys out of their money?" I asked.

"That's *one* theory," Garth said. "Right, Mr. Gray?"

"How stupid can some guys be?" I asked.

Grayson rubbed his chin. "All humans are to some degree biologically prone to intellectual laziness, emotional decision-making, confirmation bias, and other natural impulses that often obstruct critical thinking."

I smirked. "Is that your way of saying you were wrong?"

Grayson shrugged. "I wouldn't go *that* far. We still haven't proven conclusively that she *wasn't* on a mission from Krull."

"Give me a break!" I said.

"I'm serious," Grayson said. "How else can you explain what happened to the RV?"

I frowned. "I thought you said it was destroyed."

"No. I said it was *lost*."

I shot him a look. "What's the difference?"

"Well, a lot, actually," he said. "Besides the door handle that hit you in the head, not a trace of the RV could be found."

"It's like it just *vanished*," Jimmy said.

"Into a space butthole," Earl said.

"Come on, you guys!" I said, hoping this was just a joke. "What *really* happened to that stupid RV?"

"I have two theories," Grayson said. "One, the RV could've been vaporized by the phosphoric blast. Or two, we foiled Queen Kristie's plan and blew up her portal, leaving her stranded on Earth to make a living with whatever assets she was able to retain."

Grayson glanced out the window. "Think of it. My RV could've crossed over the Einstein-Rosen Bridge and is up there right now, carrying my earthly belongings and Earl's bacterial payload to distant galaxies."

Earl elbowed me and grinned like a proud papa. "My butt bacteria could be up there inoculating Uranus as we speak."

I shook my head, picturing the diarrhea-ridden RV floating around in some distant asteroid field, pinging around like a poop-laden pinball.

God help the poor alien who runs across that sorry sight. Forget biological warfare. The smell of Earl's microbiome alone would be enough to do in the entire race.

Chapter Seventy-One

It wasn't publicly known, but Garth had been able to ascertain the home address of The Amazing Randi via his network of science and conspiracy nerds.

After a short trip to Plantation, Florida, Earl parked Bessie along the shoulder of the road in front of the home where the famous magician and paranormal debunker had, until recently, lived.

I stared at the house through the passenger window. The bouquets of flowers we'd brought along weren't the only memorial offerings the great man had posthumously received.

As we climbed out to pay our respects by laying flowers on his lawn, an older gentleman came out of the house and walked toward us.

"Excuse me," he said. "Did you know Mr. Randi?"

"Uh ... yes," Grayson said. "We don't mean to intrude. We just want to pay our respects. We're all great admirers of The Amazing Randi."

The man smiled. "He always did prefer that particular title."

"I'm Nick Grayson," he said, shaking the man's hand. "This is Earl Schankles. And this young woman here is the unsinkable Roberta Drex."

The man's smile faded. "Roberta Drex?"

I winced. "Uh ... yes."

"You're kidding," he said. "I've been trying to reach you for weeks."

I blanched. "You have?"

"She was knocked out in a coma," Earl said.

I shook my head at Earl, then glanced back at the man. "Why did you want to reach *me*?"

"For an address. A colleague wanted me to mail this letter to you."

"Who?" Grayson asked. "The Amazing Randi?"

The man handed me the letter. "I'm not at liberty to say."

"Then let's go to Liberty so's you *can* say," Earl said.

The man shot Earl an odd look, then turned his attention back to me. "Let's just say it's from someone who prefers to remain anonymous." He winked at me. "Another mystery for you to figure out, perhaps?"

"But—" I said.

"No more questions," the man said. He turned on his heels and headed back toward the house.

I opened the envelope. Inside was a note. I read it aloud to Earl and Grayson.

> *It's always wise to have something important to do. Perseverance is stubbornness with a purpose. Carry on the good work, Roberta Drex. And be sure to check your bank balance.*

"What's that all about?" Grayson asked.

"I'm not sure," I said, rereading the note.

"Gimme that," Earl said, and snatched my phone from my shirt pocket.

"You *have* to know what this is about," Grayson said.

I looked up into his green eyes. "When we were on our way to Plant City, I sent some samples to the Randi Foundation. But I figured nothing would come of it. It was the day you told me Randi had died."

"Samples of the Mothman scat?" Grayson asked.

"Yes. And—" I cringed. "A small sample I clipped from your Nubbin."

Grayson blanched. "But—"

"Well, somethin' sure impressed somebody!" Earl said, shoving my phone in my face. "Lord a mighty, Bobbie!" he hollered. "Somebody done sent you a million bucks!"

"Holy crap!" I said.

But was it for the poop—or the Nubbin?

"I suffer from this obsession that I have something important to do," Grayson said.

I smiled up at him weakly. "Well, good for you."

"No," Grayson said. "I mean—that's what The Amazing Randi said. Remember me telling you that?"

"Oh. Yeah, I remember."

Grayson sighed and shook his head. "You know, Drex, I'm beginning to believe more and more like Randi did."

I suddenly felt crestfallen. "That the paranormal doesn't exist?"

"No. That the Universe doesn't care about credentials. That it cares more about *commitment*."

"Grayson's right," Earl said, nodding like a bobble-head. "I think we should *all* be committed."

I shook my head and smiled. "Earl, I couldn't agree with you more."

WE DROPPED OUR FLOWERS off in front of The Amazing Randi's house, then turned and walked back toward Bessie. Earl had sprinted ahead of Grayson and me, eager to peer at the people coming down the road with his makeshift periscope.

"Here, I've got something for you," Grayson said. He reached into his pocket and pulled out a Tootsie Pop.

I smirked. "You wouldn't be trying to sweeten me up, now that I'm a millionaire, would you?"

Grayson's left eyebrow flat-lined. "What?"

He stared at me for a moment. "I'm giving you this as a token of my *admiration*, Drex. You've proven to possess the inner fortitude required to surmount internal and external biological compulsions."

"Huh?"

"You've shown me you're pretty good at licking the hard stuff, cadet."

I laughed. "Is that your way of saying I've made the grade?"

He shrugged. "Well, maybe not an A-plus, but definitely passing, yes."

"High praise, indeed." I sighed and twirled the sucker in my fingers. "So, where do we go from here, Grayson?"

The edges of his mouth curved upward slightly. "You know, Oscar Wilde once said that if you know what you want to be, you inevitably become it. That is your punishment. But if you never know, then you can become *anything*. So, what do you want to *be*, Drex?"

I smiled up at him. "Happy."

Grayson's cheek dimpled. "Me, too."

He reached over and took my hand. I felt his spidery fingers intertwine with mine.

They fit together perfectly.

My pulse quickened. An electric tingle ran through my body. Still, something nagged me like a stain on my favorite sweater. I looked up at Grayson.

"So, tell me. What exactly is this *Experiment #5* business all about?"

"Ah," Grayson said. "The *hot bodies*."

I bit my lower lip. "Uh ... yeah."

Grayson stopped and locked his green eyes with my brown ones. Was he about to confess some deep, dark perversion?

"I've been researching Spontaneous Human Combustion," he said. "Last week, a guy in St. Petersburg woke up in his vehicle to find half his arm burned to cinders."

I never thought I'd be happy to hear about a roasted body part, yet relief washed over me like a tsunami. I pushed him away playfully. "Get real, Grayson!"

"I'm *serious*." He raised a Spock eyebrow and grinned. "St. Pete's not far from here. You in?"

I unwrapped the Tootsie Pop and smiled. "Yeah. I'm in."

"Excellent."

Suddenly, Grayson's sea-green eyes flashed weirdly. Then he grabbed me up into his arms and kissed me hard on the mouth—just like he had the night I'd first met him—that strange night nearly a year ago when I'd taken care of him after he'd collapsed outside my family's auto garage.

All of a sudden, it was déjà vu all over again.

Only *this* time, it was *me* who was delirious.

The End.

Ready for More *Freaky Florida Adventures?*
Find out where Bobbie and Grayson go from here. Check out episode 7, Smoked Mullet!
HTTPS://WWW.AMAZON.com/dp/ B09BG5JPL1

I hope you enjoyed Scatman Dues. If you did, it would be freaking fantastic if you would post a review on Amazon, Goodreads and/or BookBub. You'll be helping me keep the series going! Thanks in advance for being so awesome!

https://www.amazon.com/dp/B08MD7PRYX#customerReviews

Get a Free Gift!

INTERESTED IN MORE Florida-based mysteries? Sign up for my newsletter and be the first to learn about sales, sneak previews, and new releases! I'll send you a free copy of the *Welcome to Florida, Now Go Home as a* welcome gift!

https://dl.bookfunnel.com/ikfes8er75

For more laughs and discussions with fellow fans, follow me on Facebook, Amazon and BookBub:

Facebook:

https://www.facebook.com/valandpalspage/

Amazon:

https://www.amazon.com/-/e/B06XKJ3YD8

BookBub:

https://www.bookbub.com/search/authors?search=margaret%20lashley

Thank you! Now, please enjoy the following excerpt from: Smoked Mullet, Freaky Florida Mystery Book 7!

Smoked Mullet Excerpt

Chapter One

I could scarcely believe it.

I, Roberta Drex, was a freakin' *millionaire*!

Maybe...

Sweat trickled down the base of my neck as I stood outside Securatell Community Bank and stared at my reflection in the glass entry door. If I waited much longer, I'd be nothing but a puddle of wet clothes steaming in the midday sun.

I reached for the door, then hesitated for a moment longer.

What if...? No!

I hitched up my jeans and straightened the cheap auburn wig atop my head.

Okay. Here goes nothing...

I took a deep breath, then stormed inside. I was a woman on a mission. It was time to find out whether the account balance showing on my cellphone was real, or merely a computer glitch—some sadistic joke being pulled on me by the universe.

It wouldn't be the first time.

I marched up to a middle-aged man sitting behind a desk inside a cubicle. Oddly, both he and the walls of his office appeared to be wearing the same gray-blue fabric.

"I need to verify the funds in my account," I said, then handed him my checkbook.

"Certainly," he said, then smoothed his comb-over with a swipe of his right hand. He pecked a few keys on his computer keyboard, then his eyes bugged out like a Bugs Bunny choking on a carrot.

"Um ... Ms. Drex, it appears you have slightly over one million dollars in your account," he said, eyeing me with a tad keener interest than before.

"Could you check again?" I asked.

"Ma'am, I just verified it."

I gave him some side-eye. He flinched. Then he glanced down at his computer screen and clicked a few buttons on the keyboard.

"Yes, Ms. Drex. The money's *still* there."

"Uh-huh," I mumbled, my heart pounding in my throat. Even though I'd spent the last year investigating all sorts of incredibly outrageous and bizarre phenomena with my half-nuts partner, Nick Grayson, the idea of someone giving me a million dollars seemed more implausible than a two-headed Mothman vampire.

"Uh ... can I get that in writing?" I asked.

"Certainly, Ms. Drex." The manager pressed a few more keys, then swiveled in his chair and grabbed a sheet of paper from a printer tray. He turned back to face me, shooting me a smile he must've held in reserve for VIP customers.

I'd never seen anything like it before.

"Here you go, Ms. Drex," he said, thrusting the paper at me.

"What's this?"

"A printout of your bank statement."

"Oh. Yeah. Sure."

I should open my mail more often.

"Thanks," I said. Then I cocked my head and waved the statement at him. "You swear on your mother's grave this is real?"

He blanched and adjusted his tie. "Well ... yes, ma'am. And now that we've verified it, I'd like to inform you that we offer a full range of financial planning—"

"Save it," I said, then turned and ran out of his cubicle office and up to the first teller I spotted. She was holed up in a tiny Plexiglas booth, peering at me through cat-eye glasses. They were attached to a chain around her neck, just like the pen lying on the counter.

Geez. They don't trust people with anything *around here!*

"I'd like to withdraw fifty dollars," I blurted to the woman, then drummed my nails on the counter and glanced around, waiting for Ashton Kutcher to pop out from behind a corner and yell, "*Punked!*"

Any other day, a withdrawal over five dollars would've set off Securatell's insufficient funds alert. But not this time. And Kutcher didn't show, either. Instead, I found myself once again on the receiving end of a smile the staff kept locked away in the vault for special occasions.

"Here you go," Ms. Drex," the teller said, grinning as she counted out two crisp, new twenties and a ten.

Sweet.

"Anything else I can do for you?" she asked, pushing her pointy glasses further up the bridge of her nose.

"Uh ... yeah."

I smirked and puffed out my chest. I thought about it, but managed to refrain from resting the end of a pinkie finger to the corner of my mouth.

"I'd like to withdraw *ten thousand dollars*," I said.

"A cashier's check?" the teller asked, without so much as a blink.

"Nope. Cold. Hard. Cash."

As the teller gathered the money, the branch manager came over and attempted a Southern revival of his marketing spiel.

"Ms. Drex, that kind of money could be earning interest—"

I held my palm up like a stop sign. "Look. Thanks, but I'm in kind of a hurry. Maybe later."

"Very good," he said, then shoved a couple of brochures into my hand. "These outline some of our fine services. You can find out more details online. Or feel free to call us. We're a full service—"

"I'll keep it in mind," I said, already visualizing how the flyers would look spread out in a fan and lit on fire.

He nodded, his shoulders slumping. "Very good, ma'am."

I turned back to the teller and watched her count out crisp hundred-dollar bills until she reached one hundred.

"Should I count them again?" she asked.

"Nope. I'm good."

The teller stacked the bills tidily, then tucked them inside an envelope.

"Thanks," I said, snatching the envelope from her hand. Then I fled out the door, giggling all the way.

As I ran toward my getaway vehicle, I felt giddy. And nervous. And slightly out of control—as if I'd just robbed the place.

And to be honest, I still wasn't a hundred percent sure that I *hadn't*.

Check Out What Bobbie and Grayson are Up to Next!
Order Smoked Mullet now!
https://www.amazon.com/dp/B09BG5JPL1 [1]

More Freaky Florida Mysteries

by Margaret Lashley
Moth Busters
Dr. Prepper
Oral Robbers
Ape Shift
Weevil Spirits
Scatman Dues
Smoked Mullet

*"The things a girl's gotta do to get a lousy
PI license. Geez!"*

Bobbie Drex

About the Author

Why do I love underdogs? Well, it takes one to know one. Like the main characters in my novels, I haven't lead a life of wealth or luxury. In fact, as it stands now, I'm set to inherit a half-eaten jar of Cheez Whiz...if my siblings don't beat me to it.

During my illustrious career, I've been a roller-skating waitress, an actuarial assistant, an advertising copywriter, a real estate agent, a house flipper, an organic farmer, and a traveling vagabond/truth seeker. But no matter where I've gone or what I've done, I've always felt like a weirdo.

I've learned a heck of a lot in my life. But getting to know myself has been my greatest journey. Today, I know I'm smart. I'm direct. I'm jaded. I'm hopeful. I'm funny. I'm fierce. I'm a pushover. And I have a laugh that lures strangers over, wanting to join in the fun.

In other words, I'm a jumble of opposing talents and flaws and emotions. And it's all good.

I enjoy underdogs because we've got spunk. And hope. And secrets that drive us to be different from the rest.

So dare to be different. It's the only way to be!

Happy reading!

Made in the USA
Monee, IL
06 September 2021